RED SWARM

Jamie Hutchison

 New Generation Publishing

To my beautiful and amazing wife Karen.
She is the sun that makes my rainbow.

Kieran lay face up on the wet grass. The driving rain mixed with his blood and urine soaked clothes. A shredded piece of flesh and shattered bone was all that remained of his right leg. He could feel the cold breath from the creature as the grotesque head moved over him. Blood and mucous from his severed limb still dripped from the long piercing teeth. A prolonged hiss sounded as the jaws opened wider, wide enough to wrap around his head. He closed his eyes and prayed out loud. Our Father who art in Heaven hallowed be .... His prayers were answered with a swift death as the ferocious jaws crushed his skull. From the darkness more hideous shapes slithered toward the scent of warm blood.

CHAPTER ONE

As predicted, it was an overcast morning, low dense clouds heavily pregnant with precipitation stretched from each horizon. The November waters of the English Channel flickered between cold shades of green and drab grey. Small waves motivated by damp and chilly breezes concertinaed against the long sleek hull of HMS Sabre. On a clear day the landmarks of Plymouth three miles away would be clearly visible, today from the anchorage, without the use of binoculars, the sea, shore and sky were indefinable.

On the bridge of the Anti-Submarine frigate, the Officer of the Watch, Lieutenant Bell, checked the radar, ensuring the four thousand ton warship maintained her position. Turning, he looked at the large brass clock at the rear of the bridge; the black decorative hands indicated it was 0740.

"Quartermaster, how are we getting on with checks for the next serial?"

The QM Leading Seaman Tom Walters picked up and checked a clipboard.

"Sir, just waiting for the communicators to report back."

Lt Bell glanced at the time again, he knew the Captain would appear on the bridge shortly and he was aware what his first question would be.

"Get on to them I want these checks completed before the Captain arrives."

Tom Walters picked up a handset from the bridge console and flicked a switch to the Main Communications Office.

"MCO this is the bridge confirm all your checks are complete?"

After a few seconds the comms office replied.

"Bridge Standby."

Tom smiled to himself, all the communicators had to

do was pull up a bloody flag and they had forgotten. He could picture them now rushing to get someone up to the flag deck.

Lt Bell frowned and gave an impatient roll of his head giving another quick glance at the time.

The small loudspeaker on the bridge console brought further news from the comms office.

"Bridge, this is the MCO. The flag should be getting hoisted now."

Lt Bell opened the bridge door and looked toward the mainmast. A young sailor not adequately dressed for the weather conditions, was hastily pulling on a halyard with the blue and white flag Alpha attached. The Lieutenant watched until the flag was fully hoisted into position and returned to the warmth of the ship. As he entered he heard footsteps on the ladder leading to the bridge. He did not need to look to see who it would be.

"Good morning Officer of the Watch are we ready for the diving serial?"

"Good morning Sir. Yes all preparations are complete."

Coffee in hand, Captain John Piper walked to the front of the bridge and scanned the horizon.

"What's the forecast?"

Lt Bell felt in no doubt that the Captain had already seen the forecast, but was checking if his Officer of the Watch had taken the time to read the signal.

"Overcast with heavy showers, sea-state two for the next twenty-four hours, light winds from the west, visibility two miles reducing during showers Sir."

"Pretty dismal day then, I will be in my cabin if you need me."

On the quarterdeck stood the tall broad figure of Chief Caber McDonald. His blue waterproof jacket covered a thick woollen polar neck jumper. On his head a dark blue tight knitted hat was pulled down to his ears. His broad nose was the most conspicuous feature on his face. Just below the bridge it drifted a few degrees to the left, a souvenir from his days as a prop forward in the United

2

Services rugby team. Caber, a Chief Mechanic was also the senior ships diver. Today he was not diving but supervising the operation. Six men formed a semi circle around him. Four of them fully dressed in diving suits, the other two, the diver's assistants, clothed in bright orange waterproof suits and wearing self-inflating lifejackets. The diving team consisted of Petty Officer Stevenson and Leading Seaman Tug Wilson. The remaining two divers were both under twenty years old. Able Seaman Basher Bates who had just returned to the ship two weeks earlier from his qualifying course, this was his first operational time with the ships team. Less than ten stone in weight he looked swamped in the diving suit. His thin face with huge hazel eyes set on high cheekbones made him look nearer fourteen than his nineteen years. The remaining member of the quartet Soapy Watson, mature in both looks and manner, was already an experienced scuba diver on joining the Royal Navy. He had impressed the instructors so much on his course that they had made a recommendation that he transferred to the clearance diver specialist branch. Caber had already briefed them that their task this morning was to carry out a routine check on the ships propellers. For the second and final time he ran through the safety aspects of the dive. Finishing the brief he scanned all six men in front of him. He gave young Basher a nod of approval and was returned with an excitable smile. Happy they were ready he called out in a thick gravelly Glaswegian accent.

"Okay lads let's get in the boat and see if we kin do it without breaking anything."

Caber watched as they scaled the ladder to the waiting boat. The water looked cold and uninviting. He pulled the zipper to his jacket up tighter and rolled his woolly hat further over his ears. His chilled lips stretched just enough to suggest a smile of satisfaction that he was not diving today. Raising the hand-held radio he informed the bridge that they were now entering the diving boat.

Large radar screens provided the main illumination in

the dimly lit Operations Room. Fully manned the Ops room would hold twenty-two operators, today only four sailors manned the nerve centre of the ship. Two sat at radar consoles plotting the shipping, a third was filing signals. The final member, Tanzy Lee the Leading Hand in charge of the watch was crouched over a large chart table. Abruptly the tranquillity of the Ops Room was disturbed by an unfamiliar sound like the whining of a cat. Initially weak and intermittent it gradually became louder and more frequent, until reaching an annoying pitch. Tanzy, who was not a morning person, looked accusingly at the other three in the Operations Room. Receiving no response he muttered some obscenity and went off to track down the irritating noise. In a darkened corner of the Ops Room, which contained the sonar equipment, he located the origin of the noise. It was coming from a small loudspeaker marked UWT. He knew from talking to the sonar teams that UWT stood for Underwater Telephone and was normally used for communicating with submarines. However the sensitive acoustic device was also capable of detecting any noise in the sea be it man-made or biological. Reaching into his pocket he withdrew a small torch, running the light over the control panel he located the speaker volume he flicked it down a level and gave a satisfied smile. Returning to his previous task, he stopped and stood for a few seconds in deliberation. Reaching out he tapped the operator who was filing the signals on the shoulder.

"Go down and tell Chief Ward there is a weird noise coming over his sonar, ask him if he wants to check it out?"

As the operator reached the first rung of the ladder, Tanzy called out.

"While you are down there make a brew and if the canteen is open get me a Mars bar."

Within two minutes the slim dark-haired figure of Chief Petty Officer Sharky Ward, the senior underwater warfare rating, stood at the top of the ladder that entered

4

the Ops Room.

"Okay Tanzy, what have you dragged me up here for?"

Tanzy gave him a forced smile and turned up the volume control one click on the underwater communications.

"This racket started about five minutes ago. Do you need to know about it or can we switch the thing off?"

Sharky moved toward the control panel and turned a dial that switched between the port and starboard sensors. He listened to the noise for a few seconds then slipped on a headset and opened communications to the bridge.

"Bridge this is the Ops Room, Chief Ward speaking. We have an unidentified sound coming over the underwater comms that I suspect is sea life. Have you anything visual, like large fish movement on or near the surface?"

"Standby Ops Room" came the reply.

After a minute Lt Bell responded,

"Ops room negative on that. No movement around the ship."

The sound picked up in intensity. Sharky rotated the bearing indicator, but it appeared to be coming from all around the ship. By the tone and the frequency of it, he knew it was sea life, but he did not recall ever hearing it before. He turned a dial on the tape recorder situated alongside the sonar system, which automatically channelled the noise through it and pressed the record button. Tanzy, had now devoured his Mars Bar and was eager to get the Ops Room back to normal, impatiently he hovered behind Sharky. Eventually his tolerance cracked.

"Chief, any chance we can switch it off now?"

Sharky only acknowledged his request by the raising of his hand. He still listened to the mysterious and intriguing sound. He channelled the sound through his headset and closed his eyes, listening attentively for anything that would give him a clue to what it was. As always when deep in thought he ran his left hand over either side of his chin. Familiar with the Chief's thinking pose, Tanzy delayed any further attempts to have the volume reduced and wandered despondently back to the chart table to finish his tea. Hearing a warning pipe from the bridge that diving operations were about to take place Sharky switched his headset back to internal comms and opened a line to the bridge.

"Bridge Chief Ward speaking, fairly confident there are large shoals of fish around, would you pass on my suspicions to the diving team?"

This time the QM replied

"Roger Chief, passing message now."

Captain Piper monitored communications in his cabin between the Ops Room and bridge. Slightly intrigued in what the Ops Room were listening to. To satisfy his curiosity he stood up and made the short walk through the passageway adjacent his cabin. Entering the Ops Room and, without preamble, asked,

"So what do you think then, Chief?"

Startled, Sharky recognised the Captains voice and turned around.

"In all honesty Sir, haven't got a clue I have never heard a sound like this before. It's certainly sea life but no idea what. With a bit of luck the divers will get a visual on whatever it is."

Soapy Watson had just entered the water, the last of the divers. All four went through the process of checking their seals before submerging. The assistants held on to a safety line attached to each diver. As the divers submerged the assistants gradually released the lines out to avoid any chance of them getting tangled or gaining to much slack.

The underwater communications system still broadcasted the mysterious noise; Sharky had turned it down to a level to appease Tanzy and the other crew in the Ops room. The Captain and Sharky both sat alongside the main sonar system chatting. In mid stream of a sentence Sharky stopped and reached for the volume control of the underwater comms. As he increased the volume, all heads in the Ops Room looked toward him. The whining tone had faded, replaced with what could only be described as a hostile rasping growl. The noise reverberated around the Ops room like the theme from a cheap horror movie. Sharky glanced toward the radar screens. A few small vessels moved around, but the nearest was more than two miles away. He hastily picked up the con to the bridge.

"Bridge, confirm there is no movement around the ship?"

"Standby"

A pause of thirty seconds took place before the bridge replied.

"Ops Room, confirm no movement around the ship. Only thing visual within two miles is the diving boat just off the starboard quarter."

"Chief any ideas?" Queried the Captain.

Sharky shook his head.

"No Sir, I've never known any sea life to change frequency like that."

Sharky listened intensely to the sound radiating from the speaker. As much as he searched all his knowledge on acoustics he could not link it with anything remotely familiar.

"Sir. Got to say this has got me snookered. Only hope the divers do get a visual on whatever it is. If not I will do some analysis on the recording and see if I can gain any information from that."

Although Sharky was conversing with the Captain, he was still concentrating on the noise. In his gut he had a feeling that something was wrong. His anxiety to tie in his gut feeling with concrete evidence was making his mind race.

The Captain rose from his chair.

"Chief if you solve the mystery let me know, I will be in my cabin."

Without diverting his concentration from the noise Sharky replied.

"Yes Sir."

Just before the Captain exited the Operations Room

Sharky called out

"Sir."

The Captain stopped and turned.

"Come up with a solution already Chief?"

"No Sir, its just I think it needs further investigation."

"Well I cannot think of what else we can do Chief, with a bit of luck the divers will identify whatever it is and we will have our answer."

Sharky's faced tensed as if giving much consideration toward his next statement.

"Sir lets get the divers out."

A smile of bemusement drifted over the Captains face.

"Chief, are you serious? Do you think we have to go to those measures?"

"Sir, I have a bad feeling on this. I'll admit I have not got a clue what's out there but everything is telling me it is not good."

The deliberate and concerned tone of Sharky's reply combined with a sudden increase in the noise level from the underwater comms brought an unsmiling look to the Captains face.

"Chief, we're in the English Channel. What in this area could possibly be a threat to divers?"

"Sir, nothing that I know of but whatever is making that noise is new to me, and it does not sound friendly."

"Okay Chief, if I bring them out, how do you intend clarifying if there is a threat?"

"Sir, all I need is five minutes. Once the divers are clear of the water I'd like to transmit on the main active sonar. If there are big shoals around or large fish we should be able to pick them up on sonar."

Sharky's gaze was searching the Captains face for a decision. The rasping growl continued to sound throughout the Ops Room. The Captain paused a few seconds then decisively he picked up the intercom to the bridge.

"Officer of the Watch this is the Captain, I want the divers out of the water full haste."

Lt Bell acknowledged the Captain's order and

proceeded to radio the diving boat to recover the diver's immediately. Checking his wristwatch the Captain turned to Sharky.

"Chief you have your five minutes."

"Thank you Sir."

Sharky picked up the intercom and switched it to the ships main broadcast and piped.

"Starboard Watch sonar crew close up at the rush."

When the order from the Officer of the Watch came over Caber McDonald was stood on the stern of the diving boat.

"Sir, confirm you want us to clear the divers out of the water?"

"Confirmed with full haste."

Caber cursed under his breath and acknowledged the order from the bridge. Placing the radio down he gave the order for the diving assistants to signal the divers to return to the surface. On the bridge Lt Bell and the Quartermaster could detect that the Ops Room were getting agitated about something. They had asked twice in the last five minutes to check for anything visual. Now they were recovering the divers and closing up the sonar crew. The third member on the bridge, the Bosons Mate was sitting by the communications panel reading daily orders. He felt a tap on his shoulder, turning he met the gaze of the Quartermaster.

"Take the binoculars and go on the bridge wing and keep a look out."

"Is there anything in particular I am looking for?"

The Quartermaster shrugged.

"I don't know. If you see anything just let me know."

The Bosons Mate put on a windproof jacket and picked up a pair of binoculars, reluctantly he exited the warm bridge into the chilly morning air. Scanning the horizon all seemed normal. Lowering his binoculars, he looked down over the guardrails. Below the surface of the water, about six feet off the ship's side something moving beneath the water caught his eye. He leaned further over the guardrails to get a clearer view but whatever it was had disappeared. Contemplating that he had imagined it he began to raise his binoculars again to recheck the horizon but stopped and lowered them. As if sneaking up on someone he slowly peered over the guardrails and stared intensely along the waterline of the ship. A dark patch in the water stood out from the rest of the sea, it appeared to be moving. As if not to frighten whatever he was seeing he moved slowly toward the bridge door and waved his hand to beckon the Quartermaster to join him. A bemused Tom Walters walked out to the bridge wing.

"What?"

"Down there QM. Think there is something in the water?"

Tom Walters looked to where the Bosons Mate was pointing. About six feet from the ships side a long dark mass shifted hypnotically from side to side slowly moving from bow to stern. Turning the QM called out to the bridge.

"Sir it looks like we do have a large shoal of fish."

"Roger QM. Any idea what they are?"

"No Sir. They are too deep to get a visual on."

Before the QM had finished his reply the Bosons Mate pushed him in the back and let out a startled voice.

"Shitty death what are they?"

For a few seconds both sailors stood in awe at what they saw. The dark shape had come very close to the surface and what it consisted of was clearly visible to the two observers. Dozens of eel like creatures, red in colour with grotesque heads swam below them. Lt Bell joined them on the bridge wing, together all three sailors watched as the creatures continued to multiply before their eyes. Returning quickly to the Bridge the Officer of the Watch picked up the con to the Operations Room.

"Captain, Sir, we've just sighted a vast amount of large fish over two metres long on the Starboard side."

"Can you identify them?"

"Negative, Sir. They look like huge eels, red in colour.

10

Never seen anything like them before."

The Quartermaster who had moved around to check the port side of the ship reported even more.

"Captain, Officer of the Watch, reports that they're also on the port side. It appears we're in the middle of a large shoal of them."

"Roger, Bridge. Are the divers still in the water?"

Lt Bell looked astern and saw the first diver entering the boat. Three others bobbed on the water waiting to exit.

"Sir one in the boat, other three on the surface."

Sharky Ward checked over the sonar crew who were now closed up. He scanned the tape recorder. The recording levels indicated that it was still recording the underwater comms system.

The Captain called up to the bridge.

"Bridge, get some photographic evidence of these creatures, and get the Quartermaster to draw a weapon, if they're unidentified it may be worthwhile recovering one for analysis."

Lt Bell unlocked the weapons locker and issued the Quartermaster with a SA80 rifle and a full magazine of rounds.

Tug Wilson was the next diver due to exit the water. He had just watched Soapy Watson get onboard. Tug, with the help of an assistant pulling on his safety line, started to make his way toward the boat. At about six feet from the boat a large elongated red fish passed between him and the boat's side. It moved so slowly that it appeared to linger in his pathway for an eternity. The eel-like creature was less than a foot beneath the surface. Its body weaved like a snake. Its grotesquely large head moved from side to side. On getting directly opposite him, he caught sight of the creature's eyes, a deep piercing yellow. For a split second it appeared to stare directly back toward him. His surprise and curiosity at seeing the fish swiftly turned to uneasiness the creature's stare was filled with cold-blooded malevolence. It finally passed its body twisted and dropped deeper in the water. Instinctively he reached for his knife and unclipped it from the sheaf. The assistant who had also sighted the creature continued to pull him towards the boat. As Tug reached the side a terrifying scream came from behind him. He grasped hold of the boat and turned his head. The nearest diver to him, Petty Officer Stevenson, splashed around in a state of panic. Tug removed his mouthpiece and yelled at the boat to recover the stricken diver. Both the assistant and Caber doubled their efforts in pulling on the safety line. As he got closer to the boat the screaming intensified with pleas for help. It was then the reason became apparent. Two eel-like creatures, exactly like the one that had swam past earlier were viciously attacking him. They were both biting into the right side of his waist. The rubber on his suit had been ripped away, and a cloud of blood was surrounding the diver. A third creature joined the other two, skin and flesh was being indiscriminately ripped from the stricken diver's body. Getting the injured diver alongside, the assistants urgently grabbed him under his armpits. As he began to clear the water a creature's head rose from the sea and made a strike at the assistants. The huge jaws opened displaying rows of ferocious blood and mucous-stained piercing teeth. The surprise and shock of the attack resulted in both assistants falling back in the boat and the injured diver slipping from their grip and dropping back into the water. Before they could recover, Petty Officer Stevenson's screaming suddenly subsided, the creature that had launched the attack sank its needle like teeth deep into his throat. Blood gushed out of the gaping wound leaving a bright red tide mark along the hull of the diving boat. Further petrified screams and begging for help turned the attention to the final diver. Tug still alongside the boat, turned around and was terrified at what he could see. They were attacking Basher Bates the water around him was alive with the number of creatures ripping into him. Fear suddenly hit Tug with full force, his mind began to race and panic was taking over, nausea began to swell rapidly in the pit of his stomach. He looked toward the crew on the diving boat for assistance but they were all pre-occupied, desperately pulling on the other diver's recovery lines.

Lt Bell watched through his binoculars and was left in disbelief of what he was seeing. He lowered the binoculars and looked at the sea. Dozens possibly hundreds of creatures were heading toward the diving boat. Frantically he picked up the con to the Ops Room.

"Captain, Sir, the diver's are in trouble. They're being attacked by the creatures, hundreds of them."

On hearing the report, the Captain raced from the Ops Room to the bridge wing. Arriving, he looked astern at the diving boat and could clearly see the two divers being viciously attacked. Hastily he picked up the con to the Ops room.

"Ops Room this is the Captain go active on sonar now. Repeat, go active."

Sharky moved toward the main active sonar and turned the safe-to-transmit key to transmit. Instantly the huge three-ton transducer, on the ships keel, converted three kilowatts of electrical power into sound. The powerful sonar pulse moved through the water, bouncing off everything in its path. Immediately after the transmission the creatures changed direction away from the diving boat but a few seconds later returned back on course toward the divers.

"Sonar, Captain, switch to your minimum range scale. I want these transmissions going out as fast as possible."

On hearing the order, the sonar operator switched to minimum range scale, ensuring the transmissions went out every six seconds. With the sonar entering the water much faster, the creatures were clearly being disorientated. Their previous uniform course toward the divers was now disjointed with them heading in all directions. Anxiously, the Captain looked toward the diving boat he could still see the two divers being attacked. The sonar didn't appear to be affecting the creatures that had already reached them.

In an attempt to overcome his panic, Tug raised his

knife and drove it toward the creature biting the Petty Officer's neck. The broad sharp serrated knife entered just below the creatures head. The creature immediately freed the diver from its grip and turned toward its attacker. Tug pushed the knife deeper into the wound until reaching the hilt of the blade. Motivated by fear, he clenched down on his teeth and twisted the knife. As the blade rotated it sliced through the back of the creature's neck. The hideous partially decapitated head slid from the weapon. Tug raised the knife once more, but the lifeless creature's body drifted out of his reach and beneath the boat. Frantically Tug slipped the restraining strap on his air tanks. He gave a final glance at the stricken diver. Through a mist of blood he could see the Petty Officers head. It hung like a punch bag below his shoulders a shred of skin the only link with his body. The head moved side to side with the movement of the sea. As it swung toward Tug he could see, behind the face mask the eyes, wide open, frozen in fear.

The panic he had temporarily subdued began to rise with alarming speed. Turning toward the boat he grasped the side with both hands. Even with the loss of the air tanks he was still finding it extremely difficult to raise himself out of the water. He had managed to get his waist out of the water when suddenly he felt a grip on his chest looking up he stared straight into the eyes of Caber McDonald. Caber's huge hands had grabbed hold of his diving suit and were dragging him into the boat. Just as Tug's legs started to clear the water a creature arrived. It rose with terrifying jaws open and snapped them shut clinging onto one of the flippers viciously shaking its head from side to side. As Tug fell inboard the flipper slipped off releasing him from the grip of the creature.

The Captain thanked God as he saw a second diver get onboard the boat. He turned to the Bridge team.

"Quartermaster, use your weapon and shoot these creatures. Lt Bell, get an armed team up here now and I want them positioned around the ship shooting these bloody things."

The Quartermaster began firing into the creatures. As a bullet from the powerful rifle struck and killed one the others creatures immediately turned toward it and started devouring it. Tom Walters continued to fire into the mass accumulating around the first kill.

The boat's crew were frantically trying to recover the remaining divers. At least six of the things were attacking what remained of Petty Officer Stevenson. Every time the crew attempted to reach for his body, creatures would strike out at them. Eventually the diver's remains were no longer visible. The weight on the safety line became so heavy that it began to cut into the assistant's hands. Caber felt angry and helpless as he watched the line slip slowly through their hands and the diver sink deeper beneath the sea. The final line was being frantically pulled on by Tug and Soapy Watson. The diver wasn't visible and the line dipped steeply below the water. Caber joined them in their efforts and together they made slow progress in the recovery. As the line became vertical alongside the boat, the water became alive with the creatures. They continued to pull together and suddenly what remained of Basher broke the surface. The head was completely gone, severed at the neck. The torso was unrecognisable, parts of the rib cage protruded from the remaining pieces of the diving suit and both arms devoid of flesh and hands. A trail of intestines floated behind the body. The gruesome shock of what was secured to the line stopped the recovery. In those few seconds, creatures mobbed the remaining body parts, the line gave way and Basher's pitiful remains disappeared below the water. The two diving assistants still continued to struggle with the safety line attached to Petty Officer Stevenson, after witnessing what lay at the end of the other one their faces were full of fear and shock. Caber scanned the sea around the boat. The creatures were everywhere and massing toward the boat. He turned toward the diving assistants and placed his hands on their shoulders. He spoke to them in a calm and low voice.

"Release the line, there is nothing we can do now."

Instinctively they obeyed the command, released their grip and stood silently watching as the orange nylon line ran through their fingers. All onboard the boat looked at Caber, he looked back at their frightened and shocked gazes. Turning he walked back toward the boat's control. He yelled out in an angry and forceful voice.

"Hold on boat moving forward."

On seeing them react to his command he thrust the throttle forward. The boat responded immediately, all onboard felt the repeated thuds as the propeller hit a number of creatures. Caber quickly manoeuvred the boat alongside Sabre and under the davits. Hooking on the lifting gear, the order was given immediately to hoist it clear of the water.

Captain Piper remained on the bridge speaking over secure communications to the Flag Officer's Headquarters providing them with a brief on what had occurred. When he had finished, he called down to the Ops Room.

"Chief Ward to the Bridge."

Sharky was on the bridge within seconds. He joined the Captain who was now standing on the bridge wing looking out to sea.

"Yes, Sir?"

Sharky noticed the Captain looked tense and solemn. He spoke deliberately and the softness in his voice had gone.

"Chief, shore side want at least one of these things for analysis but every time we shoot one, the others devour it. I need ideas."

Sharky looked out over the bridge wing. This was the first time he'd seen the creatures. The sight of them left him speechless.

The Captains voice brought him back to the problem.
"Chief?"

The Chief knew of only one way to deal with submerged problems, explosives.

"Sir, we have six one-pound charges prepared in the

16

ready use locker. We could lower the boat, drop the charges and quickly recover one that has been killed or stunned by the explosions."

He knew the Captain would not be keen on putting the boat back in the water but it appeared the only alternative. Captain Piper walked back into the Bridge clearly deliberating over his decision. As he got to the middle he stopped and called out assertively.

"Officer of the Watch I want all six explosive charges in the boat. I need all the boats crew armed. Chief Ward, I would like you to go with the boats crew and supervise recovery of these creatures."

As soon as the boat hit the water it was released. The coxswain pushed the throttle on the sixty horse power engine to maximum drive. Two of the five crew carried long boathooks with sharp grapnels attached. The six one-pound charges lay in the bottom of the boat. Clear of the ship, Sharky ordered the coxswain to slow down. Picking up two charges, he pulled the pin on the first and dropped it overboard, immediately followed by the second. The coxswain once again opened the throttle to max and the boat sped away. Two underwater explosions followed behind them. Turning the boat they reduced speed and slowly moved back into the area the charges had been dropped. Eight creatures floated on the surface, some stunned, and others that looked dead. The boat manoeuvred alongside one of the creatures and both boathooks were rammed into it. One hook pierced the neck the other entered halfway down the body. Sharky gave the order to pull it inboard, as it began to clear the water; he stopped the recovery, removed his pistol and fired into its head. The two handlers then continued to pull the creature into the boat. When it hit the deck all the crew stopped and stared at the creature lying before them. The jaws were open wide enough to display rows of dagger shaped teeth. Its own blood leaked over them as if to emphasise their ferocity. Yellow cold-blooded eyes stood out like amber warning beacons against the red skin. Even in death the eyes retained a look of pure evil staring back at its slayers with absolute loathing. As re-assurance it was dead one of the crew pushed it firmly with a boathook. The pressure of the boathook against the creature resulted in a sharp serrated hook appearing from one of eight nipples on its underbelly.

"Jesus, Chief, what's that?"

Sharky crouched down to take a closer look.

"That's what you call an extremely nasty bit of kit."

Sudden movement outboard the boat detracted from the interest in the dead creature. Already other creatures had appeared and were devouring those killed or stunned. Sharky picked up another two charges and dropped them overboard. The coxswain swung the boat around and cleared the area. Twenty-five minutes later, the boat returned to Sabre with three dead creatures, all with a bullet hole in their heads.

In the Ops Room the audio from the underwater comms changed back from the growling noise to the whine. On the bridge wing the Captain watched the creatures begin to disappear from view. The sonar team reported tracking a large contact moving in a westerly direction at eleven knots. They held the contact out to 16000 yards then it faded from their screens.

The same communicator that had earlier hoisted the diving flag entered the bridge and handed the Captain an immediate signal. Without looking up from the signal the Captain spoke out.

"Officer the Watch start preparations for returning to harbour."

The warship began to weigh anchor. As the anchor broke the surface, the frigates huge twin propellers rotated and drove it slowly forward.

Sabre manoeuvred out of the anchorage towards Plymouth.

18

CHAPTER TWO

In Fleet Headquarters the signal from Sabre reporting on the morning events lay on the desk of the Sea Lord, Admiral Donald Lane. He lowered his reading glasses and his eyes fell over paragraph four for the second time.

4. At 0840 creatures similar to large eels ranging from eight to ten feet attacked divers carrying out a routine dive. Two of the diver's dead, bodies not recovered. Creatures attacked in numbers, total creatures sighted in vicinity of ship exceeded 400. Small arms and active sonar were used in defence of divers. Estimate forty to fifty creatures destroyed. Active sonar in low range scale disorientated the creatures. Three specimens recovered from water for analysis. At 0925, 45 minutes after first sighting, creatures left vicinity of ship. Shoal tracked by active sonar until 0955 heading on westerly course speed eleven knots.

The Admiral stood up from his chair and made the short walk through to the office of his Personnel Assistant, Captain John Stone. The PA had the same signal lying in front of him.

"John I want a full brief on this by tomorrow morning. Get the Captain of Sabre and any other key personnel involved up here. I also want some specialist in sea life, and find out who is carrying out analysis on the creatures recovered by Sabre."

The PA acknowledged the Sea Lord's request. As the Admiral turned and left the office, he picked up the phone and started to make a number of calls.

The sun was setting over the picturesque village of Shaldon. The fishing boats and the Teign Bridge were silhouetted against the fading light. A calm sea and still evening enhanced the serenity of the sunset. A retired couple, John and Irene walked along the deserted beach with their three dogs. The dobermans Abby and Biscuit remained abreast their owners splashing around in the water. The collie, Roscoe, as always sprinted ahead. This was the first time in nearly four months that Irene had been able to join the evening walk. Since being diagnosed with cancer her outings were restricted to hospital visits. Three weeks ago she had been given the all clear and she had now regained the strength to go out. John was hesitant about taking her but he knew it meant a great deal to her.

Roscoe had stopped about twenty yards from them and started to bark towards the sea. As they approached the collie's position, they could see movement in the shallow water and the occasional sighting of a shape that appeared to be the body of a large fish. In the dimming light it was difficult to identify what type of fish it was, but it was definitely large and from the movement, there was more than one of them. Both dobermans joined Roscoe and started to move forward into the water. The collie maintained his position on the beach and continued to bark frantically. The curiosity of Abby and Biscuit made them advance until they both stood in the water up to their chests about five yards short of the disturbance in the water. To get a closer look, John and Irene moved into the shallows allowing the gentle waves to lap against their rubber boots. They could make out at least four shapes now. As more of the shapes became visible, the size of them began to raise concerns. John called for both dogs to return to the shore. Abby and Biscuit appeared oblivious of the command, remaining in position and staring inquisitively at the movement in the water. Raising his voice in a more authoritative tone, the dogs took one step back but maintained their gaze in the direction of the fish.

From amongst the twisting shapes a head rose clearly a foot above the water. It faced both dogs and let out a threatening hiss. Even in the dimming light the yellow of its eyes radiated danger. Abby and Biscuit immediately responded and joined Roscoe in barking. The creature countered with another hiss. Opening its jaws wide it fully exhibited its long pointed teeth. Roscoe was getting more agitated, running for short distances and then returning to the previous spot, barking throughout.

The dogs owners became more frantic both shouting loudly at their pets to return to shore. John moved deeper into the water, allowing the seawater to pour over the tops of his rubber boots. As the creatures head submerged, Abby changed from a bark to a loud growl. The turning mass was now less than a yard from the dog's position. John looked back at Irene and saw she was following him. He shook his head but Irene carried on wading deeper into the water. They reached Biscuit first, John held on to her until Irene arrived and she grabbed the brown leather collar around the dark silky neck. As she took the weight of the dog, she felt a sudden yank and Biscuit let out a loud yelp of pain. Irene placed both her hands around the collar and began to drag the dog. She felt another tug, this time stronger. Biscuit's yelping was getting louder and more hysterical. Suddenly Abby let out a long and painful yelp and was struggling to break free from something. Moving to the side of Irene, John bent down to lift Biscuit from the water. Pushing his arms under the dogs belly he was about to take the weight when he felt something bite him followed by excruciating pain. Quickly recovering his arm from the water he saw the creature as it emerged still with its long teeth sunk deeply into his forearm. On breaking the water it jerked its head twice ripping of a huge lump of flesh and dropped back beneath the water. Irene let out a loud and terrified scream as blood gushed from the huge gaping wound.

A further pull on Biscuit resulted in the wet collar being yanked from Irene's grip and the dog yelping even more loudly. Abby was also in distress, flopped down on her chest, her head shaking violently, yelping and whimpering throughout.

Holding his injured arm against his chest John screamed at Irene.

"Go back leave the dogs."

Irene crying hysterically shook her head. He grabbed her with his good arm and started to lead her back to shore. They waded out with their backs to the shore, both watching and hoping the dogs would somehow break free from the creatures. Irene was only feet from the beach. She screamed as she felt teeth sink into her calf. Turning she saw a horrific sight. Behind them were more of the monstrous creatures. John rushed to Irene's aid and was frantically trying to free her from the jaws of the creature. As he kicked at its head he slipped and fell. Two creatures from behind moved forward and sunk their teeth into his neck and shoulder. Irene's screams turned even more hysterical as a second creature bit into her thigh. It swung its body around her and looped on to both her legs. Eight sharp hooks appeared from beneath its body piercing her legs. Dropping to her knees, the hooks slid up her legs slicing deep into her flesh hitting and hooking onto the bone. Another creature approached from her front and bit into her splaying arm, the teeth cut in so deep and forceful that her slender wrist bones shattered amputating the hand.

Lifting himself from the ground into a crawling position John grabbed Irene's jacket and pulled her toward the beach. All of a sudden Irene stopped screaming. John looked at her face, she was still alive but the fear had gone and he knew that she had accepted death. Tears started to stream from him. In an uncontrollable explosion of anger he managed to pull himself into a standing position and lashed out at the creatures. He got in one blow before two more creatures attacked him and he fell back to the ground. As he landed he could see his wife's body start to move away from him. The creatures were pulling her back to the water. He reached out for her, as he lifted his arm a creature bit into it. His body began to move, being dragged back into the sea. He twisted his head to look toward Irene; he caught one final fleeting glimpse of her body before voracious jaws closed on his exposed face.

Biscuit floated on the surface; the body only moving

with sudden jolts as further predatory bites tore into him. Abby's calls of distress were subdued to a pitiful whimper. A further two heads rose from the water and drove their fangs into the poor animals back and neck and she disappeared from sight. The remains of the dog's owners were towed steadily into deeper water, randomly jerking as the flesh was ripped from their bones.

The sun finally dropped behind the horizon and darkness descended on the beach. The lonely whimpering and shivering silhouette of Roscoe sat on the beach looking out to sea.

The creature lay on a long stainless steel table. It measured two point four metres and weighed forty-three kilos. The body circumference was thirty-eight centimetres, the large head measured in at fifty- eight. Steel callipers held the mouth open, displaying sharp and pointed teeth which totalled one hundred and four, the longest being just over twenty seven millimetres. The colours of the skin looked tropical, red, except for the underbelly, a golden yellow, blotted with black patches. Eight nipple like impressions lay neatly in pairs along the belly.

Three men stood over the creature, two biologists from the Ministry of Defence research facility dressed in light blue overalls. The third man a marine biologist Professor Mark Yates wore a white lab coat covering a pair of faded jeans and a red sweater. Forty-six years old, tanned from his recent work in the Caribbean, he was slim and fit looking. His greying hair still retained much of the jet-black colouring of his youth. Late that morning he had received a telephone call from the Ministry of Defence requesting him to attend the post- mortem of a strange creature that had been recovered. It was now just gone four o clock in the afternoon. Stretching his hand out to fit a surgical glove; a scar on his right hand leading from his wrist to the thumb got the attention of the other two men. Mark could see them notice it.

"Moray eel, three years ago."

He studied the creature lying on the cold steel table. On reaching the nipples on the underbelly he neatly cut two incisions into one. Using the end of the scalpel he extracted a serrated hook from it. Carefully holding it, he ran a finger around the outer edge, the point was extremely sharp. Pressing it between two fingers he twisted, it rotated. He ran his hand along the body of the creature an eel's body should be smooth and slimy. This one was like sandpaper. At the head he looked closely at the menacing teeth. Picking up a spatula he pushed down on the creature's lips, displaying a smaller, but just as sharp set.

Colin Peters, one of the research biologists, spoke out, "Any ideas?"

Mark did not answer immediately. He took a step back and looked at the creature from head to tail. The expression on his face was one of confusion. "Quite an impressive creature you have here. Nothing I have come across before. I would bet that this is a hybrid fish and guess that it did not start life in the ocean but probably a test tube.

"What makes you say that?"

"Well, you have a creature that has the characteristics of about four other fish. The hook although bigger is very similar to the giant squids. The skin is shark like, teeth barracuda and the shape is definite eel.

"A fearsome looking beast; where was it caught?"

Both researchers looked at each other.

Colin spoke.

"It was brought in by the Royal Navy, recovered by a frigate off Plymouth."

Mark touched the bullet hole entrance.

"I can see the military used their usual minimal force."

Steven James, the second researcher, turned to Mark.

"We have two more specimens both around the same size. All three were recovered from the same place."

Mark raised his eyebrows.

"Really! Two more, like this, how many did the frigate come across?"

Colin and Steven looked at each other wondering if they were divulging too much information.

Colin took the lead.

"The ship reported approximately four hundred of them ranging from two to two point five metres in length."

Mark let out a whistle he couldn't imagine what four hundred of these creatures would look like in a mass.

"Tell me, did the ship report if they remained together?"

Steven jumped in. "Yes, all of them departed together and were tracked on active sonar as a huge shoal for at least thirty minutes."

Mark's interest was in full flow.

"How did the ship come across them?"

At this question both Colin and Steven didn't provide an answer. Colin the senior of both biologists finally answered.

"I'm afraid we are not sure how much information we can divulge at this stage."

Mark smiled. He had come across the military's red tape before when asked for assistance experimenting with sea life.

The sound of a door opening diverted the biologists from Mark's questioning. An attractive dark-haired young woman wearing a laboratory coat entered the room. The scent of her perfume was pungent enough to break through the smell of the dead creature. Her name tally read Rebecca Parker and underneath the word technician. More noticeable was the tight cleavage being presented by her unbuttoned lab coat. Her breasts looked perfectly formed bringing into question their authenticity.

"Yes Becky?" Enquired Colin

Her voice was refined and clear, but with a definite hint of a Northern accent.

"Mr Peters, there is a call for you in the office from a Captain Stone, he said it is important."

As the woman turned to follow Colin back to the office she looked at Mark and smiled. Mark smiled back and watched as her shapely figure disappeared into an adjacent office.

Steven James gave a knowing smile at Mark.

"The answer is yes."

"Sorry?" Enquired Mark.

"Around six months ago she took four weeks leave. When she returned she had somewhat increased her frontage. They have been on display ever since."

"Pretty girl." Replied Mark.

Pleased that his curiosity had been satisfied.

Colin returned within five minutes.

"That was Admiral Lane's PA. He would like us, including you Professor Yates to attend a meeting at 1100 tomorrow at Northwood. I've been authorised to give you a copy of the signal the frigate sent in after the attack."

Mark looked at Colin.

"Attack!"

He grasped the signal that was being handed to him.

CHAPTER THREE

Mark drove up to the gate of the military establishment at Northwood. Two armed police approached and directed him to park his car in the bay to the left of the entrance. A further two police asked him to open both his boot and bonnet and gave the car a thorough search inside and out. Once the police were satisfied his car was no threat they handed him a pass, which included directions to the car parking area for Captain Stone's office. He entered the office of the Sea Lord's PA at 1040. Captain Stone looked early fifties with a rapidly receding hairline. Raising himself from behind the desk to shake Mark's hand, his protruding waistline advertised the effects of to many dinner parties.

"Professor Yates excellent you could make it."

"My pleasure Captain, thank you for the invite."

"No problem old chap, you were recommended by an old chum of mine, Simon Harper. Soon as I told him of the problem he said you were the best.

Mark smiled. "That was very kind of the Dean, I hope he is well."

"Fit as fiddle, now lets get you sorted for the meeting Professor."

Captain Stone led Mark into an adjacent office.

"This young lady will take you down to the conference room."

The young lady was a naval officer in her early twenties. She got up quickly from a desk which was weighed down with files, politely smiled and led Mark down a long hallway. Already seated in the conference room were a Royal Navy Captain and a Chief Petty Officer who introduced themselves as Captain John Piper and Chief Ward. Mark offered them his condolences for the loss of their crew. Over the next five to ten minutes a further five people arrived for the meeting. Two he knew already were Colin and Steven, the two biologists from the research centre. A Commander from the United States Navy whose name tally read Jeff Winters and a civilian from the Ministry of Agriculture named Tom Banks. The final person was Captain Stone himself. The Captain checked all were present and departed to inform the Admiral. As the Admiral entered the Office, all the military personnel stood and waited until he was seated.

Admiral Donald Lane wore a blue sweater over an open necked white shirt. The thick gold band of his rank shone brightly from his shoulder badges. Deeply marked frown marks charted his forehead, his steel-grey hair swept to one side. When he spoke, Mark detected a hint of a soft Scottish accent.

"Well Gentlemen, thank you for attending the meeting at such short notice. Before we start could we run around the table for introductions?"

After the introductions the Admiral continued.

"You are all aware of the reason I have called this meeting however you will not be aware that we had information passed to us two months ago from the United States regarding the existence of these creatures."

Sharky looked at his Captain who looked as surprised as him that the Navy had previous knowledge of them.

"When I say we knew of their existence, we did not consider them a threat to the British Isles therefore this attack, the first of its kind in British waters was not expected."

Mark broke in. "Excuse me, Admiral. You said the first in British Waters. Have there been other incidents recorded elsewhere?"

The Admiral nodded and looked toward Commander Winters.

"I invited Jeff to the meeting because he has information that should help us. I will leave it to him to explain."

The United States Naval Officer stood and moved toward a large map of the world that covered the whole of one wall. Jeff Winters looked young to be a Commander, his olive skin and his short-cropped dark hair gave the impression of Italian or Puerto Rican descent. When he spoke it was with a southern drawl.

"Admiral, Gentlemen three years ago the US Government were concerned that the fishing industry were struggling to meet demands, so they authorised research into genetically engineering fish."

He went on to explain that the scientists had worked toward cross-pollinating different types of fish to produce a fish that would reach maturity quickly and meet the food demand.

"In addition to the primary research the scientists were given permission to experiment with a whole raft of fish to see what genes would interact with what. We are confident, that it's from one of these experiments that this problem has originated."

He paused letting the last statement be absorbed.

"The research centre, where the experimental work was carried out is situated in Florida. Just under two years ago, Hurricane Francis slammed into the research centre and the sea flooded the experimental fish pens, allowing a lot of the fry to escape to open water."

Mark raised his hand.

"Do you know exactly what experimental fish escaped?"

The Commander referred to his notes he was holding. "There were two pens flooded, subjects 204 and 365. The first 204 was a cross between mackerel, tuna and bass; however the second was a little bit more complicated."

He paused for a few seconds and ran his finger down the page and read from it without looking up.

"Electric eel, barracuda, Squid and Red Drum fish. The scientists were trying to produce a fish that could breed and survive in very shallow water or saltwater marshes. To achieve this they introduced the genes from the electric eel that would allow them to breathe from the air."

"Why squid?" Mark asked

"Same question I asked, apparently they found in the

majority of their experiments the genes from the squid were necessary to bond the other genes."

He turned toward the map and pointed to the Florida Bay.

"The research centre is here at Whitewater Bay."

He moved his finger along the map and stopped at Key West.

"Seven Months after Hurricane Francis, we received a report that three teenagers snorkelling off Key West went missing. A partial skeleton was washed up on the beach four days later. Forensic reports stated that the bones were marked with small teeth marks all over them."

He ran his finger further along the Florida Keys.

"Over the next three months there were a total of seven reports of people missing throughout the Keys with no explanation. None of these bodies were ever recovered."

From The Keys, he pointed toward a spot just outside Miami.

"Just here is Biscayne Bay the Green Valley Stud farm lies adjacent to a wet marsh."

He picked up a folder from the table and removed half a dozen pictures and passed them to the Admiral.

"Three brood mares stabled there, all in late pregnancy were found mutilated. Little flesh remained on them."

The Admiral looked at the gruesome pictures of the horse's remains and passed the pictures around the table. Two of the pictures displayed grooves in the swamp mud, long wavy marks, all going in the same direction.

"The marks on pictures five and six are believed to be from whatever attacked the horses."

Mark interrupted, "You're saying they came ashore?"

All the audience looked at the Commander.

He nodded "Yes. Unfortunately, we believe so. The mutilation of the horses happened four months ago, since then there have been no further incidents reported Stateside."

The Admiral broke in. "But we do have a theory and some evidence to support it. Would you kindly take them through it Jeff?"

"Yes Sir. We believe that the creatures moved out of the Florida coast and picked up the Gulf Stream."

The Commander, using the map, indicated how the Gulf Stream originates in the Gulf of Mexico, exits through the Strait of Florida and follows the eastern coastline of the United States and Newfoundland and then extends into Europe by the North Atlantic Drift.

Captain John Piper broke in. "The Admiral said you had evidence to support this theory."

The Commander nodded. "Two months ago, a boating trip, whale watching off St John's in Canada, sighted a group of killer whales. They reported that large shoals of unidentified fish were attacking the whales. The description of the fish corresponds with those recovered by Sabre."

He went on to report another incident involving a catamaran anchored off St Johns Bay that was found with the crew of three missing. The boat was covered with trails of blood.

Mark raised his hand.

"Commander, how many of the fish did batch 365 contain?"

"There was a total of five hundred fry in the batch and unfortunately they all escaped."

There was a knock at the door and the young female officer who had escorted Mark to the meeting entered and handed the Admiral two signals. After the young officer had exited, the Admiral explained that he'd requested any information on suspicious deaths or incidents at sea or on the shoreline.

He informed the audience that a fishing boat had been recovered off Weymouth, which was smeared in blood with no sign of the crew. Also two people and their dogs were missing from the beach at the village of Shaldon in South Devon. So far the search for any survivors had proved fruitless. The Admiral leaned back in his chair.

"Well gentlemen, it appears the problem is now at our

doorstep, so we need solutions. Professor Yates, would you kindly take us through what you have managed to recover from the post mortem on these creatures?"

Mark rose and loaded a Power Point presentation from a memory stick. The first slide was of one of the creature lying on the stainless steel table alongside a tape measure showing it to be just less than two and half metres in length.

"This picture is one of three creatures recovered by HMS Sabre, all three were roughly the same length and weighted between forty-three and forty five kilos."

He explained that the characteristics of the creature tied in with the genes covered by the Commander. He flicked on the second slide, which displayed a close up of the serrated hook.

"Gentlemen, these hooks of which there are eight, are unique to any fish. They are very similar to those on a squid but much larger. They rotate; therefore can come in at any angle. When attacking large prey I believe they use the hooks to attach themselves to the victim allowing the head the freedom to devour the victim."

The next slide showed a close-up of the creature's head.

"This is the interesting part. The swim gills are similar to a normal fish but in addition to that, they have vascular folds in the lining of their mouths for absorbing oxygen from the air. Therefore they can breathe as easily in or out of the water."

He then pointed to a spot just forward of the creature's eyes.

"Just here are two small domes. These tie in with the creature's lateral line, which detects underwater vibrations and is capable of determining direction. It's just a guess but the complexity of these two domes and the lateral line make me believe that they're also used to communicate with each other."

He flicked to a close up of the creature's mouth.

"The head is a well constructed eating machine. The

teeth; although larger have exactly the same dental layout as the barracuda. The mouth contains two sets of teeth. There is a row of small razor-sharp teeth on the outside of the jaw. Alongside these are a set of larger dagger-like ones. All the teeth have sharp edges allowing the creature to easily cut and tear flesh from its prey. The long needle-like teeth at the front of the mouth fit into holes in the opposing jaw, allowing the mouth to close. Working on the size of the teeth and head, I'd say that one creature could devour a whole leg of beef within five minutes."

He continued to give further details of the creature's external characteristics before moving on to the report on his internal findings.

"The creature's internal organs are similar to that of any other fish except for the digestive system. Its stomach is huge compared to its overall body size, and the shortness of its intestines indicates that it has to eat a vast amount of food a day to maintain its energy levels."

Moving away from the computer console he stood at the front of the meeting desk.

"Two further things. Firstly based on what Commander Winters has told us. These creatures are hardly two years old. I would say at the current rate of growth they are capable of reaching two maybe three times this size if left to maturity. Secondly they have no reproductive organs, but unfortunately if they take the life expectancy genes of the eel they could live up to eighty-five years."

Captain Piper spoke out

"Professor, you mean we could have one of these things nearly thirty foot long."

Mark looked at the Captain

"These creatures currently move around in a shoal or as they are more eel like, swarm may be the better word. I'm saying that if not stopped you could have hundreds of them over thirty feet long swimming our oceans for the best part of the next century."

Tom Banks from the Ministry of Agriculture who had remained quiet throughout spoke.

"Professor, I assume their main source of food is fish? When you say they have to eat a lot, how much are we talking of?"

Mark thought for a few seconds.

"Taking into account the size of the stomach and intestines, I'd say they are capable of eating two-thirds of their body weight in a twenty-four hour period. At todays size around thirty kilos of food."

Tom Banks rubbed his forehead

"That's over thirteen thousand kilos of fish a day."

Mark nodded.

"Yes. They probably ended up in the English channel following the cod shoals."

"Thank you Professor." Said the Admiral and looked toward Captain Piper.

"John, I understand you have some data you wish to share with us?"

"Yes, Sir, I've brought along Chief Ward with me who took some recordings of the creatures during the attack yesterday, so I'll hand over to the Chief to take you through what we have gathered."

Sharky got up from his chair and moved toward a digital recorder that lay on the same desk as the projector.

"Admiral, Sir, these recordings were made from the underwater communications system."

Sharky switched playback on the recorder and the sound not unlike cats squealing filled the room. Mark, like Sharky, was knowledgeable on sea life sounds but he couldn't identify or relate the noise to any known creature.

"Sir, that noise was recorded about ten minutes before the attack on the divers. Just prior to the attack the noise changed to this."

Sharky switched off the recorder and selected a set point.

Switching back to play the growling sound echoed out of the speakers.

"Last night I carried some analysis out on the recordings. The first sound remained constant throughout;

however, this second sound initially started off with a spacing of .22 seconds, which reduced to .12 seconds. I believe, and it's just a hunch, that the timings reduced as the attack on the divers took place."

The Admiral looked at Mark.

"Professor, is it possible that Chief Ward is right and these creatures can communicate like that?"

Mark nodded

"Probable. They have to find food and when they do, they'll communicate it to the swarm. It ties in with my theory on their complicated lateral line."

Mark looked toward Sharky.

"Chief, I believe you transmitted on active sonar during the attack. Did it have any affect on them?"

"Yes Sir. As we transmitted it disoriented them, but it didn't affect the ones who were attacking the divers."

Mark thought for a few seconds.

"Yes. That would tie in. The creatures not at the divers would still be using their communications system for direction. When you switched on the sonar it probably acted as a jammer. Those already at the divers would not need to receive the call, so were unaffected."

Further discussions proceeded for about ten more minutes and then the Admiral spoke out.

"Gentlemen, from the information you've given me today we potentially have a major problem, not only to the United Kingdom but the world's fish population."

He took a sip of water from his glass and continued.

"I want to put a team together to come up with solutions as to how we're going to combat them. Professor Yates, I would like you to be part of that team along with Commander Winters. Commander Winters would you discuss with Captain Stone any other personnel you need in support?"

The Admiral turned to Captain Stone.

"John, I would like a daily update on this situation."

CHAPTER FOUR

The next day Mark Yates and Jeff Winters stood in the office they had been allocated. It was large, airy with ample floor space. It had an odour of new carpet and furniture polish. The walls were all painted in fresh magnolia the only items decorating them being a plastic white clock and a poster with the fire evacuation instructions.

Of the three desks available, two had computer consoles. They moved the desk with no computer to the centre of the room. On it they taped a maritime chart covering the whole of the English Channel up to the coast of Ireland. Jeff pencilled all three positions of the attacks on it.

"So, what is an American doing over here?"

"Naval Intelligence, I've been here six months now."

Mark had guessed as much and was just confirming his suspicions.

"The creatures the Admiral said the Royal Navy had prior knowledge, you must have been concerned to let them know?"

"When he said they had prior knowledge it was sent out as a general information report, so I doubt the Admiral would have been briefed on it. We never expected them to reach this far, so it was probably filed under nice to know."

"You keeping your side updated on the situation?"

"Sure am, I will be relaying any information we gain on the creatures back to Washington. I've already sent them details of your post-mortem. They will be relieved that they cannot breed. It was a major concern."

The only other person Jeff had asked to join the team was Chief Sharky Ward from HMS Sabre. He had first hand experience with the creatures and he knew that at some stage they were going to require someone with a good knowledge of sonar. Sharky had left at the crack of dawn to drive up to the Royal Navy acoustic centre and do a more in depth analysis on the recordings. By the white plastic wall clock it was just coming up to 1135 when he returned. He walked in with a beaming smile and a vibrant,

"Good morning."

Under his right arm he had two rolls of paper. He headed straight over to the table with the maritime chart on and unrolled one of them.

"Sir, Professor, I think you'll find this interesting."

The roll of paper displayed a long graph. It was annotated with frequencies on the bottom and a time scale down the side.

"What you are looking at here is an in depth analysis of the first recording before the attack."

Both Mark and Jeff nodded to acknowledge their understanding.

Sharky carried on.

"In the higher frequency spectrum there is nothing of interest, but in the lower spectrum there is a frequency tonal at around four hundred and forty hertz."

Sharky ran his finger down a dark wavy line on the graph paper.

"Notice how this line goes up and down in frequency at regular intervals?"

Jeff looked over it. "And what are all of these lines around it?"

"Oh those, that's OSN."

"OSN?" Queried Jeff.

"Sorry Sir, own ships noise. All those lines there are from machinery onboard Sabre, we just term it OSN for short."

"And you can tell that this single frequency is from the creatures?"

Sharky smiled, "You bet. It is a frequency modulated signal, the time factors tie in exactly with the recording."

Before Mark or Jeff could ask any more questions, Sharky spread out the second roll of paper.

"That first frequency was when the creatures were probably in the hunting mode. This second print out is when they changed to the growling noise, which I am going to call their attack mode."

He ran his finger down the frequency of four hundred and forty hertz again.

"See how it has changed from a wavy line to a straight line? And you see those gaps in it? Starts of at .22 second spacing reducing to .12 seconds. Bingo."

Mark asked what both he and Jeff were thinking.

"Are you saying we can track the creatures with this information?"

"Yes Professor may be a little bit difficult to track them down but once we find them a good sonar team should have no problem keeping tabs on them."

"Well Chief what do we ask the Admiral for to find these creatures?" Asked Jeff.

"Sir, you probably know about the SOSUS system, it's a underwater sensors laid along the ocean bed, primarily designed for submarine tracking, but hell they can track anything with a frequency. If we ask the Admiral to order them to start searching for these frequencies we can have the initial search underway within the hour."

Jeff proceeded to Captain Stone's office to give him an update. He returned in twenty minutes.

"The Admiral has just got off the phone to the Commanding Officer of the SOSUS station. They are setting a search on the frequency as we speak. He has also been on to Fleet Headquarters and asked for two Anti-Submarine Frigates with passive sonar arrays to be at immediate notice to sail."

"Did he say what ships Sir?" Asked Sharky.

"Yes one was Jaguar and the other Puma."

"I know both the ships Chief's I will give them a call and get a courier to deliver a copy of these graphs to them."

It was a cold damp morning, the kind of morning that you

did not want to leave the warmth and security of your duvet. Tom Davies looked down on the mudflats of Penclawdd. In the process of yawning he wished he had went to bed earlier last night instead of watching a late night episode of Law and Order.

He slipped his hand into a pocket of his worn and grubby fleece jacket and pulled out a tobacco tin. Between his calloused fingers with cracked and worn fingernails he rolled a cigarette with expert precision. Lighting it he inhaled the warm smoke. After the third puff he reluctantly continued toward the rest of the workers. There were already a dozen of then on the mud flats. He could see their tools of rakes, forks and buckets scattered around them in preparation for the dig. A tractor with a long trailer drove past, it would be loaded down with buckets of fresh shellfish by the time the tide turned. Stepping on to the wet mud he gave a shiver, it felt like his body temperature dropped with the coldness of the black slimy silt beneath his feet.

At the assembly point he noticed all the other workers had the same tired and unenthusiastic look on their faces. Three people stood out from the rest, a woman and two men all in their early twenties. From the way they were dressed, Tom guessed they were new to the job. All three wore reasonably clean jeans and their jackets did not bear the tell tale dirty cuffs from continually reaching down to the sand and mud. In his two years he had seen dozens of workers come and go. He would be surprised if all three of these made it through the week. Digging for cockles is hard work and it did not take long for people to leave in search of a less demanding role. Two of the more regular workers Dan and Sean both nineteen were never allowed to work together due to their inability to maintain a reasonable work rate unsupervised. Tom's day got worse when Sean the more arrogant of them was paired off with him. Picking up their tools they both trudged off toward their allocated spot. To the annoyance of Tom, Sean started rattling on about some bloody club he had been to the night before and he only got back at 2 am. After a minute the one-way conversation faded. Sean rustled around in his pockets and pulled out an I-phone, stuck a set of earplugs in and started nodding his head to some music. Tom thanked God that he had found some other form of entertainment.

They had been working for about ten minutes. Sean was around ten yards in front of him, still nodding away, but at least he appeared to be doing what he was being paid for. From the corner of his eye Tom caught sight of movement. About three yards behind Sean the mud began to rise until it was a long mound. Sludge slowly slid down revealing a red colouring. The mound shuddered and the whole shape of a huge eel-like creature appeared on the surface. It must have been at least eight feet long. The head still smeared with mud lifted from the ground it shook twice disposing of the residue. Its eyes flicked opened. Against the cold dark mud, the yellow piercing eyes looked on fire. Very slowly the head moved toward the direction of Sean. The young man was oblivious to what was transpiring behind him.

Tom called out but was totally ignored. At the sound of his voice the creature raised its head and opened its jaws wide. Thick saliva stained black from the mud dripped from the upper jaw. The teeth were terrifying, long pointed fangs like rows of needles packed the orifice. It began to move very slowly out of the mud toward Tom. He raised his rake and swung at the creature. Tom was not prepared for the speed the creature could move. As the rake arched toward its target, the beast in one swift movement raised its grotesque head up and back avoiding contact with the makeshift weapon.

In front of Sean the mud moved again and a second creature appeared. This time he saw it, he quickly stepped back and away from the creature emerging in front of him. On shifting his position his foot landed directly on to the tail of the first creature. The already raised head shot forward and grabbed the top of his left leg. Sean let out a scream that could only have been preceded by excruciating pain. It was so loud, that it alerted all the other diggers within a hundred yards. The sheer weight of the creature attached to his leg unbalanced him and he fell backwards. He lay prostrate, screaming and frantically trying to raise himself but unable to get a grip in the slimy sediment. The creature swung its body over Sean's chest, it shuddered and the terrified screams from him intensified. Blood started pouring from all over his body. He rolled from side to side but the creature remained locked on. The thing was continually raising its head and biting into his leg, ripping of huge lumps of flesh. Arteries and veins hung from the wound. Blood sprayed in all directions. The creatures face was covered in the thick warm liquid making its head look even more heinous and grotesque.

Tom rushed over to Sean, raising the rake he started to hit the creature. It released its bite and turned its head toward him. It hissed wildly and flashed its terrifying blood stained teeth. The power of air exhaling from the creature's mouth sent a fine mist of blood toward him. The second creature slithered towards the melee. Sean's screaming turned too hysterical crying as he saw the other creature's head come above his. Frantically he tried to drag himself along the mud but failed to make any headway. A split second before the creature struck he turned his head away in resignation of the inevitable horror. The creature snapped its jaws around his neck and shook its head from side to side. The screams and crying abruptly stopped. Tom could see the young mans windpipe protruding from what remained of his throat, blood bubbled out of it. The creature raised its head, fresh blood drained down each side of its mouth. As if savouring the warm human flesh, it held it in its mouth for a few seconds before swallowing.

The other workers had now reached the scene and all were using their tools as weapons to beat the creatures. Their efforts were continually interrupted when one of the creatures would strike toward them. Sean's face was no longer identifiable; the left side of his cheek and neck were completely eaten away. The rest of his face was just a bloody pulp. The one remaining eye was dangling from the socket. The first creature had eaten most of the flesh on the left leg and moved onto the torso. Throughout all the devastation to the young man's body his I-phone lay to one side of him, unscathed and still playing music.

It was then that Tom noticed more movement, in front, to the side and turning, behind them. The other workers also began to see what was happening and their attempts to help Sean subsided. Fear and self preservation came to the fore as numerous creatures started to slither toward them.

For a split second Tom's fear was broken when he heard the noise of a horn. He looked out over the mudflats, about four hundred yards away, the tractor and trailer was driving towards them. The other workers were shouting and waving, frantically urging the tractor on. Tom knew, even at full speed it would not make it before the creatures. Almost simultaneously three of the creatures arrived at the group, the workers kept swinging at them with their tools but they would not back away. At least a dozen more arrived, two of them made a strike toward one of the workers, it was the new female he had seen earlier. One managed to bite into her right leg. The second one snapped onto her left arm. She fell over, knocking three other workers to the ground. As they hit the ground creatures pounced onto the mangled heap of bodies. One of the men tried to make a run for it through the mass of creatures. His attempt was futile, within a few yards the creatures had brought him down. In seconds his body disappeared under a slithering mass.

The tractor was still two hundred yards away. There were at least twenty creatures at the group now, the majority of them attacking the already stricken bodies. The devouring of the humans turned into a savage frenzy. More and more creatures arrived, and started to rip the bodies apart in vehemence. Limbs were being pulled from the torsos. Chunks of human flesh were being gorged by the hoards. Blood, skin and intestines along with discarded pieces of clothing were strewn all over the slimy mud. More and more creatures were joining the onslaught. There was only himself and one other worker still standing. The creature bit him just below the knee. As he tried to escape its grip a second bit into his other leg. He fell backwards onto the cold slimy mud, more creatures bit into him, amongst his frantic screams he prayed death would come quickly.

Captain Stone opened the door to the office where all three, Mark, Jeff and Sharky were working.

"Think you should come with me."

They followed the Captain through to a room where a large television screen was showing the news. It had started with a picturesque village in Wales just a few miles from Swansea then shot to an expanse of mud flats. The newsreader went on to explain that this morning a total of fourteen people including one female were killed by unidentified creatures. Only partial remains of the bodies were found. As the report finished no-one spoke all stood in silence taking in the horror the victims must have went through. The silence was broken as the Admiral entered the room.

"Gentlemen we are going to go public on this now. I have spoken to the Ministry and they want us to take the lead on it. Professor I want you available to speak to the reporters who will be here at 1600."

At the acoustic listening station the system had been programmed to alert for any frequency coming up between 435 and 455 hertz. At 1445 a warning beeper indicated that a frequency in that spectrum had been detected. After five minutes, it was confirmed that the characteristics of the frequency tied in with those passed from Northwood. A flash signal was sent to Fleet Headquarters. The signal arrived on the Admirals desk six minutes later. Sharky Ward and Jeff Winters plotted the information on a maritime chart. The information was only a bearing from a SOSUS sensor; until two sensors could detect it they would not be able to supply an accurate range.

Mark lent over the chart.

"What time was the attack this morning?"

Sharky checked the report on it.

"Between 0730 and 0800."

Picking up a long ruler and pencil Mark drew a line from Penclawdd to the bearing given by SOSUS.

"Sabre tracked them doing around eleven knots, roughly 12 miles per hour; let's say that is their normal cruising speed and they departed Penclawdd at 0845."

Measuring out 12 miles on a set of dividers Mark moved it along the line he had drawn.

"12 miles an hour between 0845 and 1445, makes out they could have travelled 72 miles."

The lines intersected at 67 miles off the coast of Wales.

A second signal and a new bearing from the listening station arrived three minutes later. All eyes were on the chart as Jeff pencilled it in. The new bearing made the swarm moving south back toward the English Channel.

The press team consisted of TV crews from all the major channels plus eleven reporters from national papers. At the table sat Admiral Lane and Mark Yates. The Admiral introduced himself and Mark. He went on to explain that they had already formed a task group to investigate this morning's incident and they had made substantial progress in the last few hours toward coming up with a solution to eradicate these creatures.

Steve Wilson from the BBC raised his arm.

"Admiral, do you know where these creatures came from?"

"We believe they escaped from a research centre but that has still to be confirmed. So I cannot give any more information on that at present."

Steve continued, "Reports this morning said there was over a hundred of them, can you confirm that?"

I can confirm that there is a substantial number which

is believed to be in excess of one hundred."

Susan Bean from Channel 4 jumped in. "Can they breed?"

The Admiral looked at Mark to supply the answer.

"I have already carried out a post mortem on two of the creatures, neither of them had any reproduction organs, therefore they are incapable of breeding."

Susan went on.

"How long have you known about these creatures?"

The Admiral replied.

"We had suspicions of their existence two months ago, but the first confirmation was two days ago, when they were reported by a Royal Navy frigate."

The reporter from the Daily Mail raised his arm.

"You said you have a plan in force to eradicate them, can you be more specific?"

"In the last two hours we have devised a way to track the creatures, if we are able to track them, then we will be able to destroy them. The method of how this will be achieved is being worked on as we speak."

Mark and the Admiral spent a further fifteen minutes answering questions before ending the conference.

When Mark got back to the office, Sharky and Jeff had plotted another nine bearings provided by the listening station. The swarm was definitely moving south, and still on track for the channel.

"Has the listening station reported any change in the frequency?"

Sharky replied.

"No. The characteristics of the signal indicate they have been in the hunting mode throughout."

Mark looked at his wristwatch.

"It is now 1730; we have been tracking them for nearly three hours"

"Sharky if your suspicions are correct and they have not found any prey they may come ashore again."

"Agree Professor but there is another problem, when

45

they get inside the Channel they are going to go outside the range of the SOSUS sensors and we will lose contact. We need a back up system in place."

It was only when the Admiral spoke they realised he had entered the office.

"Gentlemen both anti-submarine-frigates, Jaguar and Puma sailed from Plymouth one hour ago, they should be in position to take over tracking the swarm in less than two hours."

CHAPTER FIVE

HM Ships Jaguar and Puma stationed themselves ten miles apart at the entrance to the English Channel. Their long passive sonar arrays had been streamed behind them for over twenty minutes. The sonar crews in both ships were ardently searching for the frequency of the swarm. At 2027, Jaguar reported a possible contact bearing 305 degrees. Five minutes later Puma reported the same contact bearing 040 degrees. A cross cut from both ships put the creatures sixteen miles ahead of them. Over the next thirty minutes the frequency tonal gained strength and the sonar teams had little difficulty in maintaining contact. From the information they were plotting in the operations rooms the creatures were on a course of 085 moving at a speed of 10 to 12 knots. At ten miles from the swarm, both ships brought their helicopters to a high state of alert. They were wheeled out of the hangars. On completion of flight checks they were each armed with four depth charges.

Mark and Jeff both stood in the Admirals office. Mark had requested the meeting for permission to join one of the frigates tasked to track and hopefully destroy the creatures. He suggested that now they were able to track the creatures, his knowledge as a marine biologist would be better available to the Commanding Officers of the ships. Although in all honesty he did not know what good his advice would be but he felt he needed to be closer to the action. The Admiral looked at both Professor Yates and Commander Winters.

"And you Commander do you wish to join the hunt as well?"

"Yes Sir, I would like to be of any assistance I can in destroying the creatures."

Admiral Lane picked up a signal from his desk.

"This is the latest report from Jaguar and Puma. The swarm is ten miles ahead of them. The ships are going to manoeuvre so they end up between both ships. When that happens they will attack using depth charges. That gentleman should be within the hour."

The Admiral looked at his watch.

"However! If anything does go wrong I want you two chaps to be on hand to advise the Commanding Officers. There is a helo leaving in fifteen minutes for Yeovilton. You can be transferred from there to one of the frigates I will get my staff to inform them you are coming."

Mark and Jeff both thanked the Admiral and turned to leave. Before they reached the door the Admiral spoke out.

"Commander Winters, send Chief Petty Officer Ward into see me. I will be getting him to rejoin Sabre tomorrow, if needed she will sail to join the other units."

One hour later Mark and Jeff were sat in the back of the Merlin helicopter half way to Yeovilton air station. At five miles from the ships, the creatures speed reduced to fewer than 3 knots. For the next twenty minutes there was no indication that they were moving. Suddenly the tracking frequency abruptly disappeared from the sonar screens. Puma was the first to report lost contact, shortly followed by Jaguar.

Mark and Jeff were ten minutes from landing at Yeovilton, when the message was relayed that both warships had lost contact. Mark spoke to the pilot over his headset.

"Ask them what part of the channel they were adjacent to when they lost contact?"

The helo had landed at the Air Station when the answer came through. The pilot relayed that they were adjacent to Dartmouth.

"You think they are coming ashore?" Asked Jeff.

Mark nodded

"Unless they have stopped transmitting. It can be the only reason they have lost contact."

The pilot turned to Jeff.

"Commander I have Northwood on the circuit, they want to speak to you." The pilot pressed a button in the cockpit,

"Go ahead and speak Commander, you are on line."

"Commander Winters speaking."

"Commander this is Captain Stone. From you asking where the creatures were I assume you believe they have come ashore?"

"Sir, Professor Yates believes it can be the only reason."

"The Admiral would like you take the helicopter and go down along the coast of Dartmouth and see if you can spot anything suspicious going on."

"Yes Sir. But its dark and we may not see a lot."

"Understand that but get the pilot to use his searchlight along the coast, better that than doing nothing."

The helicopter was in the process of being refuelled, another ten minutes and they would be airborne. It was less than thirty minutes flying time to Dartmouth.

They moved slowly along the coastline, the bright searchlight sweeping along the shore below. Mark, Jeff and the Aircrew man looked down for anything that would indicate the creatures were in the vicinity. With the door open it was bitterly cold and Mark was glad of the flying suit. They had been searching for over ten minutes with no sign of anything suspicious. Mark looked away from the beach toward land; it was a bright full moon night. As the light of the moon came from behind a cloud it lit up the fields adjacent to the beach. In the nearest field he saw a flock of sheep running around erratically. It was a large field with roughly two hundred animals in. The sheep seemed to be panicking, all bolting towards the far end of the field. Mark called to the pilot to bring the helo around and investigate what was going on with the sheep. As the pilot turned the aircraft, the searchlight's beam fell on the field below huge snake like figures glistened under the bright light. They were all heading in the same direction, towards the terrified animals. The sheep had now reached the far end of the field and were climbing over each other trying to escape the oncoming mass. Some animals had already been attacked and were being devoured by the creatures. The animals were becoming more hysterical. At least six had tried to jump the fence and ended up tangled on the barbed wire. Others tried to bolt, but ended up being brought down into the seething mass. Mark looked around the field everywhere the searchlight hit was alive with the creatures.

The flight observer who was sat next to the pilot was busy on the radio relaying what was happening back to HQ and the two frigates. Mark spoke to the pilot over his headset.

"If you put me down on the other side of the field and I hook you up to the fence, do you think you could pull that fence out of the ground?"

The pilot looked at him and nodded and began to lower the helicopter to within six feet of the ground. Mark jumped out rolling onto the damp grass. Out of the helicopter, the sound of the frightened sheep put a whole new dimension to the fear that was running through the poor animals. The first waves of creatures had reached the flock and were ripping into them. There was nowhere for the animals to escape they were totally surrounded in a corner of the field. This was the first time he had seen the creatures alive, they looked more evil and as murderous as he had previously imagined. The Merlin hovered just twenty feet off the ground. Mark looked up and saw the aircrew man lowering the cable and hook. He grabbed the line and pulled in about six feet of it. On reaching the fence he wrapped it around the barbed wire fence and clicked the hook on to the cable.

He signalled to the crewman to heave in. The Merlin slowly started to rise and the wire fencing began to break. As the final wire snapped, the surviving sheep tore through the gap in the fencing. Mark lay directly in their path. The petrified sheep hit him at every angle. He stumbled and fell to the ground. He tried to get up but was knocked over again. Some of the terrified animals saw him and attempted to jump over his body but only succeeded in hitting his head and body with their hoofs. In the panic and frenzy to escape most just clambered over him. When the final sheep had passed, Mark felt dazed and bruised. He looked toward the gap in the fence. The unlucky animals that did not make the escape lay dead or dying. Most of the creatures were gorging on their victims but a few were crawling over the sheep, through the gap in the fence and toward him.

The nearest creature must have been less than fifteen yards away. Another three a few yards behind. The Merlin's searchlight lit up the area; the creatures raised their heads and hissed. For the first time Mark felt for his safety. He turned to run but after one step was pulled to the ground a searing pain shot up his right leg. In the mauling by the sheep his trousers had become snared by a length of barbed wire that was still connected to a fence post. He tried to pull free but the rusty barbs dug deeper into his flesh. Sitting up he grabbed hold of the wire and started to urgently unravel it. In his haste to free himself, the wire pierced his hands. Blood poured out of the cuts making his hands wet and slippery. For a split second he looked up and caught sight of two creatures heading toward him. They were so close he could see the murderous intent in their eyes. The closest of them was only five yards away. It rose and opened its jaws just enough to display the frightening teeth. A wave of fear ran through him like he had never felt before. He intensified his effort to remove the wire. Skin was being ripped from his legs. The cuts on his hands began to pump blood at a dramatic rate. Conscious that he should be feeling pain, he did not. His self-preservation had taken over. His heart was pounding so rapidly that he felt his chest would explode. Suddenly an incredible noise surrounded him and he could feel a strong blast of heat hitting his face.

The pilot of the Merlin seeing him in trouble had brought the helicopter to less than four feet above him. The noise of the engine and rotor blades was deafening. The downdraft from the rotor blades created a powerful vortex around him.

Not only did it surprise Mark, but also the advancing creatures. They stopped and coiled back against the force of the draft and noise. The pilot's quick thinking had bought him just enough time to free himself. Getting to his feet he ran in the same direction as the fleeing sheep. The Merlin tracked his movements. At about thirty yards away from the field it came to the hover just off the ground. He ran straight toward the entrance. He could see the aircrew man and Jeff waving him in. As he jumped through the doorway he could feel the pilot was already raising the helicopter to a safe height. Pulling himself up to a sitting position he smiled and held a bloody thumb up toward the pilot. Flying above the field they could see at least sixty carcasses of sheep that were being devoured more remained obscured from sight by the mass of creatures feeding on them.

The Merlin remained over the field reporting back. HQ informed them that two further helicopters were approaching from Yeovilton and would be on the scene in six minutes. Both the helicopters joining would be armed with heavy machine guns. As if in tune with what was intended to happen, two minutes before the other helicopters arrived, the creatures turned back toward the sea. The main group were still twenty yards from safety when the armed helicopters came out of the night sky. Positioning themselves just above the beach they commenced firing into the slithering mass. When the gunfire started the creatures increased speed to escape. Mark was amazed at the swiftness they could move out of water. He could see dozens of them dead between the beach and the field. Some wounded were still attempting to make it to the safety of the sea. The helos continued firing until all movement had stopped. At first light a detachment of Royal Marines from 42 Commando arrived at the scene and cordoned of the area. The final death count of the creatures reached one hundred and sixty four.

Mark and Jeff were now standing on the bridge of HMS Jaguar; the Merlin had dropped them off on the warship prior to returning to base. On arriving onboard, Mark was taken to the sickbay and his wounds cleaned up. Although he was adamant he was in date for tetanus the young female medical assistant was even more adamant that he drop his trousers and have another. After much debate, Mark could see he was not going to win and agreed to the needle being injected into his buttock.

Jaguar along with Puma continued to trail their passive arrays in search of the swarm. Since the creatures had returned to the water no unit had gained contact. The Captain of Jaguar, Andy Spencer sat in his chair on the bridge. He turned to both the visitors on his ship and gave a welcoming smile.

"Professor and Commander welcome onboard. Did Needles sort out your wounds Professor?"

"Needles, you mean the medic?"

"Yes, a nickname the crew gave her, not many come out of the sickbay without an injection of some sort. But it helps to keep any malingering down."

Mark's face cringed.

A broad smile came over the Captain's face.

"She didn't?"

Mark nodded and rubbed the right cheek of his backside.

The Captain still smiling looked at Marks trousers that were ripped from the right knee down.

"Quartermaster get hold of the Chief Stores and see if we can get the Professor some trousers?"

The Quartermaster acknowledged the Captains request and dialled a number on the internal phone.

To help Mark passed his measurements to the QM.

"I am 32 waist 31 leg."

The QM nodded and he passed the figures over the phone as medium regular.

"Well do you think they are still in this area?" Asked the Captain.

Mark nodded. "I am pretty sure they have remained near the shoreline. If they are following the patterns of eels, when frightened they will find somewhere to hide until they feel confident enough to come out again."

A young radio operator asked permission to come on the bridge and handed the Captain a signal. The signal was from HQ, giving a detailed account of last night's action. It also advised on the next plan of attack against the creatures. HMS Sabre was sailing to join Puma and Jaguar. Once contact was gained they would track them until confident on the range and bearing. All ships helicopters were to be armed with depth charges. Sabre will go active on sonar and be handed control of all the aircraft to execute a co-ordinated drop of all the weapons simultaneously on the creatures.

"How many depth charges will that be Captain?" asked Mark

"Each helicopter will carry four so that will be twelve in total, going to be one big underwater explosion."

A chubby looking sailor came on to the bridge carrying a pair of combat trousers. He looked around and his eyes fell on Mark's torn attire.

"Sir can I assume these are for you"

"How did you guess?" Said Mark smiling.

The sailor remained blank faced and handed him a book to sign to say he had received the trousers.

At 1300 HMS Sabre arrived at the scene, she took up station five miles astern of the other two units. At 1515, HMS Puma reported a possible contact bearing 110 degrees. Two minutes later Jaguar, gained contact that corresponded to the one Puma was reporting. At 1525 Puma reported a second contact bearing 160 degrees. Jaguar gained contact on this new bearing shortly after. The Captain was in the Operations Room when Puma reported a third contact. He turned to Mark.

"We now have three contacts all with the characteristics of the creatures, any idea what is going on?"

Mark gave a worried look. "This was something I hoped would not happen, whilst they are young they will remain in a swarm, however as they mature they will break into smaller groups and eventually end up hunting individually."

"So what you are saying, if we do not take them out in a hurry, these things could end up all over the ocean, with no way of us tracking them down?"

"Correct whilst they remain in a swarm they will continue to communicate together, individually they have no reason to transmit."

The Captain called to the senior plotter.

"Which is the nearest contact to us?"

"It appears to be the one on a bearing of 165 degrees, Sir."

The Captain spoke into his microphone.

"Sonar how many contacts are you tracking now?"

"Sir, we have just gained another contact, which makes a total of four tracks, all have the same characteristics."

The Captain raised his microphone and uttered.

"Damn, at least four groups, so the most we are going to take out is twenty-five percent."

The Captain turned to his Principal Warfare Officer.

"We are going to go for the contact on the bearing of 165, inform Puma and Sabre that is the intended target."

The Captain picked up a signal pad and wrote down an update for HQ, he handed it to the on watch communicator.

"Send this immediate."

Both passive ships started tracking the same designated contact. Crosscuts indicated it to be only five miles ahead of the units. HMS Sabre who was five miles astern of Puma and Jaguar increased speed to close them. With the swarm at two miles both units were confident they had a good solution on the target and all helicopters were launched.

Sabre closed to three miles astern and was all ready to

go active on her sonar. Sharky Ward stood behind the sonar crews ready to transmit when ordered. As the contact passed by the two tracking units Sabre went active on her sonar. By the second transmission she had gained sonar contact with the target. The Helicopter Controller saw the sonar contact appear on his display and directed all three weapon carriers toward the drop zone. On his radar screen Captain John Piper watched the aircraft take up position. The sonar track was heading directly toward the centre of them. As the swarm entered the drop zone, the Aircraft Controller passed over the radio circuit.

"Standby drop, now, now, now."

On the third now, all three helicopters moved forward from the hover and began dropping their deadly cargo. Eight seconds after hitting the water, the depth charges exploded, sending plumes of water thirty feet into the air. The combined shock wave shot out, hitting the ships metal hulls with a loud thud. The sonar crew on Sabre saw clearly on their screens the huge contact caused by the water disturbance. The position of it tied in exactly with the last known position of the swarm.

The aircraft from Jaguar and Puma were directed to return to there respective units. Sabres own helicopter was tasked to go and investigate the area of the attack. It hovered in the area of impact looking for any sign that the attack was successful. The water disturbance from the explosions looked murky grey standing out clearly from the rest of the sea. After ten minutes the helicopter reported nothing sighted. Two minutes later the first creature floated to the surface. Over the next ten minutes the helo reported in excess of fifty creatures floating on the surface. Sabre increased speed and closed the area. At four hundred yards from where the helicopter was in the hover, the Officer of the Watch could clearly see through his binoculars the red of the creatures floating on the surface. Captain Piper ordered the ships boat to be launched. Onboard were sailors armed with automatic weapons, they were to proceed to where the creatures were and ensure they were dead.

Two minutes after the depth charges exploded, both Jaguar and Puma reported that they had lost contact with all the other contacts they had been tracking. Captain Spencer walked into the Sonar Room.

"Could it have been the explosion that has caused the system to malfunction?"

The Sonar Controller replied.

"Negative Sir, the system is working perfectly, it's just like they all switched off together."

For the next seventy-two hours the Royal Navy ships searched the Channel hoping to regain contact with the remaining creatures. At midnight on the third day with no contact, they were ordered to return to harbour.

CHAPTER SIX

The depth charge attack was on October 26^{th,} it was now the 4th December. Since losing contact with the swarms no other reports had been received regarding attacks at sea or shore. Royal Navy units had been tasked to search designated areas for the creatures. It had turned out to be a long boring and fruitless task for the navy and not a welcome duty.

Two weeks after the last sighting, Mark and Jeff had returned to Northwood for a meeting with Admiral Lane. They had worked out that they had destroyed nearly three hundred of the creatures. But it remained a worrisome thought that over two hundred remained unaccounted for. They summarised that the only solution could be that the creatures had moved out of British waters and returned to the deep waters of the Atlantic Ocean. Admiral Lane asked Mark to produce a report on the creatures for the Ministry to be passed to all other countries. The report was on the Admirals desk within two days.

Ten days on from that meeting, Commander Jeff Winters had returned to the United States and was working out of the base at Norfolk Virginia. Professor Mark Yates was currently lecturing at a university in Oxford, but due to fly out to Tobago in the Caribbean for some research and a few days holiday. HMS Sabre was now in dry dock for scheduled repair work and Sharky Ward was on two weeks leave at his home in Hampshire.

It was cold, wet and windy as the deep-sea fishing vessel Blue Rover rolled through the heavy swell. Waves continually breached the ships side, leaving the recovery deck awash with water. The Skipper had just ordered the nets to be hauled in. This would be the last time before they altered course back to harbour. Fishing had been pretty dismal in the last two days. The holds were only half full, but from the weight on the nets being recovered, it appeared that this catch would go someway to meeting their quota. They had already been out twenty-four hours longer than planned. If they did not leave after this catch they would have difficulty getting back before Christmas Eve.

The winch hauling in the net screeched and strained under weight. Seagulls were flocking around the boat, squawking in anticipation of the fish that were soon to appear. Six deckhands fully clothed in bright yellow waterproofs stood prepared to receive the catch. The Skipper watched on from outside the bridge door monitoring the evolution taking place. He flinched as yet another wave crashed over the recovery deck leaving the deckhands standing in over a foot of water. Although those on deck were secured with safety lines the force of the water breaching the ship was making it extremely difficult for them to maintain their footing. As the nets became vertical the winch screeched even more as it started to take full weight. A white mark on the cable passed through the pulley at the top of the derrick indicating another forty feet to go before the catch would be clear of the water. Suddenly the recovery cable began vibrating. The Skipper pursed his lips tightly and prayed they had not snagged an underwater obstruction. Last time that happened it had taken two hours to sort the nets out and a good catch had been lost. Approaching twenty feet to go the vibration on the cable became so severe the deckhands moved away to a safe distant fearing that the cable would snap. The senior deckhand looked up to the skipper, visually asking if he should stop the recovery. The skipper paused in thought for a moment then rotated his hand slowly, indicating to continue heaving in. As the top of the net broke the water, the net and cable started to shake violently, banging against the hull of the ship. It looked certain that the cable would either give way or the nets would get snagged on something. The screeching from the winch got more intense, recovery of the cable became painfully slow. Two of the crew moved over to the side of the boat to get a view of the net as it began to clear the water as they did with a sudden thud the cable bounced, the winch lost control and the net dropped back below the sea.

At the forty feet mark the cable went tight again. The winch stuttered and whined with the strain. Like a tug of war between the winch and the catch they were in a stalemate position neither willing to succumb to the other. The battle of wills lasted for few minutes then the winch slowly responded to the challenge. Painfully screeching it began to sluggishly rotate. Every few rotations it stopped as if building its strength for the next effort. At the next rotation it gradually gained momentum and maintained a steady but slow recovery. The twenty feet to go mark once again came visible. Two deckhands moved to the stern of the ship to check the nets were not snagged. As the nets broke the surface, both deckhands started pointing to the nets and shouting toward the Skipper. Assuming the nets were snagged the Skipper gave the order to stop heaving in. The senior deckhand rushed and joined the two men at the stern.

Inside the net was a mass of red shapes like huge worms coiled together. As the creatures slithered around in the mesh they got sight of their ugly ferocious heads. There mouths were opening and closing exhibiting terrifying teeth. There must have been at least six of them trapped, along with hundreds of fish.

The senior deckhand gave a hand signal that the nets were clear and the winch began to haul in the catch the last few feet. The Skipper new exactly what he had caught, he had read about them a couple of months ago and seen the television report on the attack at Penclawdd. He did not want to lose this catch, but he did not want to risk letting those things loose on his deck.

Picking up a loudhailer he shouted down to the senior deckhand.

"Get those harpoons out of the wash deck locker. I am going to bring the net in but do not release the catch. I want those things harpooned to death first."

The senior deckhand returned to the recovery deck with two poles around six feet long with barbed metal points at the end. Carefully the derrick holding the net was traversed inboard and left hanging few feet clear of the deck. A deckhand stabbed one of the harpoons into the nearest creature. As the point went deep into the creature's side it jolted and smashed its head on the top of the net. Its head came down and started biting the net wildly. Another deckhand armed with the second harpoon stabbed another. The creatures were going crazy. They appeared to understand what was happening and frantically started biting into the net. Both deckhands continued to stab the creatures, again and again, but it did not deter the creatures in their endeavour to break free. One of the creatures must have been stabbed at least six times but still tore at the nets. Out of sight of the crew one of them had bitten away enough of the net to poke part of its head through. The senior deckhand seeing this made it a prime target and stabbed it rapidly at least three times in the head. It jolted is head back and disappeared into the mass of cod. Blood started seeping from the bottom of the net on to the deck.

The other four deckhands watched on. One called out pointing to the rear of the net. The armed deckhand moved to where he was pointing. A huge ugly head was pushing its way through. He raised the harpoon and drove it with full force into the neck of the monster. With the harpoon still impaled in its neck, the creature twisted its head and gave an almighty hiss, thrusting its head forward it got within range to snap its jaws shut on its provoker. The deckhand took the full force of the bite on his right arm. With the creature still attached to his arm, he fell backwards screaming on to the water-covered deck. The momentum of his fall only assisted the creature in pulling its whole snake-like body free from the net. Still with harpoon in its neck, the wounded creature went in to a frenzied attack on the deckhand. Releasing its grip on his arm it bit into his throat. The man's screams stopped immediately, the force of the bite left the head twisted unnaturally to one side with blood pouring from it mixing with the salt water slopping over the deck. Still biting into the neck it swung is huge body over him and impaled his chest and legs with eight hooks. The second armed deckhand raced to help his shipmate. When the creature raised its head for another bite he thrust his harpoon forward directly hitting the creature fully in the left eye. He pushed it with such force the point protruded through the other side of the creature's head sending it into an uncontrollable spasm. Releasing the hooks from the man's body it started squirming frantically all over the deck. The other deckhands moved away to avoid the ferocious creature, but were held back by the safety lines attached to them. It banged against them knocking then over like ten pins. Finally ending up in one of the corners of the recovery deck it twisted into a ball. One of the deckhands moved toward it and grabbed the harpoons that were still imbedded in it. Raising one of them he rammed it with full force into the creature's head. It swished its tail and lay still.

The other creatures still captured were ripping away at the net. At least two had succumbed to the wounds of the harpoons. Three remained unharmed and intent on breaking free. Rearmed with two harpoons the crew began stabbing indiscriminately at any part of the creatures. One creature had made so much progress at breaking free of its bonds that both men turned their harpoons on it. After half a dozen stabs from each it dropped back lifelessly into the hoard of fish. Only one creature appeared to remain unharmed, after being stabbed twice it cowered back into the fish for safety. The only sign of it being still alive was a long threatening hiss coming from within the net. Both men prodded the harpoons through the hoard of fish. With a sudden act of defiance the creature swung its head against the net, the move took both men by surprise. Still with its head showing, both men gathered themselves and struck in unison impaling its head at the end of their weapons. The creature hissed wildly, streams of blood leaking from its mouth. They both stabbed the beast once more and it slid lifelessly to the bottom of the net.

CHAPTER SEVEN

It was two days before Christmas; the duty Officer at Northwood picked up the phone and called Admiral Lane at his home. The Admiral himself answered after two rings.

"Sir, duty Officer Lt Edmonds."

"Yes. What is the problem Lt?"

"Sir, there has been a sighting of the creatures, one man killed."

"Where?"

"Sir, it was at sea just off the Bay of Biscay, a deep sea trawler caught six of them in their nets. They managed to kill the creatures, but one of the crew was unfortunately killed."

"Thank you for contacting me Lt."

"Sir, there is something else."

"Yes, Lt"

"The report from the trawler was that the largest was fifteen feet long."

The Admiral paused for a while.

"Did they return with the creatures?"

"Yes Sir, I have arranged for them to be transported to the research facility."

"Good, Professor Yates is due back in the country soon, I want them put on ice until he gets back."

The Admiral put down his coffee and looked at his watch. It would be 4 a.m. in Tobago now. The old sea dog gave a wry smile, refilled his coffee cup, pulled a well fingered notebook from his pocket, and dialled Professor Yates.

Mark stretched out his arm and picked up his mobile.

"Yes?"

"Hello Professor, Admiral Lane here."

"Oh hello Admiral."

Mark looked at his phone and saw the time was 0410.

The Admiral without explanation of ringing at this time went straight into the report on the recent incident.

"Professor, I am a bit concerned that these creatures have grown nearly five feet in less than three months."

Mark agreed and did not know of any other marine creature with that rate of growth.

"Professor, I am going to contact Commander Winters, I would like you and him to pop down to that research facility where the creatures originated from and find out exactly what they were doing with those fish to get them to grow so quickly?"

"Admiral I am due back in the UK in four days."

"Yes, Professor but I thought you could delay that a day or two and go via Florida"

Mark still struggling to regain his senses from waking up agreed, to the plan.

"I will get my staff to arrange flights and transport for you. They should contact you in the next couple of hours with details."

"Admiral could you get them to delay contacting me for at least four hours? It is 4 am here right now."

At the other end of the phone the Admiral smiled.

"Good God, sorry Professor, forgot about the time difference, you get back to sleep and we will talk later."

Mark managed a smile himself, he knew the Admiral was too smart a man not to know exactly what time it was in Tobago. He looked once more at the time and dragged himself out of bed toward the bathroom. As he exited the bathroom he looked at the bed to see Jennifer, the barmaid from the diving clubhouse. The dim light from the bathroom produced a beautiful silhouette of her black naked body against the white sheets. She rolled over and opened her eyes.

"What time is it?"

"4:25"

She looked at him, waved her hand, closed her eyes and drifted off back to sleep. Mark made himself coffee and sat on the veranda of the beach cottage. His mind was now clear of sleep and he was thinking about the creatures, five feet in three months, the possibility of it amazed him, but also made him nervous. He remembered the incident with the sheep. God if they reach full maturity it would be devastating if they attacked in numbers again.

He arrived at Miami International airport at 9:20 am on December 27th. Jeff Winters flight was due to arrive at 1015. He took a coffee at Starbucks and waited for him to arrive. Jeff's plane was on time. It was nice to see him again they greeted each other like old buddies and talked and joked as they made their way to the car hire. The drive to the research centre took just over ninety minutes. Jeff had already cleared their arrival and two passes waited for them as they pulled up to the gates. The centre was an isolated building only thirty metres from the shoreline. Mark could see the fish pens at both sides of the main building. Each pen had pipes running into them leading from a brick building, he assumed to be the water purifier. As they drove towards the centre he could see the sea wall that had been breached in the hurricane over two years ago. The substantial repairs to the stone barrier stood out clearly from the much older construction. They parked the car just short of the building in an area marked for visitors. As they got out of the car two people exited the door of the building, a man in a white coat of around fifty-five and a woman in her early thirties. The woman caught Mark's attention immediately, dark haired and slim. She was dressed in a pair of jeans and a sweater with a designer logo on it. Reaching the couple, the woman moved forward and introduced herself as Lisa Michaels the senior researcher. The man was Paul Coates her assistant. Mark was a little taken aback and felt quite guilty at assuming the positions would have been reversed. As they shook hands, he detected a seductive hint of perfume from Lisa. Her hands felt soft and warm. Unaware of why he did it, he looked down at her hands for any sign of a wedding or engagement ring. The sight of her bare fingers pleased him. Lisa smiled at him as if she was reading his mind and he suddenly felt like a naughty boy that had just been found out. As they walked through the building Jeff ended up in conversation with Paul Coates, leaving Mark with Lisa.

"Professor I read your reports on the creatures, very interesting."

He smiled at her. "Please call me Mark."

"So I understand you want to discuss their abnormal growth?"

"Yes, if our figures are correct, then, these creatures are capable of growing around twenty inches a month."

"Actually we have recorded them growing nearer twenty-four inches, but those specimens were boosted with growth hormones."

They reached an office door with Lisa's name on it followed by a list of qualifications. Entering the comfortable office they sat around a large oval coffee table. Paul went over to a table where fresh coffee was brewing and prepared them all a drink.

Jeff spoke first. "Lisa, our concern is the growth rate so any information on that would be our priority."

"Certainly Jeff, you are probably aware that three things effect the growth of a fish, water space, environment and food supply?"

Mark nodded as Lisa continued.

"We were trying to develop a fish here that would satisfy the United States population. We have not got the water space at the research centre or the environment but what we can do is provide food with additional growth hormones to encourage growth."

She picked up two pieces of graph paper and handed them to Mark and Jeff.

"These graphs indicate the success rate at which certain growth hormones have worked on other fish. We have recently found genetically binding the growth gene of the common carp has achieved incredible success and we are now using that in the majority of our experiments"

Mark looked up from the graph.

"Is this the growth gene our creatures were given?"

Lisa nodded.

Mark studied the graph closely.

"One of these figures indicates that one specimen grew four hundred per cent larger."

Lisa nodded again

"Yes but that experiment also involved the use of a peptide growth hormone, so the growth factor could not be fully attributed to the growth gene"

"Did our creatures have the peptide growth hormone?" asked Jeff.

Lisa smiled "No, they just received the growth gene."

Mark broke in "So without the growth hormone would you expect our creatures to be growing at this rate?"

"Taken into account the three things to stimulate growth. We gave them the gene, but now they also have the water space and environment. So I am not altogether surprised they have maintained this rate of growth."

Jeff asked a question that he was dreading the answer to.

"How big could they grow?"

Lisa looked at her assistant.

"In all honesty I do not know the answer to that, when we discovered the creatures terrorising the Keys and Miami originated from here we stopped that particular experiment, but there is something you should see."

They exited another door in her office leading on to a long corridor. Turning into another passageway Mark was immediately struck with the smell of seawater and dampness in the air. Lisa stopped at a large metal door with a security keyboard on and tapped in a code. The doors opened electronically and they followed her inside. Inside they could hear the sound of air being pumped into water. One side of the room was completely covered by a fish tank it must have been fifty feet across and thirty feet deep. Paul Coates went over to the tank and flicked a switch at the side, the tank completely lit up.

Jeff and Mark looked on in amazement and shock. Before them was a creature at least thirty-five feet long and its body was twice as thick as a man's chest. It was coiled down in the tank, its mouth slightly opening then closing like it was gently snoring.

"I thought you stopped the experiment?" said Jeff.

"We did, this is a different version, this one is not vicious, I could get in the tank with it now and it would probably be more afraid of me. Basically it is very similar to the sea cucumber. It just eats and sleeps."

"Exactly what does it eat?" queried Mark.

"We have been feeding it fish, laced with a peptide hormone."

Lisa walked over to the tank and pointed at his head.

"If you look, very tiny teeth and on the underside no sign of those claws that the others inherited from the squid genes. This guy just swallows its food rather than biting into it."

Jeff walked over to the tank for a closer look.

"How old is it?"

"He is thirty months old, unfortunately he will not be living much longer. After the holidays he is being destroyed and his flesh is going to be checked for compatibility for the food chain."

Lisa said it so matter of fact, that Mark felt some regret for the creature. This gentle giant had been raised purely as an experiment, spending his short life in a tank and was now on death row. Even after death his flesh would be cut up and dissected, frozen and probably fed to the other experiments when of no further use.

Lisa looked at Mark observing the creature.

"You don't approve do you?"

Mark turned his gaze toward Lisa. Their eyes met and locked together for a split second. Her skin was totally unblemished and tanned. Highly defined cheekbones enhanced her deep brown eyes. He could tell by the way she looked at him she was studying him just as deeply.

"I can understand the reasoning behind your work, but

it does not make me like it. I see whole communities of fish living in harmony on the reefs, but placing something alien into that community can disrupt and destroy it. You are trying to solve the shortage of fish here, but can you imagine what could have happened if those creatures that escaped could breed? They would have decimated the world's fish population."

"I know I thought of that, it was another reason why we aborted that experiment."

He thought of the people killed so far.

"Another reason or the main reason?"

Lisa did not answer, but forced a tight smile on her face.

He suddenly felt guilty and stupid for making the remark.

A shout from Jeff got them both out of an awkward situation.

"Lisa, what do you think the life span is of our creatures?"

Lisa and Mark both walked toward Jeff.

"Taking into account the genes we used and they are now in an excellent environment with no known predators, I would say minimum forty years max around seventy-five"

She shrugged her shoulders.

"Sorry it is a big ballpark but that is the best I can come up with."

She took them around the rest of the complex pointing out other experiments that were in progress. Mark viewed a pen containing bass at least twice the normal size.

"So do you think any of these will ever end up on the dinner plate?"

She shrugged her shoulders again.

"Well with the worry over growth hormones in beef right now, even if we do come up with the perfect fish, it will probably take years to get it authorised for food production."

As they left the room Jeff and Paul Coates walked

ahead, Mark continued to walk alongside Lisa.

"Look, I apologise for the cheap comment earlier about your reasons for ending the experiment."

She looked at him and gave a forgiving smile.

"No need for the apology, I understand your feelings toward marine life and I would probably be just the same in your position."

They headed back to her office on arrival Lisa opened a drawer on her desk and handed both Mark and Jeff a memory sick each.

"This has got all the information we have on the experiments with the creatures, hope it helps."

For the next forty minutes they discussed how they expected the creatures to act over the next few months. Lisa agreed that the swarms would probably reduce in size until eventually they would break up and each creature would go it alone, the time scale for this was up for debate.

On more than one occasion Mark found himself immersed in watching Lisa, the jeans she was wearing fully complemented her shapely legs and slim waistline. Her warm smile matched her attractiveness her perfume was clean and yet seductive which could only have been designed with a beautiful woman in mind. He was comfortable and enjoying the time in her company. He hoped the chemistry between them was not a figment of his imagination. She must be nearly ten years his junior was it all just wishful thinking. He was positive that on more than one occasion their eyes had exchanged interest in each other. What if she sent these messages to all men? Imagination or not he was not looking forward to the time they would have to leave. Unfortunately a few minutes later Jeff hinted that they were going to have to depart if they were going to make their flights. Lisa walked back around to her desk and picked out a card from her drawer, before handing it to Mark she penned something on the back of it.

"This is my business card I have put my cell number on the back if you need to contact me when I am not in office."

As she handed it to him, their hands brushed together. He felt a surge of adrenalin run through his body. Once again he found himself questioning whether that was deliberate or his imagination. As they shook hands at the main entrance he felt himself holding on to her hand a few seconds longer than normal, she did not resist. She smiled at him once again and he smiled back.

On the drive back to the airport Jeff brought up a question that he had obviously been giving some thought to.

"The attack on Penclawdd?"

"Yes?"

"Do you think it was coincidence that the creatures were there when those poor cockle diggers turned up?"

"You suggesting it was a planned attack?"

"Well what the hell were they doing concealed in the mud?"

Mark thought about it, whales and dolphins are capable of carrying out co-ordinated attacks, but their intelligence levels are much higher, anyway this would not have been an attack but an ambush.

"Jeff I am sure it was just a coincidence. The creatures were probably holed up there for the night the tide went out leaving them covered with mud."

Jeff looked at Mark with a look that said he was not totally convinced.

CHAPTER EIGHT

It was a cold and wet day when Mark walked out of Heathrow airport. He had not slept on the flight back, he was going over what Jeff had brought up in the car regarding the Penclawdd tragedy. Before Jeff had mentioned it he had also considered it strange that the creatures would just happen to be where humans turned up most days. And to bury themselves in the mud, why? He would head back to his flat in Oxford, then travel down to the research centre on New Years Day; he wanted to take a closer look at the creature's brain. On stepping into his flat he stripped off his clothes, he worked out that he had been wearing them for two days. Throwing them into the washing machine he headed for the shower. Cleaned, he lay on the bed and was asleep within ten minutes.

Being New Years Day traffic was light and it was an easy drive to the Ministry of Defence research centre. As he pulled up to the parking zone outside the main building he could see two other cars parked, as he passed the first one he saw the security pass in it belonged to Colin Peters, one of the researchers he met last time.

It was he who came to reception to meet him.

"Happy New Year Mark."

"Happy New Year to you Colin."

Colin had already taken the largest of the creatures out of the chiller earlier that morning and it was on the table ready for checking.

"I have already measured it, it is a fraction over four point eight metres. All the wounds on it are from the harpoons the fishermen used to kill it."

Mark stood back and viewed it, God it looked awesome, the body on it was like one thick muscle, and the head just looked evil.

"I count sixteen wounds on it." said Mark.

"Actually two more underneath total of eighteen,

fishermen said even direct stabs to the head did not stop them."

Checking over the creature's external characteristics nothing appeared different everything just a great deal bigger than last time.

"Colin what I really want to achieve today is get a weight of the brain and spinal cord"

"You are checking for intelligence then?"

"Yes"

"Have you got the facility to do a check on the cerebral cortex"?

"Well I could call in our specialist in that field he only lives three miles away, would you like me to see if he is available?"

"Lets see what the brain and spinal cord come up with if it looks suspicious then we will call him in."

Mark and Colin both worked together on removing the brain and spinal cord, after thirty minutes both parts of the creature's anatomy lay in separate surgical dishes. Mark positioned the surgical scales on the table opposite and placed the creature's brain in first, the digital screen read out 1090 grams. Colin let out a whistle in surprise. Mark placed the tissue from the spinal cord in next, the screen flashed up 109 grams.

Colin looked at Mark and moved towards the phone.

"I will get our specialist in."

Mark left the research centre three hours later arriving back at his flat around 2200. As he entered he picked up the phone and rang Admiral Lane.

"Admiral it's Mark Yates."

"Hello Professor Happy New Year."

"Happy New Year Admiral, unfortunately we need to speak, can we meet?"

"Certainly Professor, why don't you come down tomorrow and have lunch, say 1300?"

Mark agreed and the Admiral provided him with the postcode and directions to his residence. He looked at his watch 2220, it would now be around 1720 in the States, he picked up the phone and made two more calls, one to Jeff Winters and the other to Lisa Michaels.

The Admiral's residence was just outside Chichester in West Sussex his house was a Victorian building and only accessible by a small country road. As he drove up to the large house he admired the beautiful gardens, even now in January they looked tidy and cared for. Neatly trimmed hedges bordered one parameter, whilst on the other side an old wall protected the garden from the chilly northern winds of the English winter. Pulling onto a gravel driveway alongside the front entrance Mark got out of his car and took a deep breath of the country air. The Admiral appeared from a gate at the side of the building. He was dressed in well worn corduroy trousers, a barber jacket and a pair of rubber boots. On his head was balanced a flat cap and in his right hand he carried a walking stick. As he approached the car he was joined by two cocker spaniels. Both dogs sprinted over to Mark and excitedly greeted him, a third dog an old black Labrador trailed out from the gate. The Labrador walked slowly and was clearly in the twilight of its years, on reaching the Admirals side it laid down appearing to welcome the opportunity for a rest. The front door to the main house opened and a woman in her late fifties exited she was slim and dressed in a pair of white cotton trousers and blue lambs wool jumper she looked immaculately clean and vibrant. As she walked over to where Mark and the Admiral stood she stretched out her hand to greet Mark.

"Hello Professor Yates, so nice to finally meet you, I am Mary."

"Please call me Mark, Mrs Lane"

"And me Mary"

She turned to the Admiral.

"Donald take the dogs around to the conservatory, and I will take Mark on in."

The Admiral nodded smiled at Mark and tapped both

spaniels with his walking stick and headed back towards the side gate. Both dogs sprinted ahead of him. The old Labrador, who was called Buster, got up, looked at the Admiral heading towards the gate and decided to opt for following Mark and Mary through the front door. Mark was led into a warm and comfortable room where a log fire was burning, Buster bimbled over to the fire and flopped down in front of it.

"Tea or coffee Mark?"

Mark went for the tea.

As she left, he browsed around the room. In a glass cabinet stood a photograph of the Admiral and Mary on their wedding day, he was a young lieutenant and Mary an extremely attractive young woman in her early twenties. Later photographs showed them with two children, both girls. Another was of both daughters as teenagers with a black Labrador puppy. He looked at Buster, now fully stretched out asleep and snoring. Mary and the Admiral returned together, he had changed into more comfortable clothes. Mary poured two teas then left them to talk whilst she prepared lunch.

"Well Professor, why do I have a feeling that you are not going to be giving me good news about these creatures."

" Admiral what I did not do in the first post mortem was to check the creatures brain, but in discussion with Jeff Winters and his concerns over the Penclawdd attack I carried out a full analysis on them yesterday."

"Why would the Penclawdd attack prompt you to check its brain?"

"We think the attack was possibly more than just a coincidence that the creatures were there, it is possible it may have been pre-planned."

The frowns deepened on the Admiral's brow.

"Are you going to tell me that the creatures staged an ambush?"

Mark nodded.

"From the data recovered from yesterday's post

mortem, as bizarre as it sounds, yes, it is a possibility."

The Admiral picked up his tea and leaned back on his chair.

"Go ahead Professor."

"Admiral, Elephants, have brains nearly four times the size of humans, but we do not consider them to be four times as smarter. Scientists believe a more accurate factor in determining a level of intelligence is the ratio between brain weight and the spinal chord weight. Normally a fish brain weighs less than the spinal chord. In apes the ratio between the brain and spinal chord is 8:1. In humans 50:1. In dolphins it is 40:1 theoretically putting them about on par with us."

"And our creatures Professor"

"The ratio is 9:1"

"So you are telling me that these creatures are slightly more intelligent than apes?"

"I think they are a lot more intelligent, another factor to be taken into account is the cerebral cortex that is the part of the brain where learning, memory and thinking goes on. A cerebral cortex, which is deeply folded, indicates that the brain has a greater surface area for thinking. I had an analysis and MRI scan carried out yesterday on the cerebral cortex of the creature, the folding in it points towards it being a lot smarter that the ratio between the brain and spinal cord indicate."

"Just how smart?" Asked the Admiral.

"To put it in perspective, try not to think of intelligence as we know it, our brains function towards the environment we live in, these creatures live in extremely different surroundings. For example one of your missiles may contain a highly sophisticated computer system, but that computer system is geared to one prime aim to hunt and destroy. Our creature's brains are geared to hunting for food and surviving"

"Which suggests Professor?"

"They are extremely good at it."

"Admiral look at how they responded to date. After

they were attacked in Dartmouth, they went into hiding. When they came out they broke into smaller groups. After the depth charge attack they stopped transmitting and went into deeper water. It is not exactly the actions I would expect a shoal of fish to do."

The Admiral went quiet for at least a whole minute, stood up and walked towards the bay window overlooking the garden.

Without turning he asked.

"Did you get anything from the research centre in Florida?"

"I met with the senior researcher, she confirmed that they were given a growth gene and she believes they could continue growing to at least thirty feet now they are in large expanses of water."

"Have you spoken to her about yesterdays post mortem?"

"Yes, I phoned her last night, she was as surprised as I was, but she is having her team doing a post-mortem and biopsy on a similar creature today."

Mark thought of the poor creature he had seen in the tank, he knew that its brain would be the one being sliced and diced."

CHAPTER NINE

Mark had just arrived back at is flat when his mobile rang. It was Lisa Michaels.

"Hi Mark we have checked our specimen so far it is all normal. I passed your information on to the Department, are you sure those figures are correct?"

"Hi Lisa the figures are correct, if you wish I will email you a contact at the research centre who should be able to provide you with the technical data."

"Yes, please do, I know I am going to have to provide an updated report in the very near future."

"Have there been anymore sightings of the creatures?"

"No nothing since December twenty second."

It went quiet on the phone for a few seconds as each struggled to think of something to say.

"So how was New Year for you?" Asked Lisa

"I slept through it and spent the day dissecting one of the specimens, how about you?"

"Oh I saw in the New Year and the holidays with my parents."

He smiled, pleased that there was no mention of someone else.

"Lisa, I hope you do not think I am being a bit forward but next time I am down your way, would you like to have dinner one night?"

"I would like that very much." Came the reply.

When they finished the call Mark smiled to himself, it would be nice having the time to find out more about her.

Mark poured himself a Mount Gay rum and coke and slipped the memory stick that Lisa had given him into his laptop. He went through each stage of the development of the creatures. It was getting near 2am when he came across an entry made by a researcher Tim Connors.

01 September

All Specimens are maintaining a growth rate of thirty-eight per cent above normal. To determine if this level of growth can be increased, batch number 365 will be subjected to GnRH. It is planned to carry out this trial over a 28 day period commencing on 2nd Sept.
Tim Connors

That entry was three days before Hurricane Francis hit. Mark switched to the Internet and typed GnRH into the search engine. GnRH could be used for a number of reasons but the one that caught his attention was the use of it to increase human height and the stimulation of releasing hormones from the brain.

He looked at his watch it was twenty minutes passed two; he picked up his mobile and called Lisa.

"Hi Lisa, I have found an entry in the data you gave me that the creatures did receive a growth hormone."

Lisa's tone got slightly defensive.

"I did not authorise any growth hormone."

"No it was authorised by a Tim Connors, three days before the hurricane."

Lisa went quiet for a few seconds.

"That would be early September, yes I was out of the country for four weeks, Tim would be supervising the project in my absence, but he did not discuss anything like this on my return."

"Lisa is it possible that this GnRH they were given could have stimulated brain growth?"

"GnRH is used in a number of ways, we would not know what effect it would have on less vertebrates so anything is possible."

"Look I am going to call the Admiral first thing in the morning, I am going to ask that a specimen is sent to your labrotaries as soon possible, I will get our researchers checking the remaining creatures."

"Mark, I am sorry I should have double checked that data myself."

"Forget it, hopefully we now have the answer."

After Mark's call to the Admiral, two specimens were packed and prepared for despatch to Florida; they would be on a Royal Air Force flight at 1600 that day. The MoD research centre contacted Mark and advised that a neurologist had been brought into the laboratories to carry out more extensive investigation into the remaining creature's brains. Admiral Lane requested Mark, to collate the information from both research facilities and to give him an update.

The wedding that afternoon of Sean and Diane had gone well, the weather had stayed dry and although now raining the guests were secure in the warm comfortable Riverside Club function room. The sound of laughter and music filled the room where over one hundred guests enjoyed themselves. Less than fifty yards away at the back of the Riverside Club lay the Atlantic Ocean, waves from the mighty ocean crashed on to the Galway shore. As one large wave reached the extremity of its venture on to land, it began to roll back to the ocean and in doing so it revealed a long thick sleek shape. The shape moved towards land, weaving a slow but deliberate course. More shapes appeared like they were being planted by each wave. They moved together, heading deeper inland away from the crashing waves. The final creature left the soft sand broaching the wet and thick grass; it moved deeper inland joining at least forty more of the dark shapes.

In an empty building at the rear of the clubhouse a teenage couple, fuelled by alcohol were engaged in a passionate relationship. The darkness and the rain falling on to the tin roof enhanced the eroticism of the moment for them both. The young man slipped his hand beneath the girls skirt and began to ease her panties and tights down her legs. As he successfully manoeuvred the underwear to her knees something cold and wet pressed against the back of his legs. He froze and discontinued the task at hand. In the darkness he pushed his right leg out to remove the obstruction. As his leg pushed against the obstacle he felt it move. In an instant his heightened sexual mood was replaced with anxiety. Just for a moment the obstruction released the pressure on his legs. Before he could consider his next move he was hit by tremendous force followed by excruciating pain in his right leg. He fell backward on to the adjacent wall and felt powerful jaws biting into his leg. The girl still with her panties and tights wrapped around her knees fell to the ground. As she hit the damp cement floor a grotesque head bit into the side of her neck, the warm blood from her jugular vein sprayed erratically into the darkness of the room. The young man still lay half propped against the wall screaming hysterically as he felt pieces of his flesh being ripped from his legs. His pain, fear and screaming came to an abrupt end as he was yanked to the ground.

Kieran Doherty stood by one of the exit doors watching the rain and attempting to clear a throbbing headache that had been with him since he arrived at the wedding party. From above the background music he heard what sounded like a scream followed by another. By the doorway lay a discarded cardboard box, he picked it up and used it as a makeshift umbrella and headed towards the direction of the scream. The grass was deep so he walked around the perimeter on his tiptoes to avoid the wet turf hitting his trousers. Arriving at the outbuilding he found the door half open. Moving closer he could hear sounds coming from inside, he listened for a few seconds, it sounded like dogs eating. His first thought was foxes. Just outside the door he found a light switch and flicked it on, it was a fluorescent fitting and it flickered on and of intermittently for a few seconds until it gained full power. Pushing the door open to its full extent he stood in shock, the floor was covered in blood. Two shapes lay on the floor, from one protruded a partial leg with a girls shoe hanging by a single strap, the other shape was covered in grotesque creatures. The creatures turned their heads to the open doorway, the two closest slithered towards him. Kieran dropped the cardboard box turned and ran. Less than twenty yards from the light of the exit door, his feet clipped something on the ground, he fell rolling on to the wet and slippery grass. In the urgency to get back up he slipped again dropping back on to his knees. As he pushed down on his arm to raise his body he felt excruciating pain as teeth sunk into his flesh and powerful jaws clamped around his leg. He screamed in agonising pain rolling around kicking with his free leg at the creature. Even amongst the noise of his screaming he could hear the sound of hissing coming closer to him. Sheer panic encouraged him to move. In desperation he crawled on all fours, still with the creature attached to his left leg. Noise was all around him wherever he looked shapes were appearing from the dark, all heading towards him. His mind cast back to the remains he had witnessed in the out building. He began to scream out for help, tears rolling from his eyes, urine soaked into his already wet trousers. He was still screaming as a second creature bit into the arm supporting his body weight. He dropped face down onto the wet surface. From the ground he turned his head to see a huge monstrous head with jaws open, he tried to scream but nothing came out. The creature's jaws hit his face with such force that the long sharp teeth sunk deep into his right cheek bone and pierced his closed eye.

Through the exit door that Kieran had used long red shapes slid through. A few seconds later the music from the function room was drowned out by terrified screams.

CHAPTER TEN

Mark stood in the newsagents looking at the papers on display.

The headlines did not look good, the Daily Mail led with "Massacre at Galway" and The Sun "Eaten Alive". All papers were asking what the Government and Royal Navy were doing to rid these creatures from the seas. He had been summoned for a meeting with the Admiral at 1600 today, the results from both research centres had been completed and there was to be a videoconference linked up to Florida. He walked out of the newsagents with the Daily Mail under his arm and got into his car. He arrived at Northwood by 1530 and made straight for the meeting room.

As he entered the room it was apparent that there was going to be more personnel than at the previous one, already there was a number unfamiliar faces around the table. Three ministerial looking officials who were all dressed in similar dark suits and opposite them two high ranking naval officers, one Rear Admiral and a Commodore. Colin from the MoD research centre was sat with another unfamiliar face that Mark assumed to be the specialist who had conducted the in depth analysis on the creature's brain. Tom from the Ministry of Agriculture was also there, Mark noted he was dressed exactly as he was last time they had met. The Commanding Officer of Sabre, Captain Piper entered the room, smiled at Mark and took a chair next to him. In the corner of the room stood a large flat screen television, speakers from it were strategically placed on the table along with four microphones. Admiral Lane entered accompanied by Captain Stone, once again all the Naval Officers stood until he was seated. Captain Stone switched on the television and the screen displayed two people both who Mark immediately recognised. Captain Stone spoke in one of the microphones and tested communications with

Florida. Lisa replied, "We hear and see you fine, I am Lisa Michaels the senior researcher and with me is Paul Coates."

Admiral Lane spoke.

"Welcome Lisa, I am Admiral Lane, we appreciate you have taken the time to join us, I will not do introductions for time is pressing so if anyone speaks please introduce yourself. I think we know why we are here, this problem with the creatures has now become very serious. I assume you are aware of yesterdays attack at Galway with the loss of nineteen lives?"

Mark saw Lisa nod on screen.

"We are Admiral."

The Admiral continued.

"Lisa we have carried out a comprehensive check on the creatures here, has your team got anything to add to the report that was forwarded to you?"

"Yes Admiral, I think we have found something of interest, we confirm the figures that were sent to us regarding the creatures intelligence levels, but we believe we have also found something else regarding the brain."

"Good news we hope?" said the Admiral.

Mark could see Lisa smile back at the Admiral.

"Well yes and no, we believe the creature's brain has a form of BSE, similar to what is described as Mad Cow Disease."

The Admiral looked towards the MoD researchers for confirmation.

"Do we support these findings?"

The specialist spoke out.

"Hello I am Doctor Steven Fields I must admit I did not come across this in my checks."

Lisa replied.

"Doctor, it is very early in its stages and we nearly missed it, but all our analysis points towards it being BSE."

The Admiral asked the question that everyone wanted to know.

"So Lisa, if this is true, will it eventually kill them?"

"Unfortunately until we get an older specimen, we cannot tell at what growth rate the BSE is moving at, could be months or years, in addition we only had two specimens to work with so we cannot be a hundred per-cent sure they are all effected."

Mark raised his hand.

"Hi Lisa, Professor Mark Yates for those who do not know me, how do you think the BSE will effect them, if the disease progresses in a normal manner."

"Hello Mark, well we would expect them to become even more aggressive and start to become very erratic in the way they operate, once they get to the latter stages they will become very docile and depending how fast the BSE progresses at they will eventually die. I would say that they would remain in the aggressive stage for at least twelve to eighteen months."

The Admiral broke in.

"So what you are saying Lisa that these creatures are going to continue to grow to over thirty feet and are intelligent enough to stage an ambush and there is a good chance they will turn psychopathic in the near future?"

"That about sums it up Admiral."

The Admiral looked around the table at all seated.

"Well it appears we cannot wait for the creatures to die through disease, therefore we are going to have to come up with some sort of plan to destroy them, right now I will take any ideas anybody has."

Captain Piper raised his hand to speak.

"Sir, I met with my sonar team this morning and they have come up with an idea that they could transmit noise into the sea that could attract the creatures into a specific area."

The Admiral moved in his chair.

"Go on Captain."

"Sir, the underwater specialists onboard Sabre believes that with the right equipment they could send recordings at the correct frequency out through a towed transducer that in the right water conditions could be picked up by the creatures up to 80 miles away."

Mark raised his arm.

"Admiral I have used a similar method in some of my research to attract sea life by using sound which has been very successful."

The Admiral was clearly taking an interest in the idea but added "However as you are aware we have not heard anything from them transmitting at their hunting or attacking frequencies since October, so we do not know if they will respond to us transmitting it into the sea."

"Well Admiral, maybe we can attract them with other sounds." replied Mark.

"The creatures require lots of food, we could also transmit other fish noises that would get their interest, groups of whales for example these noises along with their hunting call may be enough to get their interest."

The Admiral looked around the table for any other suggestions, none were forthcoming.

"Captain can you liaise with the Professor on what sounds may be suitable and get the sonar chaps to check the frequencies are compatible?"

"Yes Sir."

The Commodore from Fleet Headquarters in Portsmouth spoke.

"Sir, the problem I see, is how we will know if the creatures have been attracted?"

Captain Piper raised his hand again to answer.

"I also discussed that with the sonar specialists, we could use sonar buoys launched from aircraft to let us know if the creatures are in the vicinity, the plan is to modify the hunting call we are transmitting with a hidden signature, that will identify it from the real McCoy, so the operators will be able to identify what is ours and what is coming from the creatures."

"Captain when could Sabre be fully operational for this?" Asked the Admiral

"Sir, with the right support from the fleet maintenance

team we believe we could be ready in four to five days."

The Admiral turned to the two other senior Naval Officers who were from Fleet Headquarters and referred to them by first names.

"I want the work on Sabre made top priority, if it means working around the clock, make it so, I want her fully operational for this mission in three days."

Both Senior Officers nodded.

The Admiral turned towards the television and spoke to Florida.

"Lisa, I am having two more specimens flown down to you for analysis. They should be on an aircraft some time this evening."

"Thank you Admiral, my team will be ready to start as soon as they arrive."

"We will get our team looking at the remainder of the specimens to see if we can confirm they are all carrying BSE."

The Admiral turned to Tom from the Ministry of Agriculture.

"Tom I want all fishing vessels to be made aware of these creatures and to report back immediately if they come across them."

Tom nodded and scribbled something in his notebook.

The meeting carried on for another forty minutes with the discussion being mainly around the plan of transmitting the sounds into the sea and how to destroy them if they do fall for the trap. As the Admiral left, Captain Stone tapped Mark on the shoulder and asked him to drop into see the Admiral before he left. Ten minutes later, Mark was sat down in the Admiral's office in a comfortable leather chair. The Admiral sat behind a desk, which looked a genuine antique, but in pristine condition.

"Professor, I would like you to devote your time to helping us with this problem, would it be possible for you to drop any further commitments for say the next two months?"

Mark smiled.

"Admiral, I cannot see a problem, the university did have me pencilled in to do some modules, however, that is over four weeks away and I am sure they should be able to find an alternative lecturer, I will speak to them tomorrow."

"Excellent Professor, if needed I can talk to the university and will let them know you are on official government business."

"Thank you Admiral."

"Professor now you are officially on my staff, there is one thing that is niggling me."

"Yes Admiral?"

"Since these creatures broke into smaller swarms, we have seen very little of them, we had the one incident with the fishing vessel in the Bay of Biscay and the Galway incident, even taking into account that these were different swarms, that still leaves at least four swarms wandering around somewhere, where the hell do you think they have got to?"

"Admiral, I have a hunch that they have moved into different parts of the Ocean, if they are acting like eels they are extremely territorial, I would not be surprised if at least three of those groups are now out of British waters and well into the Atlantic."

"So you think there may be problems for other countries soon?"

"In all honesty Admiral I am surprised we have not already heard of any incidents abroad."

"Well let's get rid of our problem first and then start worrying about the rest of the world, when Sabre sails I would like you onboard Professor."

CHAPTER ELEVEN

Four days later Mark stepped off the train at Plymouth railway station. A sailor, wearing a cap marked HMS Sabre was there to meet him. Although Mark said he was okay the sailor picked up his suitcases and led him to a blue estate car parked outside the station. As they pulled into the dockyard, he saw six warships tied up alongside the long jetty; the grey sleek ships looked impressively powerful with the guns and missile systems adorning their decks. Sabre lay last in the row of six, from her funnel came a whisk of fumes, indicating she was getting ready to sail. He walked over the gangway on to the frigates flight deck to be met by an Officer flanked by two armed sailors. The officer stepped forward and introduced himself.

"Welcome onboard Sir, I am Lt David Wild the Officer of the Day, the Captain has asked me to escort you to your cabin."

Mark followed the Officer through the helicopter hangar and a large watertight door; they entered into a long passageway at the end they turned left into a small alcove and into a cabin that Mark would be using. The cabin was small, a bed that doubled as a seating area and a table that could be clipped back on the wall to create more room when not in use. On one of the walls was a metal cupboard with three small drawers to hold his belongings. The Officer gave him a quick tour of the area, pointing out the bathrooms and toilets which he referred to as the heads. On arriving back at his cabin both his suitcases had been placed in it, they were taking up the entire floor space. As he was looking at the stowage problem one of the crew tapped on the door.

"Hello Sir, I am the Captain's Steward, he asked me to check you were settled in okay."

"Oh I am fine thanks"

The Steward looked at the two suitcases.

"Sir, the suitcases, when you finish emptying them, if

you pull out this drawer under your bed one will fit in there and the other will go in the space at the top of your locker."

Mark thanked him for the tip. The Steward took Mark through the domestics of meal times and the nearest emergency exits, he also handed him a lifejacket to keep in his cabin. The ships main broadcast bellowed out calling the ship to harbour stations. As he unpacked and deposited the suitcases where he had been advised, he felt the movement of the warship as she moved away from the jetty.

The Captains Steward appeared once more at his cabin door carrying a blue waterproof jacket.

"Sir, the Captain would like to know if you would care to join him on the Bridge, I have brought you this jacket to use whilst onboard."

Slipping into the jacket he followed the Steward up two flights of ladders, the final one emerging on the frigates bridge. As he stepped on to the bridge, it was a hive of activity, the Captain sat in his chair supervising the proceedings. Mark stood at the back, looking through one of the windows as the ship moved towards the exit of Plymouth harbour. Swinging around in his chair the Captain smiled at him and outstretched his hand to greet him.

"Professor, welcome onboard, hope you are being well looked after"

"Extremely well Captain"

When Sabre was clear of Plymouth harbour and into the English Channel, the Captain handed control of the ship to the Officer of the Watch and took Mark down to his cabin. In the cabin, Mark could hear a speaker monitoring communications between the Bridge and the Operations room which kept the Captain updated on how things were proceeding. The Steward he had met earlier duly turned up with hot drinks, over coffee the Captain gave Mark a brief on what their intentions were.

"Professor we should be in a position to start operations

in three hours however we are going to delay until 0530 tomorrow morning, if we do get a chance to take these creatures out, I would prefer it to be daylight hours to confirm we have been successful."

Mark nodded in agreement.

"I have arranged a brief for all key personnel in the wardroom at 2100 tonight. Before that if you are happy I will get Chief Ward to take you around the Operations Room and let you see the set up of the sonar equipment."

Over the ships broadcast came the pipe "Hands to flying stations"

The Captain looked at his watch.

"That is the helicopter rejoining us from Yeovilton and on time."

He picked up a microphone and called up to the bridge to pipe Chief Ward to the Captains cabin.

Within two minutes Sharky appeared.

"Ah Chief come on in, would you take the Professor around the Ops Room and show him the sonar set up?"

"Certainly Sir."

The Ops Room was a just short walk from the Captains Cabin.

As Mark walked into the darkened room, he saw about a dozen large screens with different radar pictures on them, all were being manned. In the centre of the room was a large plotting table displaying a chart of the English Channel, a sailor leaned over it plotting the ships position. Sharky led Mark over to the far corner of the Ops Room where three large tape recorders were mounted on a table. The recorders had a vast number of wires interlocking them and leading into a large piece of equipment, which he recognised as a digital sound amplifier. A wire from the amplifier then led into what he assumed was the sonar equipment.

"Well Professor this is the dry end of the equipment, one of the three tape recorders is pre loaded with our creatures calls, the other two have fish sounds that will hopefully be enough to attract them."

Sharky handed Mark a headset that was plugged into the amplifier and switched on the tape recorder with the creature's hunting call. He listened as a clear tone of the creatures call came through both earpieces.

"The sound has been digitally enhanced, when it passes through the sonar system it will be put through two oscillators which will bring the sound down to the frequency our creatures communicate at, that frequency is what will be transmitted into the sea."

"Sharky, any idea how far the sound will travel?"

"Well based on the predicted oceanographic conditions, I believe it will be audible to the creatures at around sixty to eighty miles."

Mark and Sharky left the Ops Room and headed to the quarterdeck.

At the ships stern laid two large yellow torpedo shaped devices about six feet long.

"This is the wet end the frequency from the sonar will be transmitted through these. We have two just in case one gets a defect."

"How far will it be towed behind us?"

"About 600 yards astern of us, the depth will be based on what speed the ship is doing but probably around sixty feet. We are operating in the channel so we have to be careful of shallow water areas, if we move into deeper water then we could go a lot deeper."

Two hours later Mark was showered and changed into fresh clothes. The Captains Steward had informed him to put any dirty clothing outside his door and he would organise for it to be laundered. Mark thought he could get used to this. At 2100 he was sat in the Wardroom with around sixteen-crew member's mostly Officers but there was four Senior Ratings including Sharky. Against one of the walls was a large map of the channel with reference points marked on it. The Captain entered the Wardroom and proceeded to the front. The Operations Officer took the stage and provided the audience an introduction on the operation, the Captain thanked him and stood up to speak.

"Gentlemen, we believe that at least one swarm of the creatures we came across four months ago is still operating in British waters. When we encountered them they were over two metres long, the last time they were sighted, two weeks ago, they had increased their size to nearly four metres. Our marine specialists believe that unless stopped they will continue to grow up to eight metres in size. These creatures are intelligent and if we are to have any chance in taking at least one swarm out, we must get it right, they will not be fooled a second time. It is imperative that the creatures do not hear any sound that they could associate with any previous attack. Therefore underwater transmissions are to be strictly controlled. The only transmissions going into the sea will be the fish noises and the creatures hunting sound. Tracking of the creatures will be done completely passively by the Maritime aircraft which are on station throughout. Before I finish, I would like to introduce Professor Mark Yates who is a marine biologist, I am sure if you want any information on the creatures the Professor will be happy to discuss it with you."

As the Captain sat down Sharky stood up.

Sharky took us through the area we would be operating in, just at the entrance to the channel, our patrol area would be a twenty-five mile box, Sabre would be operating at six knots with the noisemaker streamed six-hundred yards astern. The SOSUS station had been directed to monitor the underwater surveillance system for the frequency of the creatures, they would be monitoring to the north and northwest of us. The maritime aircraft would be dropping sonar buoys to the south and southwest of us; this would provide total coverage if anything approached from the Atlantic or Irish Sea. Once contact was gained with the creatures, the maritime aircraft would start to track the contact. When they were confident of their position they would drop a full pattern of eight depth charges on them.

A young Officer asked Sharky how many sonar buoys

the aircraft would be monitoring. Sharky told him that the aircraft would initially be dropping sixteen buoys two miles apart, giving them a total coverage of over thirty-two miles. Sharky anticipated the next question of how would the aircraft know where the creatures were in relation to the buoys. The Chief explained that the buoys are numbered one to sixteen, the range prediction of each buoy is less than two miles, therefore, if buoy number seven gains contact with them, we know that the creature's position is within two miles of that buoy. On gaining contact they will drop further sonar buoys closer together to refine their position, once they have pinpointed their position they will carry out the attack.

Sharky moved on to oceanographic details of the area and the expected range prediction of the noise travelling through the water, he confirmed the expected range our transmitted hunting and fish noises would be detectable out to at least seventy miles.

Sabre's helicopter was not going to be employed as a weapon carrier but it was to have depth charges loaded ready for use in case the aircraft failed to deliver.

The Operations Officer finished off the briefing stating that the noisemaker would be getting streamed at 0530 and that all crews were to be closed up by 0500.

CHAPTER TWELVE

It was 0515, Mark stood on the dimly lit quarterdeck watching the sailors prepare to launch one of the noisemakers; he was thoroughly impressed by the professional manner in which all the team carried out their tasks. It was a cold, dark and wet morning and they had just been rousted from their beds thirty minutes earlier but appeared to be full of enthusiasm and humour towards the objective. The whole operation was carried out with very little talking, Chief Ward hardly needed to say a word to the sailors, an occasional point and nod appeared to direct them on what to do. The electrical armoured cable was attached to the nose of the noisemaker, the maintainer carried out last minute checks to ensure the power and receiving circuits were fully functional, once he was happy he indicated by thumbs up that it was ready for deployment. On getting the okay, Sharky signalled to the winch driver to start hoisting slowly, two sailors either side of the noisemaker ensured it left the deck safely. The winch continued to hoist until it was clear of the deck and hanging just below the top of the davit. Sharky detailed two of the team to turn the davit outboard which left the noisemaker hanging like a great yellow fish above the water. Picking up a microphone he reported to the bridge that the noisemaker was ready for streaming. The order came back exactly at 0530 to commence streaming. As the winch began to pay out the cable, a white spray of water was the only indication of the noisemaker hitting the water. In a few seconds it sank below the surface and out of sight.

It took nearly fifteen minutes, before a marking on the cable indicated it had reached six hundred yards. Once the required length was achieved, the maintainer once again hooked up the testing equipment and carried out further checks. Looking at his readouts he smiled and gave another thumb up that everything was working. The report went through to the bridge that the streaming had been completed and maintenance checks were correct.

By the time they got back to the Operations Room, the maritime aircraft was on task and just commenced laying the barrier of sonar buoys in the designated area. Sabre was in radio communications with the SOSUS station and keeping them updated on the operation. Ten minutes later the aircraft reported that all buoys had been laid and were ready for monitoring. The Operation Room carried out a time check with both the aircraft and the SOSUS station and informed them that they were about to start transmitting the creatures hunting signal. Within ten minutes both the aircraft and the SOSUS station reported they had detected the signal from the noisemaker.

Sharky wandered around the block of tape recorders and sonar system like a mother hen watching her chicks, he adjusted output levels and checked the depth of the noisemaker, which was registering just over sixty-five feet. Satisfied everything was working as it should, he suggested to Mark that they take the opportunity now to get some breakfast, he did not expect anything to happen for a while.

Sabre maintained a speed of five and half knots to keep the noisemaker at the chosen depth, it was now 1100 the noisemaker had been transmitting for over five hours with no response from the creatures. The Captain walked into the Ops Room and handed a signal to Mark, it was from Northwood. Lisa Michaels had reported back that the two specimens sent to them both contained the BSE in their brains, but the rate of growth of the disease was minimal from the earlier specimens and they would probably not be effected for at least another twelve to eighteen months. The Captain had highlighted paragraph two of the signal, there had been a reported sighting of the creatures, just off the Azores where they had attacked and killed two divers.

"Do you think they are our swarm Professor?"

"Possible but unlikely, I still believe that at least one of the swarms has marked their patch in and around Britain, there is still a lot of cod around and I do not think they will be moving on whilst food is readily available."

"If there is so much fish around why did they go out of their way to make an attack on Galway?"

"Look at it like a bear, a bear will risk being stung for honey, solely because he enjoys it so much, I think our creatures have a taste for warm blooded red meat, and if it means taking risks to get it they will."

"So we can expect more attacks on land?"

"Unfortunately Captain, I think as they get larger and their food intake increases, we will see a lot more, and if Lisa Michaels is correct, as the BSE takes effect they will take even greater risks."

Mark joined the Captain for lunch, as they sat in his day cabin a call came over one of the speakers.

"Captain, Sir, the maritime aircraft wishes to speak to you urgently."

Mark followed the Captain through to the Ops Room, hoping to hear that someone had gained contact with the creatures.

The Captain put on a headset and entered into discussion with the aircraft. Mark noticed a frown appearing over his forehead.

He finished the conversation by telling the aircraft to await further orders. He took off his headset and called out for everyone to listen in. The crew in the Ops Room removed their headsets and turned to face the Captain.

"The aircraft flew over us five minutes ago she has reported that we have a swarm of creatures following us about fifty yards astern. The problem is that they are too close for the depth charges to be dropped. It appears that us transmitting the hunting frequency has just made us a homing beacon for them.

Mark nodded in agreement.

"I agree Captain. I can only assume that until they find the fish or other swarm they will not start transmitting."

"Problem is Professor I need to take these things out in one go and make sure there are no survivors, the only way we are going to get that done is by depth charges. If we switch off the noisemaker they will probably just disperse, so we need to come up with some sort of plan that is going to work."

From the corner of the Ops Room a hand came up from one of the radar plotters.

"Yes Seaman Winter?" said the Captain

Everyone looked at Winter who was the ships comedian expecting him to come out with some stupid idea.

"Sir I could not help overhearing you and the Professor talking. We know they like meat, so why don't we empty the fridges, tie it all to lifejackets so it floats on the surface and while they are tucking into it, we will open the range away from them giving the aircraft a chance to blow them sky high."

The Captain looked at Winter, and then looked at Mark, who nodded.

"Seaman Winter that is a pretty sound idea, well done." said the Captain.

Winter smiled at the radar operator sat next to him and whispered,

"This is really going to piss the Caterer off."

The crew emptied the fridges of all its meat within twenty minutes. The huge joints of meat were tied to lifejackets so they would hang about thirty metres below the surface. In turn the lifejackets were linked together to provide an ideal target for the aircraft to aim the depth charges at. Mark suggested as the meat is being dropped overboard they switch from the hunting to the attacking signal on the noisemaker, which should encourage the creatures to go for the bait.

The aircraft overflew Sabre again and reported that the creatures were still astern of them they made the swarm around forty-five to fifty strong.

The Captain, made a main broadcast to the ships

company.

"This is the Captain speaking currently we have a swarm of the creatures fifty yards astern of the ship. The intention is to drop meat into the sea, hopefully this will occupy them whilst we open the range. Once we open the range, the aircraft will then drop a pattern of depth charges on them, there is a chance that we will still be close enough for the explosion to affect the ship, therefore damage control teams are to close up immediately and all watertight doors and hatches are to remain closed."

The Captain then got the warfare team together.

"At the rate those creatures eat, the Professor believes we will only have five minutes before they disperse, so we have only one shot at this. The aircraft is maintaining a distance of four miles from us, as soon as we drop the bait, I will be ordering it to make its attack run. They will be dropping the charges, whatever range we are at. When the bait hits the water we will start transmitting the creatures attack signal and the ship will be brought to maximum speed, I want everyone off the upper deck before those depth charges are dropped."

The Captain then called up the Officer of the Watch.

"Bridge Captain to avoid any possible damage to the helicopter let's get her airborne immediately."

A team of ten sailors stood on the quarterdeck, the meat and life jackets were lashed outboard. All the sailors had sharp knives in their hands. As the order to drop the bait came they began cutting the lashings. The steam of bright orange lifejackets hit the water as one and slowly drifted astern. In the Ops room, Sharky switched the noisemaker to the attack signal and on the bridge revolutions for maximum speed was ordered.

From the bridge wing, the Captain watched the floating lifejackets, they were now fifty yards astern and on his right he could see the aircraft turning for its attack run. The ship began to pick up speed, the jackets were now over one hundred yards astern and the aircraft on track for its final run. Sabres huge twin propellers were digging into the water, the speed was sixteen knots and rising. The aircraft reached her attacking height and was closing the drop point fast. With the lifejackets at just over 150 yards, the call came over the radio from the aircraft.

"Standby dropping now, now, now."

On the last now eight cylindrical shapes started dropping from the aircraft, splashing into the water around the lifejackets.

As the charges were released, the Ops Room piped over the main broadcast, "Brace, Brace, Brace" warning the crew to be prepared for the explosion. From the depth charges hitting the water to the explosion it took less than eight seconds, the resulting shock wave travelled through the ship like an earthquake. Sabre was knocked off course by over thirty degrees, one of the generators failed. All main lighting was lost throughout the ship and the emergency lighting switched on immediately. Mirrors and television screens in the after end of the ship shattered, loose equipment was thrown around. The shockwave lifted the ships stern out of the water, the propellers screeching as they broke the surface. The drop back into the water submerged the quarterdeck under four feet of water.

The Captain immediately ordered the bridge to reduce speed to five knots and called for a damage report. As the shockwave subsided, it went eerily quiet on the ship, the sound of doors opening and closing echoed throughout the ship as damage control teams went about searching each compartment for any damage or flooding. First aid teams were attending those injured. The ships engines remained in tact and the ship maintained a speed of five knots. Sharky checked the sonar system, it was lifeless and he imagined that there was no noisemaker left at the end of the cable the ship was dragging behind it. Within ten minutes the initial damage report arrived in the Ops Room; seven injured none serious.

A small flood in one of the compartments was under control and it was being pumped out. A further five minutes passed before all power to the main lighting was restored.

The Captain turned to Mark.

"Well that was something that does not happen every day."

The aircraft flew low over the area the weapons had been dropped and reported back that it was sighting a number of dead creatures floating on the surface. Sabre immediately launched the boat to make sure that they were all dead. In the process they recovered another three specimens. The sheer size of the creatures required the boat to make two journeys to complete the task. When the boat finally returned it reported the head count was fifty-six carcasses.

CHAPTER THIRTEEN

Sabre returned to Plymouth that evening; damage to the ship turned out to be minor, although the noisemaker was destroyed and the spare severely damaged. Captain Stone had contacted Mark, the Admiral would be in Plymouth tomorrow and he wanted to meet with him before he returned to Northwood. After dinner that evening, Mark wandered into the ships hangar, the three creatures recovered were still awaiting collection and lay prostrate on the hangar deck. He looked at the biggest five metres long and must have weighed over one hundred and eighty pounds. The thought of these things reaching double the size and weight sent a shiver through him. The teeth on them were now nearly five centimetres, its mouth was wide enough to take a man's head in one bite. It was just an awesome killing machine. He removed a penknife from his pocket and pulled one of the claws from the creature's nipple, eight centimetres long, that in itself could be deadly if it pierced a human body. With nearly two hundred still loose in the ocean he knew a lot more people were going to die horrible and frightening deaths, before they were finally exterminated.

The meeting with the Admiral was to be held in one of the shore offices, the big bay window gave a clear view of the dockyard. Waiting for the Admiral he watched a warship leaving harbour. He thought to himself about the experiences on Sabre the last two days and how well they responded to the situation, it gave him much faith in the Royal Navy. The large oak entrance door creaked and Mark turned from the window. As the Admiral entered it was apparent that he had just returned from ceremonial duty, still dressed in his full uniform and wearing medals.

"Good afternoon Professor, well it was good to hear the plan worked, with a little bit of initiative from the crew."

"Yes, Admiral I was very impressed how the ships

company reacted."

The Admiral continued to speak as he removed his jacket and tie.

"Well hopefully that is our problem over with for a while, however, I have been getting a lot of enquiries from abroad about these creatures."

"More reports Admiral?"

"You sound like you expected them Professor?"

"Yes, I heard about the one in the Azores, it was just a matter of time before the other swarms started being sighted."

"As well as the Azores, we have had two sightings in Canada, the Canadian sightings were only two hours and four hundred and sixty miles apart so they must have been different swarms."

"Any loss of life?"

"Apart from the two divers in the Azores, the ones in Canada were sighted attacking whales and the others came ashore just north of Halifax at a place called Tangier and killed some cattle."

The Admiral explained that it was the Americans that had contacted him, they were getting slightly concerned that they were heading back towards their backyard and wanted any information they could provide.

"Professor they also asked if you would consider going over and meeting with a couple of their chaps to discuss what we have learnt to date."

"And you said Admiral?"

"Told them it was totally up to you, but I thought you would not have a problem."

Mark smiled, he had learnt one thing whilst working with the Admiral he knew that he had politely been told to go.

"Anyway Professor it may give you a chance to meet up with that female scientist from the research centre, my intelligence reports are that you were quite taken by her when you met."

Mark looked at the Admiral and gave a bemused smile

wondering where he got his very accurate intelligence from.

The good news as he landed at Washington was that Lisa Michaels would be attending the meeting as well as Jeff Winters. His hotel was a thirty-minute cab drive from the airport, it was late when he arrived so he went straight to his room, had a drink from the mini-bar and called it a night. In the morning, he awoke early, showered and went through some of his notes that he would be discussing at the meeting. At 0700 the hotel phone rang, it was Jeff Winters.

"Morning Mark, sorry to call you this early but there was an attack by the creatures last night, seven people killed, they have brought the meeting forward to 1100."

"Where was the attack?"

"Cape Cod Bay, they came ashore and attacked a group of people night fishing."

"Any witnesses?"

"Two people were sat in a car when the attack started and managed to escape, they said that the creatures surrounded them. By the time the police got there, the bodies and the creatures had gone."

Mark walked into the meeting room with Jeff; immediately he saw Lisa sitting at the oblong table that had enough chairs around it to seat sixteen people. Lisa smiled at him. He walked towards her, she was dressed in a powder blue jacket and skirt, the pastel colour enhanced her dark hair and brown eyes. Shaking her hand he instantly detected the same fragrance of perfume he had noticed in Florida, the touch of her hand stimulated an unfamiliar but enjoyable feeling in him.

The meeting room was filling, there were four senior Naval Officers and the remainder made up of official looking people. Mark and Jeff were collecting a coffee from the refreshments table when a man approached them.

"Mark"

Turning he saw a face that looked familiar to him"

"Alan Dempsey, we carried out some work together in the Virgin Islands back in 2009."

Mark gave a wide smile as he recognised him.

"Alan did not recognise you in a suit, only ever recall you being in shorts and flip flops."

"Yes and I have put on a few pounds as well being office bound with little chance or time to go on field trips."

Alan explained that he was now a Senior lecturer at the Seattle University but was on a retainer with the US Navy.

"So I hear you have been doing pretty well taking out these creatures over in the UK?"

"Well the Royal Navy have, I have just been helping where I can."

A senior naval Officer called out for everyone to take their seats, Mark moved back to the table and sat between Lisa and Jeff. On taking his seat Mark thought that sitting next to Lisa was maybe not such a good idea, he kept getting a wisp of fragrance from her perfume, making his mind wander from the subject at hand.

An Admiral Hawkins chaired the meeting. During the introductions of those present, Mark noticed that as well as Alan Dempsey, there were two other marine biologists, a female and male, neither of which he recognised. He looked at the agenda, he was down to speak third straight after Lisa. Lisa took the audience through what she had briefed him and Jeff previously, she also mentioned the reports on the specimens that had been flown from the UK down to Florida. The female marine biologist, who was called Kate Morgan was asking her a number of questions, some of which were inferring that Lisa was to blame for the incidents.

When Lisa had finished Mark looked at her and winked, she looked a little flustered but returned a smile. It was apparent she did not expect the type of questions Kate Morgan was hitting her with. Mark was impressed that she remained cool and prevented it from turning into an argument. He had been to a number of meetings before and come across an aggressive member, but he was used to the game now.

Kate Morgan was sat opposite, just to the left of Mark, she looked at him, he returned her a look, which said, do not even think about trying that with me. Mark talked for nearly twenty minutes on what he had discovered about the creatures. He took them through the methods the Royal Navy had used to eradicate them and the success. He passed around photographs of the last three specimens they had recovered and close ups of the claws and teeth.

Alan Dempsey asked the first question.

"Mark the noisemaker, do you think it will work again?"

"Well in all honesty Alan, we were transmitting two sounds that day, the creatures hunting call and the noise of a large shoal of fish, the creatures did not transmit themselves so we cannot be completely sure what attracted them. The problem you have here in the States is the amount of coastline you have, our fishing pond was a lot smaller, but to answer your question, if we can get a good location on them there is a good chance the noisemaker will work again."

The Admiral spoke.

"Professor it appears our biggest problem is how to locate them, have you any ideas on that front?"

"Well Admiral there was an idea I was toying with, if we do not have success with the noisemaker. We could attempt to take one alive and put a transponder on it, then release it and let it direct us to one of the swarms."

Alan Dempsey was nodding; he knew as well as Mark how much success they had with transponders on sharks and dolphins.

Kate Morgan ventured a question against him.

"If we do manage to capture one, and we release it again, what is the guarantee that it is going to team up with a swarm?"

"Well.............Kate isn't it, as I covered in my brief, these creatures are extremely intelligent and I suspect they employ an extremely good communication system, I am fairly confident that a lone creature would make it back to one of the swarms with little effort."

Jeff Winters asked the obvious question.

"Any ideas how to catch one?"

"Jeff, these creatures are where the fish go, exactly the same as your fishing vessels. Six were trapped in nets off the Bay of Biscay, I think it is just a matter of time before another fishing vessel pulls one up, so we just need to let all fishing vessels know not to kill it."

The Admiral nodded.

"Sounds a reasonable idea to me, I have also spoken to Admiral Lane about acquisition of the noisemakers and sonar equipment, he suggested that as HMS Sabre is already fully equipped with the sonar equipment that she is deployed to America and made available to us if required. She sails from England tomorrow and should be here in eight days."

The Admiral tasked one of the other Naval Officers to get a notice out to all fishing vessels that if they capture one of the creatures it is to be kept alive.

After the meeting Mark, Lisa and Jeff went to a nearby restaurant for lunch. Both Lisa and Jeff were due to fly back to their offices tomorrow. Jeff had already arranged to attend a reunion with an old friend from the Navy. Lisa and Mark, both with no plans agreed to meet for dinner.

CHAPTER FOURTEEN

Mark arrived back at the hotel around 1600; Lisa was staying with a friend and would be meeting him at 1930 for dinner. The thought of having a whole evening with Lisa by himself brought a smile to his face. He sat down in the hotel reception and read a newspaper report on last nights attack at Cape Cod. Of the seven people killed three were teenagers; all boys, the other four were adults. Those that escaped reported that the creatures had come out of the sea, but as the people turned to run, there were more creatures behind them. Police stated that they had found marks that indicated that some of the creatures had come ashore about fifty yards away from the scene of attack and moved in land and ended up behind the victims. As much as Mark wished it to be a bit of bad luck that the creatures had stumbled upon the fishermen, he knew that it was too much of a coincidence that they came out of the sea driving the victims towards others waiting behind them. The thought that these creatures were co-ordinating attacks made him feel extremely uneasy.

His mobile rang it was Admiral Lane.

"Hello Professor, I heard the meeting went well?"

"As well as can be expected, considering."

"Look Professor, Admiral Hawkins was very impressed with you, asked if you would consider joining up with his team until they get a grip on the problem?"

"How long are we talking Admiral?"

"Well a couple of weeks maybe three, think they should be up with the hunt by then."

"And where will I be based?"

"We did not discuss that, Commander Winters should be able to fill you in on the finer details."

By that statement Mark knew that the Admiral had already agreed to him staying and had put the wheels in motion. He decided once again to take the route with least resistance.

"Ok Admiral, I will speak to Admiral Hawkins office tomorrow, I understand Sabre is on her way?"

"Yes thought the ship deserved a trip abroad after her sterling work against those creatures. Oh by the way Professor understand you and that lovely young American scientist are out to dinner tonight, do enjoy yourselves but go easy on the expenses."

Mark smiled to himself, as always the Admiral seemed to have a very good intelligence system.

"Thank you Admiral, I will keep you informed."

Lisa looked stunning as she entered the hotel reception, it was a cold evening and she wore a three quarter length coat. Her high heels blended into her shapely legs like they were part of her body. She beamed a smile as Mark approached. Reaching her he blurted out what was going through his mind.

"God you look amazing."

"Well thank you" replied Lisa.

"Thought we would have a drink in the lounge here before going on to the restaurant, our table is booked for 8:30."

"Suits me fine." said Lisa

As she entered the bar area, Lisa removed her coat to reveal a black dress that fully advertised the shapely body beneath it. Mark smiled again and rolled his head.

"What is wrong?" Asked Lisa.

"I cannot get over how great you look."

She gave him a slightly embarrassed smile.

They sat at a small table and talked about nothing in particular, but obviously enjoying each other's company. Mark kept getting an urge to hold her hand, but managed to control himself, although he did touch her more than once during conversation, which she did not seem to mind.

"So do you know me well enough to tell me about yourself?" Asked Mark.

Lisa told him she was 34, never been married but had lived with a partner for four years in her late twenties, that had fizzled out and had lived for her work since then. She lived just outside Miami but often stayed at her parents, who resided just twenty miles away. She had a dog and cat and her greatest love was sailing.

"And you?"

"Oh I was married for two years I lost my wife in a car accident seven years ago. Since then I just seem to work, I lecture at a university part of the year, but mostly I am on some field trip somewhere or other."

She touched Mark's hand. The feel of her hand against his felt so natural.

"I am so sorry about your wife."

"Thank you."

They had one more drink and left for the restaurant. As they departed the bar Lisa slipped her arm through his. He thought to himself, I like this woman. The restaurant was only a short walk from the hotel, Mark wished the distance was longer; he was enjoying having this beautiful woman's arm interlocking his. In the cold air the scent of her perfume warmed him. They arrived at the restaurant; it was small, pleasant and played light orchestra music in the background. As they looked at the menu, they both looked at each other and smiled; they were enjoying each other's company so much ordering the meal seemed an interruption. They eventually settled on something from the menu, which was eaten between the smiles and laughter. As he looked once more across the table at her, he could not get over how attractive he found her, not only her beauty but the way they interacted, it was like he had known her for years she made him feel so comfortable and relaxed, feelings he had not felt or enjoyed for such a long time. Although he did not want to bring the conversation around to work, he wanted to let her know that he was going to be in America a lot longer than he had anticipated.

She looked pleased and suggested that if he gets the opportunity, he should come down to Florida and she would take him sailing.

"You sounded good at the meeting today." Said Lisa.

"Oh I have been to a lot of them, you get used to playing to them."

"You will have to give me a few tips, thought I was going to freak out for a minute when that woman started hounding me."

"You were fine, handled the questions well."

She smiled at him once again

"You are very nice Mark, I have enjoyed .... no really enjoyed this evening."

She touched his hand again.

"It would be really nice if you can make it down to Florida one weekend."

"If it pleases you then that is a reason for me to make sure I come."

Lisa looked at her watch, her friend was picking her up at the hotel in twenty minutes and she had an early flight to catch tomorrow morning. Mark paid the bill and held her coat for her, as she slipped her arms inside the coat he had an over whelming urge to wrap his arms around her. They walked back to the hotel, arm in arm, she was pressed against his shoulder. Without looking at him she said that she had been looking forward to tonight all afternoon and it was all she imagined it to be. He removed his arm from hers and placed it around her shoulders, tightened his grip and said the pleasure was all his. She looked up at him and gave a beautiful smile. As they reached the hotel entrance, Lisa's friend's car was parked outside.

"I'm afraid that's my carriage"

He tightened his lips and gave a smile.

"Well until we meet again."

She held both his hands and kissed him.

"I like you Professor Yates it would be nice to see you again."

She opened the door to the car and got in, as she looked through window and waved, Mark whispered, "You will"

He was smiling to himself as he entered the hotel, he

112

could still feel the warmth of her lips.

He contacted Admiral Hawkins office early the next morning. The plan was for him to fly down to Norfolk and take up office there with Jeff and another marine biologist who was none other than Kate Morgan. Norfolk being the main US Naval Base seemed the most appropriate place to work from. There would be a USN frigate on standby to sail should it be required. Sabre would be in Norfolk a week from tomorrow.

Jeff picked Mark up at the airport. When they arrived at the office in Norfolk Kate Morgan was already waiting for them. The office made the one in Northwood look positively second rate. This was fitted with two chart tables, four computers, flip charts, whiteboards and a huge screen on the wall that the computers could be linked to. Kate Morgan walked over and shook his hand, her smile appeared genuine enough but Mark detected a slight hint of frost in her welcome. She sat down by the table with one of the computers on.

"Well I do not know where we are going to start, appears we have to wait for someone to catch one of these creatures" she said.

"Well Kate I would really like to see if we can work out how many swarms we are dealing with, I believe there is around one hundred and fifty to one hundred and eighty creatures still surviving, the group Sabre took out contained fifty-six. Let's call it sixty, making it probably three swarms on the loose."

He walked over to the chart tables.

"Jeff have you got two charts, one of the United States and another of the Atlantic?"

"Sure we have Mark."

Jeff bent down and rustled through a number of rolled up charts that were stowed under one of the chart tables, checking the numbers on them he found the two corresponding charts for those areas. Mark rolled the one of the United States out and clipped it to the chart table. He marked out all the recent attacks, the two in Canada and the one at Cape Cod Bay. Kate started to take an interest and left her chair moving over to the chart table.

Mark picked up the dividers and a pencil.

"Now what I am going to do is put further on circles on to these positions, that is from experience the creatures generally travel at eleven knots, if we mark out the possible range they could have travelled in certain periods then we should be able to see if it could possibly be the same or different swarms."

Kate and Jeff nodded.

"It will also give us an idea what coastline is at risk, by advancing the predicted range."

Over the next twenty minutes Mark plotted the attacks and put on the further on circles, he already knew that the Canadian attacks were separate groups, but he really wanted to see if it was possible for the swarm attacking north of Halifax could have made it to Cape Cod in the time scale. It worked out they could have with sixty miles to spare.

Kate went over to the computer and called up the oceanographic chart of the Atlantic.

"Mark if you give me those figures I can set up a computer programme that will automatically update the possible range of the swarms."

Mark smiled at her.

"Excellent Kate."

He knew straight away that Kate was not a person that sat around on her backside doing nothing.

Jeff looked at them both.

"Well that makes me coffee boy them, anyone want a drink?"

They both nodded.

Mark looked at the other chart of the Atlantic.

"Kate could you also plot the attack in the Azores and see if they could be in American waters?"

She gave him an unfrosted smile.

"No problem."

By the end of the day Kate had inputted the data into the computer and had the information displayed on the large wall screen. The possible position on both known swarms were indicated by a flashing diamond, moving southerly at eleven knots, there was currently two diamonds flashing, numbered one and two. The most southerly point they could have reached at this time was in the region of New Jersey. She had also worked out that the Azores swarm could have already reached American waters. Kate sat back on her chair looking at the screen and drinking coffee from a large mug. Without looking away from the screen she spoke to Mark.

"Are you guessing or do you believe they are going to move south?"

Mark walked up and stood behind her.

"A little bit of both."

Mark was warming to Kate now he was getting to know her. Not unattractive she had the look of a person who did not get out a lot. Her clothes were practical rather than being worn for effect. He noticed she did not wear perfume and her hair whilst tidy would benefit from a visit to a professional hairdresser. He decided at heart she was quite a nice person, and not the ogre he had first thought. He believed that she went for Lisa purely through the fact that she did not agree, the same as Mark, with the genetic alteration of sea life and the complications and catastrophe it could and would bring.

It was 2am and a cold but clear night at Assateague Island camp resort, Joe Williams could not sleep, wrapped up in his padded jacket he stood outside his tent smoking a cigarette. Being right here right now was probably the last place he wanted to be, but as part of the company's team building exercise he had to spend a whole weekend playing adventure games with the other fourteen participants. He was forty-three years old, the oldest in the

115

group and the only smoker, the thought of having to run around tomorrow doing some practical leadership tests failed to stimulate any enthusiasm within him.

A head stuck out from one of the other tents.

"Oh it's you Joe, thought I heard something, you know we have got to be up early tomorrow, I would get some sleep."

It was Barbara White from the finance department, who appeared to love the idea of outdoor pursuits, being half his age and a keen sportswoman."

"Just getting some fresh air."

"Looks like it puffing on that coffin nail." she replied as she stuck her head back into her tent.

He decided to move away from the campers to somewhere he could smoke without any further sarcastic remarks from the anti-smoking league. Standing by the shoreline he thought he saw something large entering the water. He stared at the area for a few seconds but did not see anything else, assuming it was a piece of driftwood or something he turned his attention back to his cigarette. Taking a final puff he decided to return and get some sleep otherwise tomorrow would be even worse than he expected. On route he stopped at one of the portable loos set up on the site. Entering he found the damn fluorescent light was not working properly, flashing on and off every few seconds. He had to relieve himself in intermittent darkness. On hearing the sound of splashing water Joe assumed he was directing everything in the general direction, his targeting was confirmed true as the light came on for a few seconds before lapsing into darkness again. Just as he was coming to the conclusion of his business, he felt a thud against the loo, he stopped and listened but nothing more. He thought if anything it would be one of the ponies that wander this area of the park. Zipping himself up there was another thud. He stood still for a few seconds, hearing nothing more he slowly opened the door. It was dark and he did not see any ponies. As he went to step out the fluorescent light flicked on, on the

116

ground about six foot from him were what he assumed to be at least six huge snakes, slithering across the grass. As the light reflected against them, all six turned their gaze towards him, the closest two raising their heads and letting out an aggressive hiss. One of them turned and started to move towards him, Joe quickly stepped back into the loo and closed the door shut. The creature slammed against the door three times before it went quiet.

Joe whispered "Jesus Christ" to himself. He stood there not knowing what to do; he checked the bolt was over on the door, his stomach was churning. He tried to recall in his head what he had just seen but it appeared too incredible. Sitting down on the toilet seat he lit another cigarette all of the while his ears listened intensively for any further noises from outside.

Without warning the silence was broken with screaming and shouting from outside, he knew then that those vicious looking creatures must have been sighted at the campsite. The screaming turned hysterical. People were shouting and begging for help. Moving towards the door he slowly unbolted it, gradually pushing the door open just enough for him to look outside. The screaming and shouting grew louder than ever, he could hear a woman crying amongst the terrified shouts for help, it sounded like they were being massacred.

The fluorescent light flicked on again and a beam of light shot out, there was no sign of the creatures. Opening the door further he caught sight of a figure running from the direction of the campsite. It was a woman, she was dressed in something white and looked ghost like as she ran screaming across the grass. Suddenly she slipped and went sprawling to the ground about twenty yards from him. Joe opened the door fully and ran towards her. He had covered half the distance when the shapes of two creatures started heading directly for her. She started to pick herself up but in her haste to get moving she slipped again. On the damp grass the creatures were moving very fast. Joe reached her and grabbed her arm and started pulling her back towards the loo, he recognised her immediately as Barbara White. Both creatures were less than five yards behind them, she was screaming and stumbling in her effort to escape them. They reached the door to the loo and Joe pushed Barbara inside, as he went to slam the door shut a creature rammed its head into the gap. It was hissing and snapping and trying to squeeze through the gap. The light continued to flick on and off. Suddenly as the light illuminated, the creature stopped hissing, its evil yellow eyes stared at him, after a pause, it rolled its head as if to get a full view of the area inside, it breathed slowly and deeply. Once again it settled its gaze on Joe and let out a slow terrifying hiss. As if to install further fear it opened its jaws wide enough to fully display the ferocious teeth within. Suddenly the light went out again and the creature renewed the battle to break into the container, Joe kept all his weight firmly against the door. Barbara was cradling herself and crying in the farthest corner, her head buried under her arms.

"Barbara I need help." Joe shouted.

It was too dark to see her, but he heard no movement.

He screamed out at the top of his voice.

"Barbara I need some fucking help now."

The light came on again, she looked up.

"Barbara go into my pocket and get my lighter out."

She stood up and moved around the small room sticking to the farthest wall from the creature. Just then a second creature banged against the door, surprising Joe and allowing the trapped creature to move his head slightly farther in. Barbara moved back to her corner.

The creatures jaws were less than six inches away from Joe's body.

He looked at her.

"Barbara please help me I cannot hold this door much longer."

She got up again and moved towards him. She stretched her hand out and reached inside his jacket pocket withdrawing the lighter.

The lights went out again and the creatures continued to ram the door. As the light came on again she was still grasping on to the lighter with both hands like is was a precious diamond.

"Go over and pull out a lot of toilet paper, I want you to set light to it and throw it between the gap in the door"

She moved back towards the toilet roll holder and started pulling off the paper.

"Barbara I need you to speed up." Shouted Joe.

The second creature's head could now be seen trying to push in between the gap.

Standing with a pile of toilet paper in her hand she flicked the lighter; it seemed to take forever before the paper caught light.

"Now throw it to the gap Barbara."

She threw the burning paper towards the gap and it fell a foot short. The creatures appeared to understand the plan and put in renewed effort towards breaking in. They started hissing wildly and banging the door with their bodies. Joe knew that if another creature turned up they would break through.

Barbara started ripping more paper out, pulling it until the roll was empty, she held the lighter to it and it ignited. Through hers tears she looked at Joe, he nodded to her and she threw the burning paper towards the door. It landed inches away from the creature, as the flames began to rise they struck the offending head. The creature began to hiss wildly, shaking its head side to side; Joe felt the creature start to pull away, he released just enough pressure from the door for it to escape; as it did he slammed the door and pushed the bolt over. With the door closed he stamped out the burning toilet paper which left a rancid smell of burnt paper in the confined space.

Barbara went back to the corner sobbing and cradling herself. Joe took off his jacket and put it over her, sitting down beside her on the floor he put his arm over her shoulders.

He noticed the screaming from outside had now

stopped; after a further five minutes he heard more noises. It sounded like something was being dragged along the pathway. The noise continued for nearly fifteen minutes then apart from the sobs of Barbara, went deadly quiet.

They sat there for over an hour, he looked at his watch it was now 3:15am. Barbara had now stopped crying but did not say anything. At 4am it was still quiet. Joe reached into his trouser pocket and pulled out a packet of cigarettes, he picked up the lighter from the floor and lit up. Barbara raised her head and looked at him.

"Joe, Can I have one of those?"

He gave her the one he had already lit.

At 5:55am Joe stood up and moved towards the door, Barbara looked at him and rolled her head. He raised the palm of his hand and moved towards the door, he pulled the bolt over and opened the door a few inches. It was just beginning to get light and the visibility allowed him to make out the pathway to the campsite. He turned to Barbara.

"I am going to go outside, shut the door and lock it. I will come back and get you if it is all clear."

He opened the door just enough to look around and check all was clear. As Joe slipped outside Barbara closed and locked the door. On the pathway that led to the campsite, he could see dark smears all over it. Walking hesitantly towards the campsite, he could see the tents were in disarray, not one tent was erect. Reaching where the first tent had stood Joe found the canvas covered in blood; pieces of ripped clothing were strewn around with no sign of any bodies. Last night there were over a dozen people here, now he could not see anyone. Moving deeper into the campsite he saw an arm sticking from under a canvas. He rushed toward it. On reaching it he could tell it belonged to a woman, an engagement ring shone through the blood covered fingers, he lifted the canvas and was met with a horrifying sight, all that was attached to the arm was part of a rib cage and some internal organs that dangled from the centre. He felt like vomiting and retched

120

twice, nothing came up from his stomach. Gathering himself he slowly walked around the whole campsite. He could find no sign of life anywhere the arm and partial torso was all that remained of his work colleagues. Amongst the carnage he found the spot where his tent had stood. Under the bloodstained debris he found his rucksack smeared with congealed blood. Pulling the zipper open he reached in and pulled out a mobile phone walking back towards Barbara he dialled 911.

CHAPTER SIXTEEN

For his stay at Norfolk the US Navy had provided Mark accommodation within the Naval Base, it was a tidy two bedroom flat, with all the amenities and a pleasant ten minute walk from the office they were using. Kate Morgan had been provided one in the same block. It was now 7:10am; he had been up since 6:00 he had showered but still wandered around with a towel wrapped around his waist. He sat at the breakfast bar eating a slice of toast and sipping his second coffee of the day. Mark had spent most of last night thinking about how they could deal with the creatures if no fishing vessel managed to capture one. Even then they will only have a chance of detecting one swarm. The problem was still buzzing around his head when the doorbell rang.

Opening the door Kate walked straight in.

"You watching the news?"

She walked over to the television and switched it on flicking through the channels until she got to the station she wanted.

"They attacked a camp resort at Assateague Island early this morning."

The news channel was showing pictures being taken from a helicopter of the campsite. The area looked devastated, Mark could see streaks on a pathway leading from the campsite, which he knew were blood smears.

"How many killed?"

"Thirteen missing, they have not found any bodies yet, two people survived, the missing people were all adults, eight males and five females"

"Where exactly is Assateague Island?"

"About one-hundred and ten miles north of here, I cannot be sure until I get to the office, but this could be another swarm."

"Help yourself to coffee, I will go and get dressed."

When they got to the office, Jeff was already there,

Kate went straight over to the computer and brought the tracking chart up on screen.

"The attack was around 2am, if our figures are correct the most southerly track would still be over one hundred miles away, unless they increased speed, do you think that is possible Mark?"

"No it will be a different swarm, don't ask me how they do it but they knew people were there, they would have been in that area long before the attack took place, Kate can you start another track for swarm number three?"

Jeff reported that two warships were sailing from Norfolk to carry out active sonar sweeps of the area in search of the creatures. Mark did not expect them to have much success, the creatures knew all about active sonar, and they would probably avoid the warships if they heard it.

"You think they are that smart?" Asked Kate.

Mark nodded.

"Oh these creatures are smart and they learn very fast, do not under estimate them."

"Mark, the bodies where do they go, you think there would be skeletons or something left behind"? Queried Jeff.

"Its a guess but they know the longer they are on land the more danger they are in, they eat what they can, tear what is left into pieces, and then carry it off into the sea."

Mark cast his mind back to the pictures he had seen on TV that morning; the campsite had appeared a good one hundred yards from the shore.

He turned to Kate

"Could you look up what time high tide was in Assateague Island?"

Kate flicked on to the web and called up the times tables.

"High tide was at 2:11am this morning"

She looked at Mark.

"You thinking what I am thinking?"

"Yes, check out the tide in Cape Cod, and then call up

the British ones for Galway in Ireland and Dartmouth for the dates of the attacks."

Within two minutes she had the results.

"All of them were at high tide."

Mark grimaced.

"Shit, how did I not notice that, check the Canadian attack at where was it.........Tangiers."

She tapped on her keyboard and swung around on her chair towards him.

"Yep, high tide"

"So they come ashore at high tide when the sea is closest to the prey, Kate how long will it take us to get to Assateague Island?"

"8:45 now could be there by lunch time if we leave now"

Mark turned to Jeff.

"Can you make sure we have clearances to attend the scene?"

Jeff nodded "No problem."

Mark and Kate arrived at Assateague Island at 12:10pm; they drove to within two hundred yards of the scene of the attack and parked alongside two police cars. The entire area was roped off by reels of plastic stripping and the entrance to it was guarded by two police officers. Reaching the guards, Kate explained who they were and the purpose of their visit, one of them radioed to someone else who gave them the all clear to enter. As they entered, Mark walked along side the pathway he had seen on the news, the blood stood out clearly from the light grey cement, the wavy streaks were all heading in the same direction, towards the sea. At the campsite, there were six people wandering around, two of them were writing on clipboards, others had started to dismantle what remained of the tents and placing the personal belongings of the victims into heavy duty green plastic bags. A woman approached them; she introduced herself as Sandra Kent, the Detective in charge. She looked everything Mark envisaged an American cop would look like, badge slung over her neck and a gun clearly visible at her waist. Kate and Mark returned the introductions and the nature of their business.

"Sandra, have you interviewed the two survivors yet?" Asked Mark.

"Yes, one male and one female, the guy only survived because he was in the john at the time, the woman said that she only managed to get away from the creatures because one of her colleagues was fighting them off with one of the tent poles and all the creatures turned on him giving her a chance to run, she was then pulled inside the john by the guy."

"Did she give any indication of numbers?"

"Not exactly, it was dark, but she said it sounded like all the tents being attacked, so well into double figures, earlier today we counted at least fifty-two trails in the mud."

"Thanks Sandra, we are going to look around if you don't mind?"

"No problem."

Mark tapped Kate on the shoulder and pointed in the direction of the sea, as they got there he stood by the high tide mark and looked back. At high tide the campsite was less than forty yards away. He looked around, he was recalling the attack at Cape Cod when they had come ashore at different parts of the beach. Walking along the coastline he looked for any tell tale signs that they had carried out the same manoeuvre here. Reaching the part of the beach that was adjacent to one end of the campsite, he saw the marks, at least six grooves in the soft sand. He looked at Kate, frowned, turned around and waved for Kate to follow. He walked to the end of the beach adjacent to the other perimeter of the campsite where in the sand still remained four clear grooves.

"See what I mean Kate, these things are good at what they do."

"You saying they surrounded the campsite?"

"When one of the survivors said they were attacking all the tents, I figured they must have approached from different angles, they carried out a pincer move, you try to escape from one group, you would just run into another one."

On the way back to the car they stopped and told Sandra Kent of Mark's suspicions.

"As a police officer, if that's the case, I would have to say that they did not pick this spot by accident, they must have had a reason."

"You saying they checked it out first" Asked Kate.

"All I am saying is that if we were dealing with humans, to pull it off, I would have expected them to have checked the layout first, but they are not human so maybe they just got lucky."

"They seem to get lucky too often for it to be a coincidence." Said Mark

Mark pulled out his mobile phone and called Jeff. He asked him if he could get hold of blown up satellite pictures of all the areas that had been attacked, including Galway and Dartmouth

Kate asked what he wanted them for.

"I am doing exactly what Detective Kent would do if she was dealing with humans, looking for common denominators."

On the drive back, they realised they had not eaten so they stopped at a steak house. Over the meal, Kate brought up Lisa Michaels.

"You looked pretty enamoured with Lisa Michaels at the meeting, are you and her an item?"

"No we are just friends, only met her once before."

"Well looked to me like a couple of love birds, you did not take your eyes off her, and she was sending out flares for you to come and get her."

Mark smiled.

"We just get along fine"

Kate laughed and had to put her hand to her mouth to

avoid a piece of meat she was chewing popping out.

"I think you and her may get along a lot better given half the chance."

Mark smiled again but in his mind hoped it was true.

"You have a wicked sense of humour Kate, are you involved with anyone?"

"Nah I have a sort of on off relationship with this guy, but he is sort of married so it's not going anywhere."

"What is sort of married?"

"Ok he's married, but we both get what we want from each other so if everyone is happy, it's ok with me."

"So you are not looking for a long term relationship?"

She laughed again, this time with no food.

"Not unless you are offering, you looked quite cute in the bath towel this morning."

Mark rolled his head and laughed.

"You definitely surprise me Kate, I will keep it in mind and thanks for the compliment."

When they arrived back at Norfolk they stopped off at the office, it was gone 5pm and Jeff was still there.

"Hi guys thought I would hang around till you got back, anything to report?"

"They used the same tactics as at Cape Cod, approached them on all sides so they could not escape." answered Mark.

A cringe came over Jeff's face.

"Wow this is scary, Mark."

Kate cut in.

"Yes and Mark also reckons they may be doing a recognisance of the area before they attack."

"That true?"

Mark nodded.

"It's the only explanation. The chance of them attacking like that, without knowledge of where the target is does not work out."

Jeff picked up a big brown envelope from his desk and handed it to Mark.

"Got these directly off the base intelligence centre, it's the satellite pictures of the attack areas. I have put in a magnifying glass in case you need to take a closer look at them."

"Thanks I will take these back to my place to study tonight."

Before they left that night Mark checked on the computer as to how far south the swarms could have reached, right now they could be just over one hundred miles south of Norfolk.

He realised that at sometime today there would have been a swarm right opposite their position.

CHAPTER SEVENTEEN

Mark stopped at the PX stores on the way back and bought a bottle of Mount Gay rum and a six pack of coca cola, when he had to do a lot of thinking he found rum an excellent stimulant. As an after thought he picked up a ready-made meal, just in case he got hungry.

He was on his second rum and coke and had been looking at the satellite pictures for over an hour, he did not know what he was looking for, but was hoping there would be something that would indicate to why these particular sites were chosen for attack. He finished his drink put the magnifying glass down and went for a refill. On return he stood over the photographs lining the tabletop, he scanned over each one slowly, as he reached the one with the magnifying glass on he reached to move it, as it lifted he noticed a dark spot being magnified, it was in the sea. He sat down and pulled the photograph closer to him, it was just a darker shade than the surrounding area it could have been anything. He picked up another photo and scanned the sea area with the magnifier; there were dark areas on this one. He went through the rest, the one from Cape Cod had quite few of them; them he realised they must be buoys. It was getting late, it had gone 2am and the rum was taking affect, he was tired, tomorrow he would check what buoys were in the areas, the saying grabbing at straws passed through his mind.

Kate was at his door at 8am, popping in for a coffee before going to the office. Mark was fully dressed ready to leave.

"Damn Mark I was hoping I would have caught you with the towel still on."

She wandered over to the photographs still spread out on the table.

"You find anything on these?"

"Not sure but would you do me a favour when we get

129

in, call up the charts for those areas and see what buoy indicators they have, especially that one"

He pointed to Galway.

"Sure no problem, you think they can read buoys as well?"

She laughed. Mark smiled.

Jeff was not in when they arrived at the office, Kate got straight onto checking what buoys were sited where the attacks took place.

"Well that one in the Galway waters is a Sewerage dumping area."

She tapped away on her keyboard again.

"Tangiers we have three, Hazard buoy, Sewerage and Electrical Cables."

She tapped again.

"Cape Cod whole bunch of them."

"Any sewerage?" Asked Mark.

"Yep"

"And Assateague Island?"

Kate tapped away once more on her keyboard.

"Just the one sewerage."

Kate looked up at him from her Keyboard.

"You think this has anything to do with why they picked those areas?"

"Have not got a clue, but it is the only common denominator in all the areas."

"Tell you what Kate, could you tap some more into your computer and plot all the sewerage outlets from here to Charleston?"

"Sure, may take a while though."

Jeff turned up the office at 9:45am; Admiral Hawkins office had just contacted him, he would like an update on any progress towards tracking the creatures down.

Mark and Kate looked at each other.

"Well apart from there being at least three swarms in American waters and they attack at high water we have not got too much to tell him" said Mark.

"Well he is getting a lot of questions asked of him over the attack at Assateague Island, he needs some answers."

Jeff looked up the plotting screen; Kate had already plotted about a dozen buoys.

"What are these new reference points you are plotting?"

"I checked through those satellite pictures you gave me for anything common to all attack sites, the only thing I could come up with was that they all had sewerage outlets in the vicinity, but it may be just a coincidence."

"Mark you must feel a little bit more confident than that, otherwise you would not be bothering to plot them."

Mark walked over to the screen and ran his fingers through his hair.

"Well let's say that they associate for whatever reason sewerage with warm blooded food, there is a possibility that they would come ashore directly opposite the outlet looking for prey, but that is only a hunch."

"Mark I like your hunches, tell me for instance, if your hunch is correct what would be your plan?"

"Well Jeff, we know they come ashore at high water, and there is a possibility they pick areas with sewerage outlets, I would find a remote sewerage discharge area, have other sewerage pumps switched off along that stretch of coast a couple of hours before high tide, and have a little surprise party waiting for them, if and when they came ashore."

"Sounds good to me Mark."

"You are not honestly going to go to the Admiral with that plan are you?"

"Well what do you want to wait for, some other poor bastards to get eaten alive to see if there is a sewerage discharge opposite, or have a go for it now and hope we are right? Far as I can see we have nothing to lose."

"Think I agree with Jeff on this one." Said Kate.

Mark stared at the computer-generated screen and nodded his head.

"Yes I can see your point, Kate how long before you

get those buoys plotted?"

"Why don't you two guys go and get the coffee and some doughnuts and I will be finished before you get back."

When they returned Kate had just finished.

Mark looked at the reference points all running down the coast, there was a lot, to many he thought.

"Kate could you put up the predicted position of group three in say thirty-six-hours?"

Kate tapped away and the number three diamond pointer started flashing just past Wilmington. Mark looked at the area there were three buoys marked, one opposite Carolina Beach another opposite the city and one opposite Cape Fear. Cape Fear's discharge was the closest to deep water.

"Kate what are the times of high tides of Cape Fear tomorrow night and the next two nights?"

Within a minute she had the information.

"3:11am, 3:26am and 3:31am"

Mark turned to Jeff.

"Right if we are going to go for this, Cape Fear looks as good as any place, we are going to have to move fast on this if we are going to be ready for tomorrow night."

"Ok if you write me a list of what you need I will get on to the Admirals staff and see if they can meet your order on time."

Jeff was on the phone for over thirty minutes speaking to different people, he turned to Mark and handed him the phone.

"The Admiral wants to speak to you."

"Hello Admiral."

"Professor are you sure these creatures are going to be that far south?"

"Admiral I am not sure on anything, but I have a feeling that the swarms are all moving south."

"Ok Professor, you will have all the equipment and

personnel you have asked for in the timescale, good luck."

"Thank you Admiral"

He turned to Kate.

"I want to be down there first thing tomorrow morning to check over the site, you coming or staying here?"

"What and miss all the action, I am with you."

Jeff would stay in Norfolk until he knew all the equipment and personnel had arrived on the site.

They left for Cape Fear two hours later, once they were out of Norfolk the roads were fast and the scenery pleasant. Mark kept thinking he may be going on a wild goose chase and the idea about the buoys totally wrong, but he knew that Jeff was right they could not wait for a swarm to attack again at the expense of human life just to confirm his hunch.

Kate could see Mark was deep in thought and did not ask any questions of him until they were nearly an hour into the drive.

"So what is the plan?"

"Well tomorrow morning Kate, you an I are going for a boat trip to a sewerage buoy."

"Jesus you Brits really know how to impress a girl."

He smiled, Kate's sense of humour did a lot to make him relax.

"Then we are going to travel directly back from it and find out the best landing spot for the creatures."

He went on to explain that he had requested enough movement sensors to cover around two hundred yards, they would be placed along the landing point to detect anything that passed through them.

"That's where you come in Kate, I would like you monitoring them."

"From a safe distance and somewhere warm, I hope?"

"In the back of a van probably."

"Who is going to be the bait?" asked Kate.

"There will be around twenty marines playing campers, I have also asked for two underwater transducers to record any sound transmitted in the sea. One will be suspended below the sewerage buoy the other will be just off the shore. If they do send reconnaissance creatures ashore first, they must transmit something back to the main group."

"At high tide it's going to be very dark out there at night, you got lighting?"

"Yes, the floodlighting control will be in the van with you, when they get far enough away from the sea you will hit the switch and illuminate them for the marines to kill."

"Well sounds a good plan, lets hope the guests turn up."

They arrived at Cape Fear early evening, they booked into the first hotel they came to, it was out of season and there were lots of rooms available. At reception Mark picked up a couple of the brochures advertising fishing and boating trips, from his room he rang one of the numbers he got a boat for 9am the next day.

CHAPTER EIGHTEEN

Mark was up early, too early for breakfast and took a walk down to the seafront. He watched the waves rolling in over the beach and the seagull's beachcombing for whatever the tide had left behind. The chill in the sea breeze soon cleared any remains of sleep from his head. The scenery was not unlike his hometown in Devon, as a child he would spend hours discovering things on the beach and rock pools, writing and drawing down what he had found. He still had the drawing books. On days when he needed reason to go on he would pull one out and look at the childish sketches of crabs and shrimps to try and recapture some of that perfect world. He had looked at those books a lot when he had lost his wife. The drawings depicted a different world an uncomplicated world without human interference into the balance of the sea, a world absent of genetically formed fish that killed and devoured human beings.

Walking back towards the hotel he passed a couple with their dogs, he thought of the couple at Shaldon who were killed, just out for a stroll with their pets, yet some scientist thousands of miles away messing around with nature caused them to die horrible deaths. It was hard to picture Lisa Michaels as that scientist, she was bright, beautiful and fun to be with she did not portray the picture of a self-indulgent unsympathetic scientist who could wreak havoc on the world.

When he arrived back at the hotel, he found Kate already at the breakfast table. She looked wide-awake and full of enthusiasm, she wore a pair of blue jeans and a multi coloured woollen jumper that could only have been knitted by an aging relative. Her hair was tied back in a ponytail with a large bright pink elastic band holding it in place.

Mark smiled at her.

"Well you look ready for action"

"Ready and willing Mark, you did say there would be twenty marines?"

She gave him a cheeky smile and winked.

After breakfast they still had a full thirty minutes before the skipper of the charter boat was due to pick them up.

They sat on the hotel veranda, looking at the sea view. Kate looked at Mark and saw from his face that he was thinking of the horrors that were swimming the depths beneath it.

The Skipper walked into the hotel spot on nine. He was in his early fifties, although still a bit chilly outside he was wearing shorts, t-shirt and flip flops. After introductions he led them to a pick up truck. It was only a short drive to the jetty where his boat "Sea Shell" was tied up. She was in pretty good condition, recently painted in a light and dark blue decor the wooden deck was also freshly sanded and varnished. They followed the Skipper into the wheelhouse Mark pointed out on a chart the buoy he wished him to travel to. The Skipper did not ask for reasons, he started up the engine, Mark and Kate slipped the bow and stern lines. Twenty-five minutes later, the sewerage buoy was clearly visible to them. On reaching it the Skipper manoeuvred the boat around it a couple of times and then brought Sea Shell to a stop. Mark looked at the chart again and asked if he would head towards the land directly opposite the buoy. The Skipper nodded and started the boat moving again. He handed Mark a pair of binoculars, looking through them he could see a sandy beach, no buildings were visible within half a mile of it, it looked an ideal position.

Mark turned to the Skipper.

"You familiar with that part of shoreline?"

"Sure, know it well."

"Is it accessible by road?"

"Yeh you can drive right up to it, you may need a four wheel drive if its wet, but the forecast is pretty good for the next week so you should be okay with a routine car.

The skipper took the boat to within thirty yards of the beach, turned slowly and manoeuvred adjacent as to give

Mark a good look at the area.

When they arrived back at the hotel a police officer was waiting for them.

"Professor Yates?"

"Yes Officer?"

"Hello Sir, I understand the military are carrying out an operation in an area of Cape Fear, I have been requested to provide you with any assistance you may need."

"That's very kind of you Officer, we will need restricted entry to part of the shoreline for possibly three days. Lets grab a coffee and I will take you through the details and afterwards we will go and survey the area."

At 11:45 am the first truck arrived at the beachhead. It carried all the movement sensors and floodlighting. The crew of four technicians wasted no time in unloading the equipment and setting it up. At 13:30 two military trucks arrived with the detachment of marines and their equipment, they were followed in by a large vehicle, which contained all the monitoring equipment. By 1600 all the movement sensors were in place and tested. One underwater listening device was placed fifty yards from the shore and the other dangled thirty feet below the sewerage buoy. Each floodlight had its own heavy-duty battery that would provide power for up to four hours.

The marines set up the campsite thirty yards from the high tide mark to give them a good field of fire. Mark with the Officer in Charge of the marines walked the beach and assessed where the creatures would approach from if they carried out the usual pincer attack. The tents were placed strategically to allow each one to have good visibility. Mark then phoned Jeff to ensure the other two sewerage discharges in the area would stop pumping between midnight and 4am.

It was gone 7pm when everything was in place. Kate would be in the monitoring station and keep all the marines updated by the radio earpieces they were wearing. In the event of the creatures turning up, the switching on of the floodlights, would give approval for the marines to open fire. Two camouflaged sniper trained marine sentries were fitted with night visions goggles and placed as to have full view of the beach area. They would also be responsible for calling for the floodlights.

Mark went into the monitoring station and checked the underwater listening devices were functioning correctly.

"Well Kate, think we are as ready as we will ever be, let's hope they take the bait."

She held her hand up with her fingers crossed.

The sea was calm and very little wind; the crew of the deep-sea trawler had just finished supper and were getting dressed for recovery of the nets. When all were on deck, the winches were powered up and they began to heave in. As the net broke the water, the crew all moved back, inside was what looked like a giant eel, it was slithering all around the net looking for an opening and continually hissing. The crew knew exactly what it was the Skipper had briefed them on the shipping report from the navy, he had also made a contingency plan if one was caught. The catch remained outboard the vessel, two of the crew opened up the hold, one other went to check all internal doors below were secure. The Skipper then ordered the net to be traversed inboard until it was over the hold. The creature was going crazy trying to bite its way out. Once the net was in the hold, the skipper ordered it to be released. The creature and all of the catch dropped into the hold. Immediately the crew closed the hatches. The deep-sea fishing vessel Clare Louise altered course towards Norfolk.

Mark and Kate sat drinking a warm drink that just about passed for coffee, it was 1:30am the listening devices and movement sensors remained quiet. It was time for another radio check and Kate called out to all stations to report back.

At 2:37am, the underwater listening device at the buoy started receiving a noise not dissimilar to a bird chirping; this went on for about three minutes and then stopped.

Kate spoke into the microphone.

"All stations, we have picked something up from the listening station at the buoy."

She received copied from the two sentries and the marines IC.

Nearly twenty minutes passed with no further incidents.

At 2:56 the listening device near the beach detected the same chirping sound. Kate passed out the information to all stations.

Two minutes later one of the sentries with the night vision goggles reported possible movement on the beach. A few seconds passed before he reported in again.

"Confirmed movement on the beach, approaching campsite from south."

The movement sensors then indicated that something had just passed through them.

Mark and Kate were both biting their bottom lips.

The other sentry reported in.

"Confirmed movement on the beach to north of campsite."

The technician in the monitoring station, pointed to a second movement sensor confirming the sentry's report.

It was deadly quiet, Mark could feel the tension in the air, he knew these two creatures were the advance party to recce the campsite. The sentry reported in again.

"Southerly creature heading back to sea."

The northerly creature still remained ashore.

The sentry reported in again.

"Northerly creature returning to sea."

A minute passed with no reports, and then the underwater listening device by the shore detected more chirping sounds.

Immediately the listening device at the buoy detected the same sounds.

Mark nodded to Kate and whispered.

"I think they are coming in now."

Kate called for all stations to standby, suspect creatures on their way to shore.

Five minutes passed, ten minutes with no movement, then at fourteen minutes both sentries reported in.

"Multiple movements on beach, we have five creatures approaching from south and six from north, mass of them moving through centre of beach"

In the monitoring station all the movement sensors were flashing.

The sentries reported that all the creatures appeared to be clear of the shore. Clearing the sand they moved on to the grass heading towards the campsite. They were 10 yards from the campsite when the order to hit the floodlights was given.

Kate hit the switch. The whole campsite was illuminated; the light made the red creatures wet bodies glisten under the brightness. Immediately the marines engaged them with automatic weapons. For the first few seconds the creatures were caught in hesitation whether to continue advancing or retreat back to the ocean. Most of them raised there heads towards the offending lighting and hissed wildly allowing the marines perfect targets.

The noise from the gunfire was horrendously loud, in the first ten seconds of shooting half the creatures were dead or lay dying on the ground. Others that had been wounded were trying to crawl back towards the safety of the sea. The marines were now up on their feet and advancing towards them. All the creatures that could move were attempting to escape but were being slowed by the amount of bullets entering their bodies. Only two made it back to the beach but were ripped to pieces by a hail of bullets before reaching the safety of the ocean. The gunfire reduced and finally turned to intermittent shots as the marines ensured that all the creatures were dead. After ten minutes the marine officer reported all clear. Mark and Kate left the safety of the monitoring station and went to witness the area of devastation.

By the time they arrived the marines were piling the carcasses together. Blood and pieces of flesh were scattered all over the area.

The Lieutenant came over to Mark.

"Professor initial count is fifty-six dead, oh and Professor the guys said to make sure you invite them to your next fishing trip."

"Will do Lieutenant, your guys have done a fantastic job."

Kate looked in awe of the creatures lying before her, this was the first time she had seen them in the flesh.

"Jesus Mark, they must be nearly twenty foot long, look at the teeth on that one."

Although it was nearly 4am, Mark called Jeff who had asked to be informed of any success whatever the time.

He answered after four rings.

"Hello Commander Winter."

"Hello Jeff, good news fifty-six dead, tell the Admiral tomorrow his marines were excellent."

"I will be telling him now he wants to know whatever the time, well done Mark oh and Mark more good news, we have caught a live one, fishing vessel is bringing it direct to Norfolk, should be with us by 9am."

CHAPTER NINETEEN

At 5:55am as the sun rose, the marines began to dismantle the tents and load their equipment back on to the trucks. In the middle of the grass verge bordering the campsite and beach lay a mound of dead creatures over three foot high and twenty foot wide. Seagulls were already hovering above the carcasses and picking up small pieces of flesh scattered around the area of devastation. Four of the least damaged creatures had been separated from the rest and wrapped in canvas ready for transportation to the research centre. Mark had done a preliminary check on them, the largest was just short of nineteen feet and the head had a circumference of twenty eight inches. The longest teeth positioned at the front were now two and half inches long. Mark looked at the yellow eyes, even dead they maintained the look of total malevolence, the body no longer functioned yet the eyes still appeared to be watching, taking in everything going on around them. The Lieutenant approached Mark and informed him that they had been instructed to burn the remainder of the carcasses, then dispose of any remains into the ocean.

Mark nodded; already he could see marines dousing the carcasses in petrol.

"Your men must be tired Lieutenant?"

"Yes, there is a relief party coming down to take over the disposal and recovery of the sensors, they are thirty minutes away, as soon as we hand over we will head back to base."

After thanking each of the marines, Mark went over to the monitoring station and retrieved a recording of last night's underwater communications.

Thirty minutes later, Mark and Kate were on the road heading back to Norfolk.

"You need a shave." Said Kate.

Mark looked at himself in the car mirror.

"I need the whole works, feel like shit."

His mobile rang. It was Admiral Lane.

"Hello Admiral."

"Just ringing up to congratulate you on last night's success Professor. Admiral Hawkins just got off the phone to me."

"It went well Admiral, but we were lucky."

"So what's the next plan, understand they have caught a live one."

"Yes Admiral, hopefully we can get a transponder tagged to that, release it and track it to another swarm."

"Well you appear to be doing a bloody good job over there Professor."

Mark heard a female voice in the background.

"Professor, Mary says hello and you must come to dinner when you get back."

"Tell her I would love to come to dinner."

The Clare Louise was at the entrance to Norfolk harbour, the creature contained in the hold had been banging and barging the hatches for most of the journey back. They had placed restraining chains to the top of the hatch to ensure it had no chance of forcing them open. The deep sea fishing vessel was called up by the harbourmaster to proceed direct to a jetty normally restricted for warships. As they secured alongside the jetty a naval Commander was the first to cross the gangway, it was Jeff Winter.

The Skipper came down from the bridge and shook hands with Jeff.

"Well Commander, just what are your plans to get this thing out of my hold?"

"Sir, a marine biologist and a veterinarian will be with us shortly, the plan is to tranquillise the creature and hoist it out into a secure container. I have also been informed to tell you that the navy will reimburse you for a full hold of fish and fuel costs plus any damage incurred by the creature."

"Thanks good news Commander, I am ex navy myself,

always happy to help when I can."

The marine biologist Alan Dempsey and the vet Kevin Beck walked on to the deck of the Clare Louise ten minutes later. The vet carried the rifle that would deliver the tranquilliser and anaesthetic to the creature.

Jeff turned to the Skipper.

"Do you think we can loosen those retaining straps on the hold just enough to raise the hatch a few inches and let the vet get a tranquilliser dart into it?"

"Commander, one of the hatch doors down below has a viewing port in it, it is only the diameter of a small plate, but if we broke the glass in it, I think that would be the safer option."

The Skipper escorted Jeff and the vet below decks to the door where the viewing port was. They looked through it but it was misted on the other side and nothing was visible through it.

"Is this big enough Kevin?" Asked Jeff.

The vet nodded.

The Skipper left and returned with a heavy hammer.

He signalled for Jeff and the vet to stand back and smashed the hammer against the glass; it took three hits before the reinforced glass gave way.

As soon as the glass smashed the creature rammed its head against the opening, they could feel the rush of air from its breath. It turned its head to the side, the three men watched as the yellow eye peered through the opening at them. It stayed in that position for a good thirty seconds, staring directly at the three men, the eye looked pure evil and all three felt a chill run through them. As if it had taken in enough information, it suddenly rammed its body against the door once more and moved back.

The vet loaded the dart into the rifle.

"First of all I am going to give it a tranquilliser which contains diazepam that should relax it, in about twenty minutes I will give it another dart containing propofol which is an anaesthetic and will put it to sleep."

"You sure these drugs are going to work on it?" Asked

the Skipper.

"Well I am going to give it enough for a horse, which is heavier so they should."

The vet stood back from the viewing port and laid the barrel of the rifle on its rim. He aimed, and fired, the dart hit the creature's body about four feet from its head. Immediately the dart pierced the body it went berserk. Slamming its body against the bulkheads and door, its head raised high off the ground, mouth open and showing the full extent of its vicious looking teeth. It carried on rampaging around the compartment for over two minutes, gradually its movement began to slow until finally it returned to the far end of the hold and coiled up. The creature remained quiet for the next twenty minutes, Kevin loaded the rifle with the propofol dart and fired it into the creature, it jerked twice but remained coiled in the corner.

"Give it fifteen minutes and the anaesthetic will have taken effect, should stay under sedation for at least four hours."

Back on the upper deck the Skipper looked at the vet and Jeff.

"Who is actually going to go in there with it?"

"I believe I am the lucky guy." Said Alan Dempsey.

Fifteen minutes later, Alan Dempsey looked through the viewing port. The creature lay still in the far corner. Behind him was Kevin Beck they were both dressed in blue overalls and wearing heavy-duty leather gloves. Alan carried with him a rope strop. Slowly Alan turned the handle of the door. As the door creaked open there was no movement from the creature. He stepped inside, the deck was wet and slippery, fish were scattered all around. He moved tentatively towards the coiled shape in the far corner. As he reached it, he pushed its tail with his foot, no movement. He bent down and slipped the rope strop around its tail end, pulling on it until the strop tightened. Alan waved to Kevin to join him, they both began to pull on the strop uncoiling the creature so it lay flat and straight on the deck of the hold. Satisfied it was fully sedated he signalled for the hatches of the hold be opened. A crane hook was lowered into the hold; Alan and Kevin rolled the creature onto a long canvas, they secured four more strops around it and hooked them on to the crane. The canvass package was hoisted clear of the hold directly into a secure metal container on the back of a waiting truck.

At 10:30am Mark and Kate arrived back at the base. Mark called up Jeff immediately and asked how they were progressing with the one that was captured. Jeff informed him that the creature had successfully been sedated and was currently being transported to a medical facility to have the transponder fitted.

"Who is fitting the transponder?"

"Alan Dempsey."

"Good choice, look I am shattered, I am going to get some sleep, should be awake around 3pm, if I am needed feel free to call."

CHAPTER TWENTY

In the medical facility, two stainless steel tables had to be pushed together to take the creatures nineteen feet; even then three feet of its tail flopped over the end. It had been nearly ninety minutes since the creature had been put under anaesthetic.

Kevin Beck checked that it remained fully unconscious, he inserted a hypodermic needle into the creature and started drawing blood samples requested by Lisa Michaels.

Alan Dempsey held the transponder which looked the shape and size of a disposable lighter it would be tagged on to the creatures back. He held the transponder in place and fired in the first surgical staple. He looked at the head of the creature to see if there was any movement; the creature remained unresponsive. He fired a further two staples in and checked the transponder was fully secure.

Unnoticed, from one of the creature's nipples, very slowly, a white serrated claw began to emerge; the movement of it was intermittent as if it was causing much pain and effort to extract. Alan starting at the head ran his right hand down the body of the creature, the feel of power in it was awesome; the streamlined shape was perfectly formed to move through the water with minimum resistance. He thought to himself that if this creature were not so deadly it would be a wondrous sight to see it swimming the oceans. As his hand continued to move along the body it drew adjacent to the creature's first nipple, he felt a shiver under the creature's skin; he looked towards Kevin as if to speak, before he uttered a sound the creature's claw fully extended and rotated towards his hand. The claw jerked and stabbed the back of his hand just short of the index finger. It passed through his skin and flesh and rotated again, crunching and breaking bones, penetrating right through to the palm. Alan was screaming in pain, and trying to break free from the claw. The creature began to shiver and vibrate as if trying to come back to life. With great effort and determination its head rose from the steel table, it twisted and clamped its jaws shut on Alan's arm, the force of the bite and the weight of the creatures head, snapped his bone in two, the arm flopped like a broken doll's. The creature bit down once more and Alan fell back, screaming in pain. As he looked up he could see his arm still hanging from the creature's claw. He went into shock cradling the stump of his right arm which was pumping out blood at a dramatic rate over the floor. As if completely exhausted from the effort of the attack the creature's head dropped back down on to the table and returned to a state of unconsciousness. The severed arm remained hanging on the claw like meat on a butchers hook.

The two assistants in the room dashed forward and pulled Alan clear of the area; Kevin Beck ran towards the creature and stabbed it with a needle full of anaesthetic.

Mark's phone rang at 11:30am.

"Mark it is Jeff, I know you have just got to sleep but there has been an incident, the creature attacked Alan Dempsey, it severed his right arm."

"Jesus, Jeff I thought the bloody thing was unconscious."

"It was, it had enough anaesthetic in it to keep a horse down for four hours, it just seemed to come alive for a few seconds."

"How is Alan?"

"He is in hospital sedated, they could not save his arm it was too badly damaged."

"Does Kate know?"

"I was going to ring her next."

"Ok does the transponder still need to be fitted?"

"Alan fitted it, just needs checking."

"Ok I will be ready in fifteen minutes, send a car for me."

Mark was in the medical centre in twenty-five minutes accompanied by Kate Morgan. As they walked into the room Kevin Beck approached them. He was desperately trying to explain to them that there was no way that the thing should have been able to become conscious. Mark laid his arm on his shoulder and said there are lots of things that these creatures did that broke the rules and it was not his fault. As re-assurance Kate nodded in agreement.

Kevin told them that after the attack he gave it another injection of anaesthetic, which took it well above the recommended dosage for its weight.

Mark approached the creature and checked the transponder; it was secure and just required checking that it was fully operational. Walking over to a table in the far corner he switched on the receiver. He turned a dial to transmit and flicked a self-return switch. This sent out a transmission to the transponder, within a second the equipment indicated that the transponder had replied. He tested it twice more and then gave the thumb up that all was ok to Jeff.

Mark walked back towards the creature he looked at its head. Alan's congealed blood still remained smeared around its mouth.

It was immediately prepared for transportation back to the dockyard. This time it was secured into a wire cargo net and transported by the same secure container to the awaiting USS Delaware. The Delaware was a small but fast minesweeper. Onboard the ship the Operations Room had been fitted with all the tracking equipment.

The creature, still in the wire cargo net, lay on the sweep deck. The net was hooked up to a davit ready to be winched outboard.

On the bridge, Mark, Jeff and the Captain of the sweeper were looking over the chart of the area that they intended to release it.

Mark turned to the Captain.

"This transponder is the best we have, but it has its limitations. If it goes below 110 metres it is unlikely you will receive a signal from it, also it has to be within six miles of you."

The Captain nodded and Mark continued.

"The information coming back to you will be displayed on your console but it will also be transmitted via satellite back to Norfolk."

"How long can that transponder operate for?" Asked Jeff.

"Battery life will be around six weeks."

They agreed in order to obtain a good initial track on the creature, the best option would be to release it in an expanse of water less than sixty metres deep this would give them consistent tracking long enough to identify what course it was heading on.

The Delaware would sail south along the coast and once they considered the creature had regained consciousness and they were in suitable water it would be released. Mark and Jeff departed the ship the Delaware sailed immediately out of Norfolk.

On returning to their office, Kate had already set up the screen that would receive the tracking information from the satellite. As they walked in she told them that she had just spoken to the hospital, Alan was still sedated.

"Well what's the plan?" Asked Kate.

Jeff replied.

"We have two options really, if we are confident the creature has teamed up with another swarm we can try and take them out with depth charges, or we can track them down the coast and wait until they look like they are going to come ashore again and take them out on land."

Kate looked at Mark.

"And what plan do you prefer?"

"If we are confident it has teamed up with a swarm, I would go for the depth charges. If we have any doubt we will track it along the shoreline."

Jeff explained to Kate that two helicopters with a detachment of marines were on standby to move down the coast just in case they came ashore.

At 1610 the creatures eyes opened and it stared around its surroundings. One of the deckhands moved towards the cargo net. The creatures head slowly turned watching the sailors every move.

USS Delaware was now fifty miles south of Norfolk and in water less than sixty metres deep. The captured creature appeared to have regained all of its senses and was trying to move around in the net. Even the net being made of wire had not deterred it from trying to bite its way out. The Captain radioed back to Norfolk and requested permission to release the creature. On permission being granted, the cargo net, which was held by two hooks, was winched outboard and slowly lowered to just above the water. The creature sensing the close proximity of the sea started to become more agitated and aggressive in its attempt to escape.

The Captain ordered one of the hooks to be released allowing one side of the cargo net to fall free and the creature to slide into the ocean. The crew watched as it swam shallow for a few seconds then dived deeper and out of sight. On the bridge the Captain gave the order to transmit, the sonar transducer below the ship sent out a short single pulse, less than ten seconds later the transponder replied. On the Delaware the digital screen displayed the creatures current depth, and position. The same information was displayed three seconds later on the screen in Norfolk.

The information was being updated every ninety seconds. Initially the positioning of the creature was erratic with no clear course being assumed, after fifteen minutes and ten more updates, a course was beginning to be plotted it was heading south.

CHAPTER TWENTY-ONE

The tracking had been going on for just over two hours the creature remained on a southerly course travelling at an average speed of eleven knots. The transponder had only failed to reply twice, which was an excellent percentage over the time scale. The marines and two helicopters had been positioned one hundred miles ahead of the current position and placed on standby.

Based on what they had learnt so far about the swarms, Kate had marked off all the sewerage dumping areas a hundred miles ahead with the time of high tide for that area. Mark watched the data being fed into the computer, the last three reports had the creature slowing down and the course becoming erratic, three minutes later the computer indicated that it had changed course towards land.

"Do you think it has teamed up with a swarm?" Asked Jeff

"Too soon to tell, there is no sewerage buoys in that area and high tide is over four hours away."

The next three reports put it back on a course of south speed eleven knots.

"What do you think that was about?"

"Looks like our guy just pulled over for dinner, probably found a shoal of fish." Replied Mark

Kate spoke out to no one in particular.

"Well he seems pretty determined on his course, must be heading somewhere."

Mark walked closer to the screen before he answered.

"Or he is in communication with a swarm, he has covered twenty-five miles now and barely moved a degree of course, he is homing in on something, believe me."

Jeff had arranged some comfortable chairs and a settee to be put in the room next door. Both Kate and Mark had only had an hour's sleep in the last thirty-six and it appeared it was going to be another long night. Kate had already retired to the settee and was fast asleep when Mark came in. Sitting down on one of the armchairs, he sipped on a lukewarm cup of coffee and thought about the creature with the transponder. These beasts were pure killing machines even the great white shark came nowhere near to them. He imagined it now cutting through the ocean like a dagger heading towards possibly fifty more of them. He put down the half empty cup, laid back on the chair and fell asleep.

During the next five hours, the creature appeared to break for food twice more but continued on its southerly course at an average speed of eleven knots. It was 3:30am when Mark re-appeared from the rest room. Jeff was sat at a table his head in his hands focussed on the screen.

"Anything happening?"

"Nope it has stopped a couple of times for food, but otherwise same course and speed throughout."

Mark looked at position indicator, it was thirty-six miles north of the marine's position. Delaware was still three miles astern from it. The next sewerage buoy was four miles ahead and high water would in forty- five minutes. The creature swam past the buoy and high tide maintaining the same course and speed.

At 5:15am, it slowed down to virtually three knots, it remained at that speed for over thirty minutes and by the course alterations appeared to be going around in circles.

Kate appeared yawning from the rest room.

"Anything going on guys?"

"This looks promising I think he may have teamed up with a swarm" Said Mark

"What makes you think that?"

"It is swimming in circles and only doing three knots which is not fast enough for chasing fish, so I would say there is a strong possibility it is interacting with a group."

It was another fifteen minutes before the transponder reported the creature had increased speed to 9 knots and resumed a southerly course. Mark sat back on the chair and watched the progress of both the creature and the Delaware. The previous manoeuvres were indicative of joining up with a swarm but it would be good if he could confirm his theory in some way.

The only way he was going to do that was to use active sonar and see the size of the sonar echo returned, it would be chancy. On hearing active sonar they could alter course and go into deeper water and the transponder may fail to reply. The thought was drumming around in his head it was like playing a game of poker would he go all in and use active sonar. He played with the idea for ten minutes and finally decided he would take the chance. He remembered a conversation he had with Sharky during his time on Sabre. He had explained about how the helicopters can use active sonar but it is not as powerful as surface ships. What if they were to use less powerful sonar with a different transmission type?

"Jeff could we get hold of an Anti- Submarine helicopter?"

"Cannot see a problem with that, you thinking of using active sonar?"

"Well it will give us a definite answer if we are tracking more than the one."

Although it was only 6am, Jeff got on the phone to the air station and spoke to the Duty Officer. The conversation lasted less then five minutes.

"The Duty Officer will get back to us as soon as he speaks to the Flight Controller."

Ten minutes later the phone rang, it was the Flight Controller, they could have a Seahawk helicopter ready to go in forty-five minutes. Mark handed Jeff a piece of paper with co-ordinates of where he would like the helicopter to take up station. Jeff read it out to the Flight Controller who said he would get back with an estimated time of arrival. When the he returned the call he advised the helicopter

154

could be on station by 0830. Mark beckoned to Jeff to hand him the phone.

"Hi, Professor Mark Yates here, when the helicopter gets on station the Delaware will direct them into position. The objective is to see how big an echo will be returned, so as soon as the helicopter gets contact and has established echo size they are to stop transmitting, we do not want to spook them into going deep."

The Flight Controller confirmed the instructions.

The Seahawk helicopter took off from the air station at 0705. It carried dipping sonar, which it would lower into the water and send out a single pulse transmission. The sonar would be operating in a low range scale therefore the transmissions would go out rapidly. If it gained contact quickly it could be transmitting for less than two minutes. On the Delaware the Captain received the message that a Seahawk helicopter would be joining them at 0830, they were to direct it one mile in front of the transponders position.

It was now 0825, on the ships radio the Seahawk's call sign came over calling up the Delaware. It was three miles away and requesting an operating area. The Delaware passed out a course for the helo to position it one mile in front of the creature's current location. The huge Seahawk helicopter altered course towards the reported area, three minutes later it went into the hover and began to lower its sonar into the ocean to a depth of thirty metres. Two minutes later, the helicopters sonar operator sitting in front of his screen switched to transmit. Thirty metres below the surface of the ocean, the cylindrical transducer sent out a single ping into the ocean. The first transmission displayed a possible contact 1800 yards away. The second transmission confirmed the contact now at 1720 yards. The contact was strong and heading towards them. At the third transmission they were content that is was a large contact moving at a speed of 8 to10 knots. They transmitted once more for final confirmation then stopped transmitting.

The winch operator began to recover the sonar

transducer from the ocean, on clearing the water, the Seahawk altered back towards the air station.

Back in Norfolk they were monitoring the radio reports from the Seahawk and all eyes were on the next transponder report.

It flashed up on the screen the creature remained heading south at a speed of nine knots.

Mark clenched his fist and said a long pleasurable yes.

"Well that confirms it we have a swarm of them."

Mark smiled, not only did they confirm that it was a swarm, but they did not react to the Seahawks dipping sonar.

Mark poured Jeff and Kate a coffee and sat down at a table with them.

"Well guys, as I see it, we now have an opportunity to go in and depth charge them, anybody disagree?"

Both Jeff and Kate agreed that it was too good an opportunity to miss.

At 0915, Jeff got in contact with the Admiral's office, less than five minutes later Admiral Hawkins phoned back personally.

Jeff answered.

"Commander, switch me to loudspeaker"

"You are on loudspeaker Sir" Replied Jeff.

"Well, this looks like all we could have prayed for. Professor how many depth charges was the Royal Navy using against these beasts?"

"They carried out one attack using twelve and another using eight, all dropped simultaneously Admiral."

"Well I think we will go for the twelve want to make sure none of these damn creatures get away."

Mark followed up.

"Admiral, these are pretty difficult to kill, after the attacks Sabre deployed the ships boat with armed sailors, to make sure they were all dead."

"Good idea, we will inform Delaware to carry out that task. Commander my staff has spoken to the Air Station there is three Seahawks being prepared for the operation,

156

they should be ready in the next twenty minutes, I want you to liaise with them direct and pass them their instructions."

"Will do, Sir."

"Keep me informed, I want to know the result as soon as the attack has been carried out, happy hunting."

Jeff turned to Mark and Kate.

"Well I never thought I would end up taking Seahawks for live depth charge attacks."

Both Mark and Kate smiled.

"So Commander, what's the plan?" Said Kate.

"Well I do not want to look like I am copying the Royal Navy, but the way they conducted the first attack against them with the helicopters forming a net and being directed to drop the depth charges when the swarm entered it looked pretty impressive, think I will go with that."

"Sounds like a plan to me." Replied Mark.

Jeff called up the Delaware on the radio and passed the intended attack information to the Captain. The Delaware was to direct the three Seahawks to one mile in front of the swarm and order them to drop their depth charges once they entered the kill zone.

By 0955, the three Seahawks took off from the air station carrying a payload of four depth charges each; there in flight time would be one hour twenty-five minutes getting them on station at 1120.

Mark looked at the computer screen; that would put them roughly in the area opposite Cape Hatteras; they were going to be very close to the ocean shelf and deep water. He did not know what brought it on but suddenly he felt slightly sick in his stomach that something was going to go wrong.

"Kate would you put up the exact location the creatures will be at when the Seahawks arrive?"

Kate tapped four keys on her keyboard and a red flashing cross appeared at the predicted position.

Mark looked at it; they will be less than a mile from the ocean shelf.

"Kate what depth of water will they be in?"

"90 metres but if they turn it drops down to 750 metres pretty rapidly."

Jeff looked at Mark.

"Something wrong?"

"Just wish they were not so close to deep water, if they get spooked for any reason they could go deep extremely quickly."

The Seahawks were still thirty minutes from the operating area and the swarm were still maintaining a southerly course. Suddenly the transponder began to report a change of course. The creature was swimming erratically and to all effect it looked like it was another food stop. Mark prayed that if it was a shoal of fish they would not pursue them into the deeper water.

All three of them watched as the reports from the transponder came in. The course alterations had put the swarm within half a mile of the ocean shelf. The transponder failed to reply once, then twice, on the third time it responded putting the creatures back on a course of south speed nine knots.

Mark looked at the new position they were extremely close to the shelf and very deep water.

The Seahawks were now only seven minutes from the area and were in communications with the Delaware. Mark, Jeff and Kate all sat silently deeply immersed in the communications between the ship and helicopters.

Delaware passed out the position for the attack and the three Seahawks adjusted their course to take up the attack positions.

Mark looked at where the Seahawks would be delivering their attack, Christ he thought they are directly on the edge of the shelf.

"Kate what is the depth of water in the attack zone?"

"120 metres but a stones throw away it drops to over 700 metres."

The three Seahawks went into the hover over the area of the planned attack.

Delaware was counting down the range to them.

1800 yards, 1700 yards, 1600 yards, 1500 yards, at 1400 yards the swarm began to slow down to about four knots. The next range call was 1330 yards then 1300 yards. The next report made them still at 1300 yards and the course was beginning to become erratic. The next report from the transponder still made them at a range of 1270 yards from the Seahawks.

Jeff looked at Mark.

"Have we got a problem?"

"I do not know but I do not like this." Replied Mark.

The next transponder report made the swarm doing three knots and still swimming erratically at just over 1200 yards from the attack zone.

Kate spoke out.

"Mark, you said these creatures learn fast, have they come across helicopters before? For three Seahawks must be pretty noisy that close to them."

"Oh yes they have come across helicopters before, and it has always been a nasty experience."

Mark turned towards Jeff.

"Jeff I agree with Kate, I do not think they are going to walk into a trap this time, I have a feeling they are going to go deep pretty soon."

"Any suggestions?" Questioned Jeff.

"Tell the Delaware they are not falling for it bring the Seahawks to the swarm and drop the charges"

Jeff immediately relayed the message to the Delaware and Seahawks.

As the three Seahawks moved forward they got to within 800 yards of the creatures, when the transponder reported the swarm had increased speed and was heading towards deep water. The next transponder report gave them a speed of 14 knots and at a depth of 120 metres, which also put them directly over the ocean shelf.

There was one more transponder report before the Delaware called out to the Seahawks to drop the charges.

The Seahawks immediately began to vomit the depth

charges into the ocean below. Delaware reported multiple explosions.

It was four minutes later when the first sighting of a creature appeared floating on the ocean surface, after seven minutes the helicopters reported twenty two of them on the surface. Some of them were still alive and obviously concussed because they were still jerking around as they floated on the surface.

Delaware quickly had the boat in the water with armed sailors and heading towards the creatures. Before the boat arrived two of them had recovered sufficiently enough to swim drunkenly around on the surface, before diving down to the ocean depths. A total of twenty creatures were delivered a shot to the head by the armed sailors, two of those were hoisted onboard the Delaware to be taken back to Norfolk for further analysis.

"Only twenty killed." Said Jeff.

"Making probably up to thirty escaping." Replied Mark.

A message came in that none of those killed had a transponder attached therefore Delaware was going to remain on a southerly course at a speed of nine knots for the next twenty-four hours in a hope of picking it up again.

Mark thought it unlikely. The transponder was extremely sensitive and would probably have been damaged in the attack.

Jeff gave Admiral Hawkins office a call and relayed the disappointing news.

CHAPTER TWENTY-TWO

The grey sleek shape of HMS Sabre sailed into Norfolk harbour. The British warship looked quite different from her American counterparts that she passed. The United States navy warships sat much lower in the water and bristled with an array of weapons. Sabre with her single barrelled gun on her forecastle and the two missile systems mid ships, stood much higher in the water. Her light grey paintwork was immaculate and glistened against the morning sun. Sailors dressed in full blue uniform gave her a look of stateliness as she slowly sailed in with the white ensign fluttering proudly in the breeze. Mark looked on at Sabre's entrance and felt quite patriotic by the appearance of the Royal Navy. Around him stood other spectators and the comments he was overhearing supported his impression that Sabre looked an impressive and professional warship. As the ship got closer to the harbour wall, he saw Captain Piper on the bridge wing holding a microphone in his hand relaying orders to the bridge. Sailors stood around the upper deck holding large rattan fenders to protect her side as she approached the berth. The coming alongside was a smoothly executed manoeuvre and within five minutes the ship was secure enough for a large crane on the jetty to lower the gangway onto the flight deck. Mark looked down towards the quarterdeck, he could see two familiar yellow shapes of the noisemakers fitted securely into metal brackets. As the gangway was secured he also noticed that the armed sentries who were usually sailors had been replaced by two Royal Marines.

Twenty minutes later Mark was seated with the Captain in his cabin drinking tea, also present was Sabre's Operations Officer Lt Commander Steve Dodds.

"I noticed you had Royal Marines on the gangway"

The Captain nodded.

"Yes, we have embarked twelve marines for this

deployment, Admiral Lane thought they may come in useful at some stage."

Mark took them through the previous two weeks operations against the creatures and the significant points he had learnt.

"So how many creatures do you think are left then Professor?" Asked the Operations Officer.

"I think there is one swarm still undetected probably around fifty strong, and the creatures we attacked yesterday probably have around thirty survivors."

"And any idea what our next move is going to be?" Asked the Captain.

"Right now I have not got a clue, they are stationing marines near some more remote areas where sewage discharges are, but it is a big coastline and the missing groups could be anywhere between here and Florida by now."

"Well, Admiral Lane has told me to provide any assistance we can, so if you need us we are ready."

"There is one thing, I would like Chief Ward to do some acoustic analysis on the tape recording from Cape Fear, I have the clearances for him to use the analysis centre here in Norfolk."

"No problem, I will get the Chief to get in touch with you, will tomorrow morning be ok?"

"Tomorrow will be fine."

The acoustic analysis centre was situated about ten miles away from the naval base. Mark and Sharky entered the heavily guarded main gate, security here was extremely high. At the entrance they had to go through a double glass door. As they entered both doors closed, they remained trapped between the doors until their security clearances were checked. On exiting they were given numbered passes marked *visitor* and were then instructed to wait until a Petty Officer from the analysis section arrived to escort them. Their escort arrived and led them through a long passageway. Reaching the end of the passageway they entered a large room filled with computer screens and a number of tables most of which were covered with long sheets of graph paper. The air-conditioning made it quite chilly which Mark gathered was for the benefit of all the electrical equipment and computers rather than those working in there. There were seven naval personnel in the room; four were working at computers and three studying graphs at a table. As they proceeded into the room, one of them a female officer at the table turned and walked towards them, she was tall and had her blonde hair tied back in a tight bun. Reaching them she offered her hand and introduced herself as Lieutenant Commander Emma Wright the senior acoustic analysis officer. Mark and Sharky returned the introduction and gave her a brief explanation of the reason behind their visit. Mark handed the tape recording to Emma who in turn called to a Petty Officer who was working at a computer to take the recording and run it through the spectrum analyser. She then led them over to two large computer screens at the far end of the room. On the screens were marked sections for different frequencies, the lowest being zero to fifty hertz building up to a maximum of ten kilohertz. The Petty Officer who had taken the recording informed Emma that it was set up and ready to run. She pressed a button marked run and lines started to appear at the top of the screens dropping in a waterfall fashion towards the bottom of the screen. Sharky appeared to know exactly what he was looking at, but for the benefit of Mark, Emma talked him through it.

"Professor, we are running your recording through the spectrum analyser, what you see at the top of the screens is any frequencies that are being detected on it."

"So all these frequencies are coming from the creatures?" Asked Mark

"No. The ocean is filled with lots of noises, most of these frequencies will not have anything to do with the creatures.

"Oh like OSN?" Replied Mark

Sharky smiled at Mark, quite impressed he had remembered. Even Emma looked a little surprised at him using sonar terminology.

"Yes like OSN, what we are going to do is identify and isolate the actual frequencies that the creatures were transmitting on."

Emma turned a dial at the side of the screen that made the recording run at triple speed.

"Professor, I am speeding the recording up, we are used to looking at these screens and can manage to analysis at three times the normal speed."

Emma kept switching from high speed to low speed as she detected any suspicious frequency. Fifteen minutes had passed and nothing of any interest was detected. Emma and Sharky were now both seated in front of the screens and Mark sat on the edge of a table behind them.

Without looking away from the screen, Sharky asked Emma to switch back to slow speed, and pointed to a line appearing on the screen. The line was much darker than the other frequencies being displayed and had abruptly started where as the other frequencies were there throughout. As quickly as it started the frequency stopped.

"Is that a possibility?" Asked Mark.

Without answering Emma used a set of markers on the screen to measure the transmission time of the frequency.

"Three point six seconds, three hundred and fifty two hertz." She said to no one in particular.

Emma and Sharky started to talk amongst themselves regarding the suspect frequency. As the frequency dropped down to the middle of the screen, Emma switched the screen to freeze and the picture froze.

Emma turned to Sharky.

"You check the higher spectrum from 1 kilohertz up, I will check the lower."

They both started flicking through the screens, checking for any frequencies that had started and stopped at the same time as the one they had spotted.

"Something here at 7 kilohertz, same characteristics."

Emma looked over to Sharky's screen and nodded.

It was a much thicker line than the first one but appeared to start and stop at the same time.

"Looks definitely from the same noise source" Replied Emma.

It was less than five minutes before Emma and Sharky had completed a full search.

Emma pressed two buttons on the screen and the two frequencies detected appeared enlarged. She pressed a button at the side of each screen and a photograph of both screens was despatched from a printer situated at the side of the computers. She stood up and laid the photographs on the table that Mark had been sat on.

"Well Professor, these frequencies are what we call abrupt starts and stops, which generally means that something or someone has transmitted the frequency for a very short period of time."

"Like transmitting on sonar?"

"Yes, a possibility, but this is not sonar, see how it bends with time, it is what we call a frequency modulated signal, that means it is changing frequency all of the time, this one starts off low and goes up in frequency."

"You think it is the creatures?"

Emma called over to the Petty Officer and told him to rewind it and switch to loudspeaker. From the speakers came a sound similar to the noise you hear when you put your ear to a large seashell, suddenly a chirping noise broke through the background noise, it was the same as Mark had heard at Cape Fear.

"Is that the noise you heard before Professor?" Asked Emma.

Mark nodded.

"Well it looks like that confirms this was the frequency that your creatures were transmitting on."

"But there was a lot of it going on, for at least a couple of minutes when I first heard it."

As Mark spoke more chirping noises came over the speakers.

165

"Looks like you may have missed the first transmission and we are now listening to what you heard that night."

Emma and Sharky moved back towards the screens.

She called over for the recording to be rewound back to where the chirping had started and switched the screens to run.

They left the loudspeakers running and as the recording reached the chirping, at least six different lines started to appear on the screens, all around the three hundred and fifty hertz and seven kilohertz mark. Once again, they let the frequencies reach the middle of the screen, froze it and took two more photographs.

Emma laid the photographs on the table, looked at them for a few seconds and then passed them towards Sharky. After a few seconds she spoke to Sharky.

"You thinking what I am thinking?"

Mark waited in anticipation to find out what both sonar analysts were thinking.

Sharky nodded.

"At least four different frequencies, and three different characteristics, they look like they were having a good old chat to one another."

Emma nodded in agreement.

She turned to Mark.

"Professor, now we have isolated the frequencies, I am going to run the computer to search for any similar frequencies on the tape. What I need you to do is write down the sequence of events of that morning. If we are correct, we may be able to isolate to some degree what the frequencies meant."

"You mean you could translate the language they are using?"

"Roughly, we can look at your sequence of events and try and establish what would be the likely discussion going on and identify what frequencies were used."

Emma called over two analysts one male and one female; she spoke to them for a couple of minutes then turned to Mark and Sharky.

166

"I am going to make this a top priority task, I will have my team working on it throughout the night we should be able to give you an answer by this time tomorrow."

Mark spent the next twenty minutes writing down every detail he could think of from the attack at Cape Fear. They thanked Emma and arranged another visit for the next day. On the way back to the base, they pulled over and went into a bar for a beer.

As they each drank a Budweiser, Mark brought up a something he had noticed at the analysis centre.

"You looked a bit surprised when you heard the noise the creatures were making."

Sharky nodded.

"It surprised me how different it sounded from when we first came across them, I have never known any species of sea life change so acoustically before, it just worried me a little that every time we come across them something changes."

Mark thought back to the first recordings of them, the whining and growling noises, and then something dawned on him.

"Sharky, when we first met them, they were theoretically still babies just like human babies they had no set language, but as they have grown they have learnt to talk. I think the creatures have now matured enough to communicate clearly enough to one another."

"So you agree that they can communicate beyond what is normal for sea life?"

"Oh I think these creatures are very capable and will evolve well beyond the communication levels of even the dolphin."

CHAPTER TWENTY-THREE

Back in Norfolk, Mark lay on his bed, he picked up the phone and pressed fast dial to Lisa Michaels. He had not spoken to her for over a week, he had felt like ringing her on a number of occasions but something always seemed to be going on that resulted in him not calling. The phone rang twice and then he heard her voice, the sound of it made him smile and a picture of her on their night out in Washington appeared in his mind.

"Hi Mark, thought you had forgotten me?"

"No that would be extremely difficult."

They talked for over twenty minutes, on nothing in particular but just enjoying the sound of each other's voices.

"So when am I going to see you again?" She asked.

"It is very difficult to set a date without the chance of having to cancel. I never know what our next move against the creatures is going to be."

"Well its Tuesday today why don't we make a date for this weekend and if it turns out you cannot make it, I will understand."

Mark thought for a few seconds, he could get down to Florida and be back in Norfolk in a few hours if he was required.

"Ok let's say I fly down Friday for the weekend, do you know a good hotel?"

"Do not worry about a hotel I will pick you up at the airport, just call me when you know your flight times."

"It will be nice to see you again Lisa."

"And you Mark"

When he finally hung up he had forgotten all about the problems with the creatures, his mind was fully occupied thinking of Lisa Michaels and the possibility of a whole weekend with her.

Three hundred and twenty miles away to the south, just

outside Jacksonville, Victoria Cotton sat on a wooden bench looking out towards the ocean. Her eyes were red from crying, tears and mascara marks stained her cheeks. Earlier that night she had been with two girlfriends, both were much prettier and slimmer than her and both were now in the company of two young men. Victoria was short at just five feet one inches and weighed nearly one hundred and ninety pounds. Twenty-two years old she had never had a boyfriend. Still living with her parents, it had been her mother who had pushed her into accepting the invitation from the two girls from work. She knew that mentioning it at home was a mistake. All along she had suspected they had only invited her to drive them there and back. The thought of it brought more tears to her eyes realising now it was the truth. As soon as they had entered the club they had left her to join up with some other people. She should have stayed at home chatting to her friends on the internet. Those people were her real friends, although Victoria had never revealed to them what she really looked like and when asked to send a photo had chosen one of her younger sister who was much prettier and slimmer.

In the background the music from the clubhouse played. Looking at her watch there was still forty-five minutes to go before the arranged time to meet up with the other two and taxi them home. The thought of leaving without them went through her mind but that would only make things difficult at work on Monday. Victoria shivered, the sea air brought a chill with it and it was beginning to feel cold with just a long skirt and thin blouse on. She decided to head back to the car park and spend the rest of the time listening to the radio in the comfort and warmth of her car.

Getting up from the bench, something caught her eye, a long dark shape was passing over the narrow pathway that led towards the clubhouse. The illumination from the small solar lamps that edged the pathway reflected against the shape making it glisten as if it was wet or oily. Standing perfectly still her eyes followed the shape until it disappeared from sight into the borders of evergreen shrubs. Victoria stood motionless for nearly a whole minute, breathing quietly, concentrating on the spot where it had crossed over. Although the quickest route back to the car park was along the same pathway where the shape had crossed, fear advised her senses on a detour to avoid that route. Her short plump legs walked as quickly and quietly as they could towards her car. Every few seconds her head turned to check there was nothing following her. On reaching the car her imagination of what the shape was had reached a level that made her very frightened. Quickly getting into the vehicle she immediately locked all the doors. Slipping the keys in to the ignition the radio came on, The Rolling Stones, Love is Strong was playing, she liked the Stones and this was one of her favourites. Listening to the music began to ease her fear and anxiety. Casting her mind back to what she saw, maybe her eyes were playing tricks on her, it was dark and she had been crying. By the time The Stones had finished she had convinced herself she had imagined it all.

Ten minutes had passed and the windscreen began to mist up. Reaching into the glove compartment she withdrew a box of tissues. Singing along with the music on the radio Victoria pulled a few from the packet and wiped the excess moisture from the windows. Whilst wiping the front windscreen, movement outside made her stop and stare. What looked like a gigantic snake was slithering along the lawn towards the clubhouse. Transfixed on the snake like figure her attention was suddenly diverted on hearing laughter and voices. Looking around four young people were exiting the clubhouse and heading towards the car park. On turning her gaze back to the snake she caught sight of another moving around the parked cars. Her eyes flicked back towards the first one, there were at least six more shapes joining it, all moving directly towards the entrance of the clubhouse. The four teenagers were unaware they were heading directly towards them. In her urgency to warn them, her hand pressed down hard on the car horn. The prolonged noise caused the young people to stop and look around, it was then they noticed the danger they were heading toward. Both the teenage girls let out terrified screams. For a moment all four froze, their brains trying to absorb the unbelievable, flight took over and in unison they turned and started running back towards the entrance of the clubhouse.

The window began to mist up again Victoria hastily pulled out more tissues and rubbed frantically trying to clear the moisture. On clearing enough to view she could see that the creatures were within a few yards of one of the teenagers. The closest creature to them began to pursue them, for its size it moved at incredible speed. To her astonishment it lifted from the ground and sprung forward through the air, just before landing it opened a huge set of jaws and snapped then shut on one of the female's legs. As it landed back on the ground, it twisted its head lifting the girl into the air and slammed her down on the hard cement car park. The leg firmly held in the creature's jaws separated at the thigh, the remainder of the body spun away landing a few yards away. Victoria could see the girl's body still moving, her arms flaying in all directions the rest of the body was in an uncontrollable spasm.

The other three teenagers continued to run, suddenly they all stopped. At least four of the creatures blocked their way to the entrance. In a panic they turned to look for an alternative escape route. They were then presented with the full horror of what had happened to their friend. The creature that had attacked her had virtually devoured all of the amputated leg. Protruding from its mouth was the upper part of the limb which the creature quickly dispensed with. One of the males turned and ran to the left of the clubhouse disappearing out of sight. The other two hesitated for a moment then both followed the first. A few seconds later Victoria could clearly hear a female's petrified scream from the direction they had fled followed by a male voice crying for help.

She looked on in horror at the dismembered body of the first girl that had been attacked. The creature that had devoured her leg swung its head around and grabbed the girl by the waist. It bit into the girl with such ferociousness that it cut the body in half in a matter of seconds. The upper torso and head fell away as the creature feasted on the remaining leg.

At the clubhouse the huge snake like shapes began to enter the doorway. Victoria turned the ignition and the small car's engine immediately responded, as she flicked on the headlights to full beam, they illuminated the front of the clubhouse. What she saw left her shaking in fear, there must have been thirty of the snake-like creatures. Above the sound of the music from the club came frantic screaming. Suddenly one of the large bay windows smashed and a chair that had been thrown through it landed on the lawn outside. From the broken window a young man appeared, he jumped on to the lawn below and held out his hand to help a long blonde haired female who was exiting the same way. As the girl jumped her skirt got snagged on the broken window frame. Both she and the young man were now pulling frantically to free it. Without warning the skirt broke free and they both tumbled over onto the grass. From the surrounding shrubbery three creatures appeared moving at speed towards them. The young man was the first to get to his feet and grabbed hold of the girl's hand pulling at it to hasten her recovery from the ground. As the girl finally rose, Victoria noticed that her dress had completely been ripped off. For a second the fear and horror of what she was witnessing left her, she found herself transfixed on the girls figure. In a mixture of jealousy and attraction she stared at the girls shapely legs leading up to the tiny panties. Amongst all of the horror she was seeing she felt embarrassed and guilty at feeling sexually attracted to her.

More screaming brought her back to reality. She could

172

see the young couple were now on their feet. Just as they were about to make their first stride towards escaping a creature got close enough to strike. Its jaws snapped around the girl's leg and she fell to the ground. The young man was using both hands pulling at her arm trying to release her from the grip of the creature. Suddenly the girl's body broke free which resulted in the young man falling backwards. Victoria saw that she had only been released by the amputation of her leg, which was now being devoured by the creature. As the couple lay on the ground a further two creatures arrived, one of them approached the young man from the back, it opened its jaws and snapped them shut around his head, with a twist of its body, it ripped the head and neck from the shoulders. The second creature moved towards the screaming girl, it bit into her right arm and started shaking her body, the arm separated from her torso and her screaming remains were thrown through the air, landing just short of another creature. The girl landed face up on the grass, between the crying and screaming, Victoria could hear her shouting for her mother. Her cries for help were ended as the closest creature bit into her head.

People were now rushing from every exit of the building, all were running straight into the waiting creatures there was no escaping them. She pushed the car into gear and accelerated. Just as the car moved forward a fleeing couple ran straight in front of it. Victoria instinctively swung the steering wheel to avoid them. The severe alteration of course brought the car into a collision with a parked truck. As the cars contacted, she jolted forward banging her head hard against the top of the steering wheel. Blood flowed from her forehead down the side of her nose, dripping from the chin on to her new blouse. In a panic she pushed the gears into reverse drive, suddenly the driver's side window exploded over her followed by a searing pain in her left arm. Her body was slammed against the inside of the door. There was a loud crack and the pull against her body subsided. All that remained of her arm was a bloody stump. Through her screaming she saw a creature with its head raised less than three feet away from the car devouring her severed arm. The evil looking eyes returned the stare then swallowed the final remains of her limb. Victoria pushed away from the door towards the passenger seat. The creature moved closer to the window and let out a terrifying hiss pushing its grotesque head through the window. It was so close to her she could smell her own blood on its breath. It drove its head down and grabbed hold of her leg pulling her body towards the car window. Screaming and crying she could feel herself being lifted and her leg being dragged through the window. Her body moved along the dashboard and brushed the volume control of the radio turning it up to maximum. The music blared out. Her oversized buttocks reached the broken window and became firmly lodged in the small opening. The creature increased the strength behind the pull and started shaking its head side to side. Victoria's screaming was being drowned out by loud music from the radio. Agonising pain passed completely through her body as she began to move through the window. The broken glass and metal ripped and sliced through her skin and flesh. Skin was being torn from her buttocks all the way up to the nape of her neck. A final hard pull from the creature brought her crashing onto the car park. The creature started to drag her along the ground. Through her tear filled eyes she saw dozens of creatures moving away from the clubhouse all of them were dragging human body parts. Many of them being carried away were still alive. One of them a dark haired girl was screaming and begging for help, she appeared to have all her body parts intact and was trying to grab anything that would stop her from being taken. As if annoyed with the noise the creature dragging the girl lifted its head and swung her body in a high arc slamming it down on the hard cement. Even above the surrounding noise Victoria could hear the crack as the girls head made contact with the ground. The creature continued to drag Victoria along, the hard cement changed to grass followed by sand. She could hear the waves crashing against the shore. As the first wave met her damaged body the saltwater burnt into her exposed flesh like acid. She screamed like she knew this would be the last noise she would ever make. In those last few moments she reflected on her life. Tears streamed from her eyes as she was dragged beneath the waves.

CHAPTER TWENTY-FOUR

It was the highest death count to date, the latest figures reported sixty-four people missing all aged between eighteen and twenty-seven years old. The number of fatalities was expected to rise. Emergency telephone numbers were being inundated with calls from people reporting missing friends and relatives. A partial hand and the right side of a female torso were all the creatures left behind to associate the blood soaked areas with the butchery of humans. Mark, Jeff and Kate all watched in silence at the television coverage of the massacre. Around the police perimeter there were hundreds of people many were visibly crying. Already a large number of flowers and wreaths were being laid alongside the main entrance to the clubhouse.

Mark turned away from the screen and looked at the area of the chart of the attack, two sewerage buoys.

"We are going to have to warn the public in all areas with sewerage buoys."

Jeff nodded.

"The Admiral has already discussed it they are having a press conference this afternoon. The national guard is being positioned around the high threat coastal areas."

As the news report changed to another headline, Kate turned to Mark.

"Mark, over sixty-four people missing with a good chance of that rising, I know these creatures are getting bigger but if our swarms are on average fifty strong it seems a lot of people to go missing in one attack."

Mark nodded slowly.

"I have been thinking about that, even at the size they are now I would not have expected that amount of killing, we know they generally eat everything they kill, but there could be an explanation."

"Which is?" Asked Jeff.

"The swarm we attacked with the depth charges has

joined up with the other one that would make them around seventy to eighty strong."

Kate exhaled a large breath.

"Jesus! If that many of them came ashore, no wonder those kids were massacred."

Mark nodded his head in agreement.

"Kate I think you can delete all the other tracks on the computer, and start a new track on this attack."

Mark wandered over to one of the desks and sat down and started doodling with a pencil on a notebook . After about five minutes he got up from the desk and looked at the computer screen.

"What are you thinking?" Asked Kate.

"I am wondering why they would join together? They are intelligent creatures and they must know they are more vulnerable in a large swarm. But there is one possible reason."

"Which is?" Asked Jeff.

"One of the creatures is dominant and controlling the others."

By the end of the day the final count had risen to seventy-three confirmed missing and the warning to all coastal areas had been transmitted. The telephone rang and Jeff answered it. Mark and Kate listened and watched Jeff as he spoke and nodded. He put down the receiver and turned to them both.

We will be able to confirm if your theory on how many of them were involved in the attack, they have viewed the security cameras from the nightclub; the whole massacre was captured on film. Copies of the footage are being sent up to us, should be here sometime this evening.

Mark took two very important telephone calls that afternoon, the first from Emma Wright. She reported that they had recovered a lot of data from the recording and were pretty confident they had isolated certain frequencies associated with specific communications between the creatures. Mark explained to her that last nights attack has

177

delayed him making his planned return to the analysis centre today but would try to be there early tomorrow. Emma fully understood and hoped to have further data for him by the time he arrived.

The second call was from Lisa Michaels, her team had completed a full autopsy on the creatures recovered from the recent depth charge attack and reported that the BSE damage to the brain had advanced. She considered it was now a strong possibility that the creatures were entering a period that would make them very erratic and extremely aggressive. Mark wondered how more aggressive they could actually get, but he knew what Lisa meant. Right now they killed for food, now or in the near future they would start killing for no reason.

At 1830 the footage covering the attack arrived in Norfolk. Mark, Kate and Jeff sat in a conference room with a large LCD television. On the script that arrived with the recording, the first sighting was at 0116, when a creature was sighted moving over the walkway towards the nightclub. They forwarded the recording to that time and watched the dark shape move tentatively but with deliberation towards the nightclub, they could also see a small rotund female figure in the distance looking towards the creature. Eight minutes later the same security camera picked up one returning to the ocean. The footage ran on for another nine minutes before the creatures began to appear. The security camera detected twenty-two moving over the walkway. The picture changed to another camera, which showed more of them moving towards the building from another angle. As the last creature moved out of the cameras view, the picture switched from the walkway to a view of the car park and nightclub entrance. In the car park they could see movement all around the cars, the picture changed again to one of the garden areas showing even more creatures slithering along the grass. The lights from the nightclub entrance gave a clear view of the first attack on a group of teenagers; they all sat in silence as they watched the horror and butchery unfold.

The way the young people were dying was horrific, one of the female's faces appeared clearly on the camera, and the fear on her face was terrifying to those watching. Cameras inside the building showed a scene of devastation, carnage and slaughter as the creatures attacked and devoured the young victims. Without saying anything Kate got up from her chair and left the room, Mark and Jeff did not acknowledge her leaving, both sat silently, occasionally lowering their heads to look away from the horrific killings the creatures were inflicting on the young people. The footage ran on for another fifteen minutes, throughout it the creatures were killing and devouring their prey. As in unison the creatures stopped and started to move out of the building, all of them dragged with them bodies and body parts. The camera switched once more from inside the building to the entrance. The doorway was crammed with a seething mass of creatures leaving and dragging their kills. Mark looked at them in horror. He could see that not all of the people they were dragging were dead. A few were still moving and screaming but any attempts to break free were futile. He watched as one young man being dragged by his leg held on to the doorway with both his free hands. The creature released the leg, turned and snapped its ferocious jaws onto the teenagers head, the body went limp. Releasing the head it returned to dragging the body along by the leg. As the creature twisted its body around to continue, Mark pressed the remote control and froze the screen. Jeff looked at Mark for an explanation.

"Jeff look at its back."

"I see a white mark." Replied Jeff.

"That white mark is a transponder, this is the creature we had in Norfolk and it confirms that the two swarms have merged."

Mark kept the screen frozen for a few more seconds, during that time he thought that this thing killing these young people had been lying on a table in front of him and now it was eating humans alive. From the picture on the screen he could see those cold eyes, the same evil stare he had witnessed before.

They both left the conference room and joined Kate in the office; she still looked visibly shaken by the horror of what she had seen and her eyes were red from tears. None of them mentioned the contents. Mark sat alongside Kate and put his arm around her shoulders.

"Come on I will walk you back to your room."

When Mark and Kate arrived back at their accommodation he took her into her room and made her a drink. She gave a forced smile and thanked him. He stayed with her for about thirty minutes, very little was said during that time. It was gone 2200 when he finally entered his own room. He picked up his mobile phone and it showed one missed call, the number was Admiral Lane's, he pressed call.

The Admiral answered the phone in a sombre voice and expressed his sorrow at the amount of human life lost in the attack at Jacksonville. Mark took him through what they had found out and hopefully they would get some sort of breakthrough from that knowledge. The Admiral already knew about the analysis that was going on with the recordings from Cape Fear, Mark assumed it must have been from an update Sabre had passed to him, but he never ever questioned where the he got his information. The Admiral asked if he was happy to stay and carry on. Mark assured him that he would stay as long as he could be of help.

"Professor, you know if it was not for you a lot more people would have lost their lives."

"Thank you Admiral, but let's hope we can kill this remaining swarm as quickly as possible without the loss of more innocent people."

"Professor, I am putting Sabre fully at your disposal. If you need her assistance to take that swarm out, just call me."

"Thank you for the support Admiral."

At the end of the phone call Mark poured himself a neat

rum, he took a large gulp from it and held it in his mouth letting the alcohol release the full affect.

CHAPTER TWENTY-FIVE

Mark and Sharky arrived at the Analysis Centre at 1030, Emma Wright was there to meet them at reception, she was out of uniform and looked extremely attractive in a pair of Levi jeans and Nike sweater, her hair was down and flowed to its full length of about four inches below her shoulders. Mark noticed a slight scent of Chanel No 5 from her; it was a perfume that his wife Cindy often used and he had never forgotten the aroma from it.

"Please excuse the casual dress, I am travelling to a hockey match this afternoon."

"We have not brought you in on your day off have we?" Asked Mark.

"No I had to come in to clear some paperwork this morning anyway, never seem to get the time for that when I am actually on duty."

She led them into a different area of the analysis centre from the last time they had visited. It was a much smaller room and to enter it Emma had to key in six numbers on to a coded keypad. In the room there were four comfortable looking chairs alongside two large desks. Each desk had a computer screen in the centre of them. On a shelf above the computer screens were what Mark assumed to be digital sound enhancers. Emma opened a wall safe and withdrew from it a small compact disc.

"Ok, what I have here is a disc with every frequency that has been recovered from your recording, we have been through the scenario you wrote Mark and tried to tie in the frequencies with what we assumed would have been the dialogue going on between the creatures."

Mark and Sharky nodded in acknowledgement.

As she was speaking Emma slipped the disc into one of the computers.

"To cut a long story short, we believe we have isolated frequencies that relate to key words or possibly meanings."

The information was now loaded. On the screen it

appeared as tables displaying two columns of figures. One column contained frequencies and the other number of times detected.

Emma pointed to the first column.

"This column here indicates the frequencies detected and the second column the number of times it was used."

A frequency of three hundred and fifty hertz was by far the most common with one hundred and thirty two detections.

Emma pointed to that frequency.

"This frequency here is what we believe to be a start, stop signal to a sentence or message. Very similar to the old Morse code when you would prefix with a start or end a message code."

She went on to explain that all the other frequencies detected had this start and stop frequencies either side of them. Emma hit the mouse and the screen moved on to page two. A third column appeared. In the third column were headed words or phrases. The frequency she had just explained had the words start and stop alongside it, other frequencies had the words such as safe, go, come, here, leaving, back and food alongside them. Mark could see three of the frequencies had no words but question marks alongside them. Emma explained that the computer programme they used gave every frequency a percentage on the likelihood of the correct meaning any percentage that fell below thirty five percent was given a question mark.

She hit the mouse once more and a fourth column appeared with percentages shown. Mark noticed the start stop signal had a percentage value of ninety-two, the next highest was eighty-one percent which was adjacent to the word safe. The words come, back, food and go were all in the high seventies.

Emma went on to explain that they had built up a conversation from Mark's scenario and the computer had applied a computer generated voice to it.

She tapped the left hand key on the mouse and a

monotone computer voice came out of the speakers, it started by informing them that the following recording is classified and the date and time it was produced.

On the screen appeared a start box, Emma move the mouse over it and clicked.

The computer-generated voice began.

Time 0238   Start Go Shore Stop

Time 0243 Start Here Stop

Time 0244Start Go Stop

Time 0250Start Back, Safe, Food, Stop

Time 0256Start Back, Safe, Food, Stop

Time 0257Start Coming Stop

Time 0258Start Go Stop

Emma explained that whilst there were a lot more frequencies being transmitted the computer had only used frequencies considered higher than a seventy percent chance of being correct.

Sharky asked Emma to click back to the frequencies detected table. As it appeared on the screen, Sharky looked down it for the frequency at seven Kilohertz they had detected. Alongside it was just a question mark.

"So no idea what this high frequency is?" Asked Sharky.

"No idea but it appears to be around during most of the recording."

"Any ideas Sharky?" Asked Mark.

"Just one, it could be a friend or foe frequency, when they are communicating at a low frequency, they can confirm it is from a genuine source if it has this high seven kilohertz signal backing it up. Similar if ships were communicating with each other we would expect them to authenticate with a coded signal."

Emma smiled and nodded.

"That would make sense." She said

Mark nodded.

"Sounds exactly something like these smart bastards would have in place."

Mark and Sharky left the Analysis Centre at 1145 and headed back to Norfolk, they stopped at the same bar as they had used previously on their visit.

"So Sharky can we use this information to our advantage?"

"I think so, the creatures cannot be a hundred percent sure they are the only remaining swarm, what if we transmitted a signal calling for them."

"Do you think they would fall for that, they have walked into traps like that before and they usually learn fast?"

Sharky nodded slowly and gave a devilish smile

"That is the thing. They do not need to come to us. If they reply we could pinpoint their exact location from the transmission, all we would need is two ships minimum to detect the transmission and we could cross fix their position and track them for as long as they continued to transmit."

Mark and Sharky ordered another drink each and talked over the possibility of transmitting a signal to the remaining swarm. By the time they had finished their second drink they were both entirely enthusiastic about the plan. Mark raised his arm to get the Bartenders attention and order another two beers.

"Hold on a minute Professor one of us has to drive back."

"We can get a cab back and pick up the car tomorrow we are only five miles from base."

Sharky gave him a thumb up and took a long drink from his beer.

Half way through the third drink Mark's mobile rang it was Kate Morgan.

"Mark where are you?"

"Oh hi Kate, Sharky and I are having a few beers in a bar called . . . . . . .Sharky what's this placed called?"

Sharky looked around and saw a sign saying The Hogs Head.

"The Hogs Head" loud enough for Kate to hear.

"Well you could have invited me and Jeff if you were having a few drinks." Kate sent back.

"Well it was sort of unplanned, why don't you join us, the bar is about five miles outside the base on the main highway."

"Ok we will get a cab down, be there in about thirty minutes, stay sober until we get there."

Mark and Sharky were finishing their fourth beer when Kate and Jeff entered the bar. Kate wandered over to Mark and squeezed his shoulders.

"You enjoying yourself?"

"Having a great time, what are you drinking?"

"I will have a beer for starters." Answered Kate.

"Same for me." Followed Jeff.

Sharky stood up and introduced himself to Kate she gave him a big friendly hug.

"Heard a lot about you Chief, and its all good."

As the round of drinks arrived, Kate put her hand over Mark's glass.

"Before you have any more give us an update on what you two have been doing today?"

"Well Sharky has come up with a pretty good idea" Replied Mark.

Mark took them through what had gone on at the Analysis Centre and the plan to use the information.

Both Kate and Jeff looked at each other and passed looks of agreement.

Nearly two hours and a number of drinks later all four of them were laughing and joking. Of all of them Sharky appeared to be handling the amount of alcohol they were consuming the best. Mark had already spilled most of one drink over his trousers and Kate, who had started on large Jack Daniels three rounds previously, was laughing and giggling. Mark got up to go to the toilets and had a definite swerve to his walk. Kate looked at his efforts at walking straight and turned to Sharky.

"It is good to see him relaxing for a change, he needed a break."

Sharky smiled back at her and nodded.

It was nearly 7pm and Jeff thought it a good idea to order food. Fifteen minutes later four huge burgers and fries were placed on the table. All four tucked into them as if they were starving.

They enjoyed the hospitality of the Hogs Head for another three hours, Mark was beginning to fall asleep and Jeff had his arm around Kate telling her some story that he found very amusing, but no one else understood because he never finished a sentence without bursting into laughter.

Sharky who was still managing to drink his beer, had a definite list to starboard and was leaning heavily on Mark's shoulder.

"Think it is about time we headed back." Sharky managed to say as he downed the last beer from his glass.

Kate and Jeff managed to nod in agreement, but Mark remained oblivious to the suggestion, his head resting on his chest, with eyes now firmly closed. Sharky called over to the bartender to order a cab.

CHAPTER TWENTY-SIX

Mark woke at 5am his head was throbbing and his mouth felt and tasted like the Sahara desert. He got out of bed and headed for the kitchen, searching in one of the drawers he found a packet of aspirins and knocked two of them back with a full glass of water. He never realised water could taste so good. He looked at the kitchen clock, five past five, he stood for a minute undecided on what to do. As if coming out of a trance he refilled the glass tumbler and took another drink of water and headed back to bed and submerged under the duvet. Three and a half hours later, he was brought out of his sleep with a ringing noise. He lay there listening to the noise, his brain trying to establish what it was, as if finding the right memory cell it alerted him to it being his mobile, he emerged from below the duvet and picked it up. It was Lisa Michaels.

"Hi Mark, I assume from what happened you will not be able to make it this weekend?"

Mark was still trying to gather his thoughts.

"Well I am not sure Lisa, should know by end of today."

"You ok Mark you sound a little bit odd, I didn't wake you did I?"

"No I'm fine." He replied still trying to get his brain into full gear.

The doorbell rang.

"Lisa there is someone at the door can I call you back this evening?"

"No problem I will look forward to it."

As they were saying their goodbyes Mark wrapped a towel around himself and headed for the door, he also realised he was extremely desperate for the toilet.

He opened the door to Kate.

"Morning Mark, God you look like shit?"

"Morning Kate, thanks, make yourself useful and make the coffee, I am going for a shower."

He was turning towards the bathroom before he finished the sentence.

Fifteen minutes later, he appeared with a dressing gown on still drying his hair with a towel.

He sat down to a freshly made coffee and took a long slow drink of it. He looked across the breakfast table to Kate and smiled.

"Thanks Kate I needed that."

"No problem thought you might need a little help this morning to get yourself in gear."

Kate did not look like she had touched a drop of alcohol last night; she was wide awake and looked full of life.

"How can you look so bouncy this morning?"

"Oh, I have always been lucky, drink does not seem to leave many after effects with me, although I have been up a couple of hours, I also had a good breakfast of bacon and eggs" Replied Kate.

Right now Mark's stomach felt like it had a giant fur ball in it and the thought of Kate's breakfast made the fur ball turn three hundred and sixty degrees.

"Let's not talk about food eh."

Kate smiled. "More coffee?"

"Yes please."

They both arrived at the office just after nine-thirty; Jeff was already there, a large mug of coffee in his hand and looking slightly fragile. He raised his hand to acknowledge them as they walked in and went back to his drink.

Kate shrugged her shoulders.

"Jesus, you guys do suffer after a night out."

Kate poured coffee for herself and Mark and joined Jeff around the table.

Jeff pushed a signal across the desk to Mark.

"This is the latest report from the Jacksonville attack and also an incident witnessed yesterday."

The signal said that the final toll at Jacksonville was now ninety-two people presumed dead. It also reported that at 1720 yesterday, two fishing vessels, seventy -six miles of the coast of Saint Augustine, recovering their nets full of fish had witnessed the nets being attacked and ripped apart by extremely large eel like creatures.

Kate looked at the computer track on the screen and confirmed that it was probably the swarm that had attacked Jacksonville. She lined the cursor up on the position of where the fishing vessels reported the incident and typed in UPDATE SWARM 1 TIME 1720 and hit the return key. The numbers 1720 appeared on the spot where the incident happened annotated with the date underneath. Circles indicating the swarms possible position based on a speed of 12 knots from that time, radiated from it.

Mark nodded in agreement.

"Kate could you put in a line from the Jacksonville attack to the fishing boat incident and work out the average speed they would have been doing to get there?"

"No problem."

She tapped away on her keyboard and answered within seconds.

"Speed would have been 7.2 Knots, slower than normal"

"I would have expected that, they had just gorged themselves and also taken food back to the ocean with them, I think they would have been hanging around the coast of Jacksonville for an hour or so."

When he said the word food he realised he had been referring to the young people the creatures had dragged off with them. He felt the same as if he had made a racist comment, but at the time could not think of a more sensitive word to use. If Kate and Jeff had thought it insensitive they did not acknowledge it, maybe he was being too critical of his statement.

A knock at the door interrupted his thoughts, as he turned the door opened and Admiral Hawkins walked in followed by Captain Piper and Sharky. Jeff immediately stood up from his chair and came to attention; the Admiral waved his hand in a manner, which indicated for Jeff to stand easy.

"Good Morning team, I was just visiting HMS Sabre when I was informed that Chief Ward was coming over to discuss the way ahead with the creatures, thought I would listen in."

"It is very nice to see you again Admiral" Replied Mark.

Jeff and Kate a little in awe of the Admiral both smiled in agreement.

The Admiral moved into the room and sat on a chair that dominated full view of the room, Captain Piper sat just to the left of him.

"Any chance of a coffee Commander" Asked the Admiral.

"That's my department Sir, how do you take it" Replied Kate.

"White none please Kate."

Kate took the orders from both Captain Piper and Sharky and went off to make the refreshments. When she arrived back the Admiral changed the conversation from idle chat to a more serious level.

"Team, yesterday I had to attend a meeting with the Vice President, we are extremely concerned about these creatures operating in American waters especially after the attack at Jacksonville. There are a couple of questions I need full clarification on. Firstly, can you assure me there is no chance of these things breeding and secondly how many do you estimate remain alive?"

The Admiral directed his questions at Mark and he responded.

"Admiral, the initial autopsy showed that they had no reproductive organs, so they cannot breed, I will speak to Lisa Michaels and get her team to confirm this if you wish. To the second question I believe the current number of creatures that remain are minimum seventy to a maximum of ninety. There is no way that we can give you an accurate number however I believe that all the remaining creatures are now operating as one swarm."

"Good that's what I will take back to the Vice President. Next I need to know what the next plan of action is?"

Mark took the Admiral and Captain Piper through what they had learnt at the analysis centre and the idea Sharky had come up with. Captain Piper looked towards his Chief and nodded in approval.

"Chief Ward and I went through the logistics of what would be required and we need a minimum of three anti-submarine frigates to track them down and achieve a good attack solution on them. This time when we do go into attack them, we believe using maritime aircraft rather than helicopters would be the better option, they are faster and can carry a bigger payload of weapons."

The Admiral nodded in agreement.

"Just run me through how you are going to detect them please?" He asked.

"I think the Chief may give you the better answer Admiral."

Sharky, took the Admiral through what they had learnt at the analysis centre and how he believed they could transmit some of the known frequencies and hopefully get a response from the remaining creatures. He continued to give a detailed brief to the Admiral with such enthusiasm that Mark thought Sharky could have sold the Admiral a used car at the same time.

The Admiral thanked Sharky and turned towards Captain Piper.

"John, sound feasible to you?"

"Sir, it worked pretty well in UK waters when we were just using basic frequencies to attract them, this is a little bit more complicated for we are now using discreet frequencies that they actually communicate on. If we can get them to respond there should not be a problem pin pointing them, the gamble is will they respond."

"Well as I see it we have very few options, so we will go with the plan, Commander my staff will get back to you this afternoon with two ships to support HMS Sabre. When would you like to hold a briefing?"

Jeff looked at Mark.

"Tomorrow morning say 1100." Mark replied.

Captain Piper offered the Sabre to host the meeting.

Mark nodded "Sounds good to me, thank you Captain."

Mark, called up flight times to Miami, there was a flight leaving tomorrow that would get him there at 1932. The meeting tomorrow was to be held at 1100 on Sabre, he assumed it to be over by 1300. He thought what the hell and booked a return ticket on line; he would catch a flight back Sunday night.

He dialled Lisa, she answered after two rings.

"Hi"

"We are on, I will arrive around seven thirty tomorrow evening."

"Excellent, I am really looking forward to seeing you again."

Her voice sounded full of enthusiasm and excitement. A picture of her flashed across Mark's mind.

"I am really looking forward to seeing you to. Are you sure you can find me somewhere to stay?"

"Well I have four bedrooms so you can pick anyone you like."

"Oh fine, won't the neighbours talk?"

"Only if they have binoculars, the nearest lives two miles away."

"It sounds nice, until tomorrow evening then."

"Really looking forward to it, I will be at the airport to meet you."

When they finished the conversation Mark smiled to himself, God he was really looking forward to seeing her again.

Sixteen people sat around the long highly polished table in the wardroom of the British frigate. From Sabre there was the Captain, the two Principal Warfare Officers one of which was the Operations Officer and Sharky Ward. Two Officers accompanied both Captains from the two American Anti-Submarine frigates, USS Diamond and Arrow. Emma Wright was present along with two Officers from the air group for the maritime aircraft. Mark, Kate and Jeff made up the remainder.

Captain Piper opened the proceedings by giving them a brief history of the creatures and the action carried out by the Royal Navy against them, he then handed over to Mark to take them through the proceedings since the creatures had left British waters. He covered the keys points and then rapidly moved on to why they were all here today.

With the help of Sabre's Warfare team he had already drawn up a plan of the intended operation. He explained to the audience that Sabre was fitted with a highly sophisticated sonar suite, capable of transmitting and receiving low and high frequencies out to long ranges. The plan was that Sabre would transmit frequencies that the analysis centre in Norfolk had identified as specific communications between the creatures. It was hoped that on hearing these frequencies the swarm that attacked Jacksonville would reply. On them replying to the signal Diamond and Arrow would then detect the transmissions on their passive sonar systems, allowing a cross-fix to give an accurate position of them. The computer programme from the analysis centre would be downloaded into Sabre's computer system to allow translation of what the creatures were transmitting. Once sufficient tracking of the swarm had been completed and their position pinpointed, then the three maritime aircraft would be called in to carry out the depth charge attacks They would be carrying eight depth charges each making the total number of ordinance being dropped as twenty-four depth charges. Captain Piper stated that although the amount of explosives being used appeared excessive, the information they will be receiving will have a time delay error and not totally accurate. The amount of ordnance dropped and the area of devastation should compensate for any minor inaccuracies in the swarms position. For the next thirty minutes discussions and questions were debated, it was agreed that all three Anti-Submarine frigates would sail south on Monday morning.

CHAPTER TWENTY-SEVEN

The plane arrived four minutes early at Miami airport, as he exited arrivals he saw her standing there, the smile in her eyes equalled that of her mouth, she did not attempt to conceal her excitement, waving eagerly towards him. Marks enthusiasm matched hers and as they reached each other they joined in an intimate hug and gentle kiss. Holding her he took in the whole scent of her perfume the fragrance was seductive yet clean and innocent. Her tanned olive skin, enhanced with dark flowing hair gave the appearance of Italian ancestry. They walked from the airport hand in hand smiling at each other.

The drive to her house, took just over forty-five minutes, they talked about nothing important the creatures did not come into the conversation once. As she drove she took one hand off the steering wheel and laid it on his. He cupped her hand and squeezed it gently. Mark felt it strange that he had barely been with this beautiful woman more than a few hours previously yet he felt as comfortable as if he had been with her for much longer.

The house looked stunning, a block paved driveway, shaded by palm trees led to an arched courtyard. As they exited the car, the scent of orange groves was in the air. Around the courtyard were large plant pots with colourful and exotic plants in them. A cat meandered from behind one of the plant pots; it wandered over to Lisa and its tail rose high and rubbed against her.

"This is Alice."

Reaching down she gave the black and white cat a scratch on its head.

As they approached the door, Mark could hear the barking of a dog from within.

"And that noise you hear is Oscar don't worry he is big but a real teddy bear."

As the door opened a large but extremely healthy looking Alsatian greeted them. He rushed to Lisa, tail wagging and started licking her hand. It then turned to Mark. Oscar gave him a curious look and sniffed him and when satisfied he was not a threat continued with his enthusiastic greeting for Lisa.

Lisa, Mark and Oscar followed by Alice entered the house which was just as stunning inside as the exterior.

Mark looked on from the hallway into a huge lounge area it was brightened by large French doors and arched shaped windows. The furniture looked expensive and comfortable, the plain beige walls complimented the colours. The flooring was highly polished wood and on the farthest wall was a chimney with a huge open fire. The fireplace looked purely ornamental and either side of it in the inglenooks stood exquisite statues of bronze horses.

"Lisa this house is amazing."

"Yes it is beautiful, I grew up here, it still belongs to my parents but they have another house further up the coast they prefer, so they allow me to use this one."

She led him through the lounge area, still escorted by Oscar; the cat had detoured to another room, which Mark assumed to be the kitchen. Lisa opened the two large French doors to reveal a gorgeous lawn and swimming pool; all around it lay more plant pots with an abundance of colour flowing from them. Beyond the garden a white wooden fence bordered a field of orange trees.

"Do you look after this yourself?"

"Good God no, I have a gardener who comes around three times a week, the place would look like a desert if it was left to me."

Mark wandered out farther into the garden area and sat down on a rattan chair with comfortable blue cushions on.

"What would you like to drink?"

"Cold beer would be fine if you have got one."

"Think I can rustle one of those up, Coors ok?"

"As long as it's wet and cold."

Lisa was gone less than five minutes before returning with two cold beers, she sat down on a recliner chair next to him and took a sip of her beer. Mark watched her as she drank her beer, she was truly a beautiful woman he took a long drink from his and laid his hand on hers.

Forty-three miles off the coast of Florida drifted a twenty-seven foot fishing boat. The blue paint on its side was faded and badly deteriorated the whole structure of it looked in a poor state of seaworthiness. It was showing a definite list to port and the occasional wave breached the side allowing seawater to drop into the bilges. A dark and dirty hand grasped the throttle controlling the forty cc engine that was struggling to maintain any headway against the prevailing current. Huddled in the boat were a total of fourteen people, all of Cuban descent. Around them were holdalls and black bags containing personnel effects. Of the people onboard six were men, five women and three children, one of which was still being breast fed by its mother. The other two children were both female and under five years old. The boat stank of petrol from the cans of fuel lined down the centre. They had left the coast of Cuba under darkness twenty-six hours ago, since then they had travelled just forty-seven miles, barely two miles an hour and just over half way to their goal of reaching the United States. As if hitting a rock the boat jolted sharply to one side, the man steering the boat looked to the side that had sustained the hit, as he did, the boat jolted again, this time it reverberated from below as if there was some obstruction beneath them. The passengers were all aware of the mysterious obstruction and began to stare over the side for evidence of what it was. The man controlling the boat shrugged his shoulders towards the passengers indicating he could not see anything. The boat regained its previous slow momentum and began to continue on its designated course. The tired and bedraggled passengers sat back again in their cramped and uncomfortable positions. On the low lying port side, a woman in her early thirties, slim and not unattractive even in her current squalid conditions sat slightly higher than her fellow passengers. As she began to close her eyes she felt a splash of water hit her back, before she could turn a huge open jaw rose from the deep and clamped shut on her right shoulder. The gruesome head of the creature dropped back into the ocean dragging the petite body with it. It happened so quickly the woman did not even have time to let out a scream. Only the man driving the boat had witnessed the whole horrendous event. The other passengers were only aware the woman had disappeared from the vacant position that was left. Assuming she had fallen overboard they looked outboard to see where she had gone. What they witnessed sent terror and panic through them, three gigantic creatures were biting into her body she was literally being ripped apart. Both her legs were torn away and being devoured by two of the creatures, the remainder of her body was firmly in the jaws of the other. As from no-where further creatures appeared. The woman's head parted from the rest of her body, it floated free for a few seconds, before it was devoured in one bite.

Around the boat, creatures began to appear from everywhere, they were circling the boat, barging and bumping it. The boat began to rock. Passengers were screaming and trying to get away from the sides. One woman had her eyes closed and was praying loudly. A man picked up a boathook and drove it towards one of the creatures, as he raised it for a second time one of the monstrous beasts rose from the water and bit into his right arm pulling him towards the waiting mass. His body was torn to pieces in seconds all that remained of him was a mist of red in the ocean which was quickly dispersed by the turbulence the creatures were creating. After the second kill, the creatures appeared to go into a mad frenzy; the barging against the boat became more intense, the boat started rocking severely from side to side. A woman stood up to make it towards the opposite side, as she did, the boat took a heavy knock, she fell backwards and her back hit the side of the boat, a crack that could only be associated with a breaking bone sounded above the screaming and chaos in the boat. She lay balanced, her

199

head and shoulders hanging outside the security of the boat. Her eyes opened wide and transfixed to the creatures swimming only inches from her head, the scream she emitted brought home the full terror that was being endured by her. Before she reached the final climax of her scream it was cut short as a creature bit and twisted her head dragging her body beneath the water. The port side of the boat was now only a few inches above the water line and two creatures launched themselves at it, the weight of their bodies hitting the boat made it list even more dangerously towards being flooded and capsizing. Both the creatures made a grab for the nearest passengers, the targets were men, one was immediately dragged to his death, the second was bit on the leg and was being held by two other passengers to stop him being dragged overboard. The tug of war with the creature lasted only a few seconds, the creature with the left leg firmly in its jaws bit in deeper, swung its head and the limb was dismembered just above the knee. The skin was ripped up to the groin before it broke free. Blood gushed out from the wound at a tremendous rate, leaving the man screaming and writhing on the deck of the boat.

From the helm of the boat, Jose Torres the boat owner watched in horror at what was happening. He had opened the throttle to maximum on the outboard but the combined weight of the people onboard and the water coming in was not allowing the boat to make adequate speed to escape. In his oil covered hand he picked up a hard wooden club from below the bilges and moved forward. As he reached the first passenger, a woman; he raised the club smashing it against her head. As the woman began to fall he pushed her towards the side and let her body fall into the water and the awaiting jaws. He raised the club again this time against one of two remaining men, the victim raised his arm to protect his head but he was too late to stop the crude weapon making contact with the right side of his face, he fell over the side and a terrifying death quickly followed. The remaining passengers all moved to the front of the boat to avoid the swinging of the lethal club, Jose lashed out wildly with the weapon, in the tight proximity of the boat it connected with a woman's neck, the force of the club hitting her propelled her body straight over the side.

The one remaining man put himself between the killer and the woman and children, as Jose swung the man ducked and drove his body forward grabbing Jose around the waist. They both fell over into the blood and petrol soaked deck. As the men fought, the woman got up and laid the baby between the two children. Free from the baby she reached inside her jean pocket and removed an oblong shape, pressing a button on the side of it and a four-inch thin piercing blade appeared. She moved towards the two men, Jose Torres had broken free from the wrestling and was beginning to stand up, he never made it. The woman drove the knife into the side of his neck; he tried to reach for the weapon but the woman removed it and stabbed him again in the throat. He dropped back on to the deck of the boat, a gurgling noise came from his mouth that was leaking bright red blood and froth.

The woman helped the man who had protected her to his feet and indicated to him to throw Jose over board. After disposing of the body the man rushed to the stern of the boat and took control of the throttle. The woman moved along the boat throwing all the holdalls and bags containing personal belongings overboard. As she reached the man with the amputated leg she found he was dead, she rolled him to the side of the boat. She was having difficulty trying to get the body over the side, as one of his arms flopped over the side a head rose from the water and yanked the torn body overboard. The creatures continued to barge the boat, but the boat was now moving through the water much faster. The woman looked towards the man at the controls of the outboard and nodded, as she did a creature rose from the water and closed its jaws around his leg, it dropped back into the ocean and the man was gone. Without anyone at the throttle the boat began to slow and manoeuvre around in a circle. Moving towards the stern she took control of the outboard bringing it back onto a steady course and opened the throttle to maximum revs. The boat was now making speed through the water and the creatures had stopped ramming it. For the next twenty minutes the boat proceeded at maximum revolutions until the engine began to smoke and splutter. The engine misfired twice and stopped. Drifting along with the current, the woman left the stern and joined the children, she took the baby in her arms, removed her breast and offered it to the child, as the baby suckled she wrapped her arms around the two young girls.

CHAPTER TWENTY-EIGHT

The sun was setting and Lisa moved around the lounge switching on table lamps. Mark sat on the comfortable leather sofa and watched her captivating barefooted figure moving around the room. As she settled down beside him, her tanned legs brushed against his and a surge of excitement travelled through his body. Resting his arm over hers their fingers interlocked. She laid back and placed her head on his shoulder. Without looking up she spoke.

"It is good to have you here I was worried you would not make it."

Her closeness mixed with the fragrance and warmth of her body had aroused him to a stage where he had to kiss her. He turned his head and placed his hand on the side of her face, their lips merged together with such a natural movement. The kiss started as warm and tender but quickly developed into one of heated passion. His hands drifted underneath her loose top, running them across her bare back. She pulled gently away from the kiss and raised her lips and kissed forehead. Looking into his eyes she ran her fingers along his right cheek. Her fingers settled on his lips, he could smell and taste the full fresh scent of them. Slowly she stood up. Pulling his arm she led him towards the bedroom.

The fishing boat continued to drift, the woman and three children remained huddled together, darkness began to fall. She listened attentively for any noises other than the lapping of the waves against the boats hull. The baby was asleep and both young girls had not spoken since she had sat with them. Pulling a dirty blanket from beside her she laid it over the infants. When darkness finally came, the only illumination was from the full moon. Watching the moon in full brightness brought some comfort to her. A few minutes passed before a thick cloud totally engulfed the moon and shrouded them in total darkness. A sudden thud on the bottom of the boat made her aware that both infants were awake for she felt them both move tighter against her. The baby stirred in her arms, she held it closer her breast. Five minutes went past with no further noises, the moon was bright again and the woman's eyes had adjusted to the darkness giving her some visibility beyond the boat. Suddenly the boat surged to one side, as if something had deliberately pushed it sideways. One of the girls let out a frightened whimper, the woman held both of then tighter. Darkness engulfed them again as another cloud obscured the moon. From out of the obscurity of the night came a noise, a long breath being expelled like that of a snake. The moon reappeared, she strained her eyes to see anything beyond the boat, nothing was there.

It was gone midnight and they had returned to the lounge, Lisa lay propped against him dressed in a white cotton gown, Mark wore only a pair of jeans, they both held a glass of chardonnay in their hands. He ran his fingers affectionately through her hair. She laid her hand on his left knee slowly moving her fingers over it.

Mark could see Lisa was deep in thought.

"You worried about something?"

She looked up at him and smiled.

"Just a little, I think I enjoy your company to much."

"Well if it helps I enjoy your company too."

"No what I mean is, I am slightly frightened about missing you too much when you have to leave."

He dropped his hand from her hair and gave her a tight hug around her shoulders.

"I can always come back."

She tightened her grip on his knee.

"I hope so."

Mark finished his drink and placed it down on the coffee table he took her drink from her and placed it next to his. He brought her face to his and kissed her very gently. He placed his mouth next to her ear and whispered.

"I will always be around for you that's a promise."
She returned the kiss and whispered in his ear.
"Let's go back to bed."

It had been nearly two hours since the last noise was heard. She was beginning to doze when she heard a voice.

"When can we go home?"

It was one the girls.

She replied very quietly.

"Soon we will go home."

"What is your name?" Came the reply.

"My name is Rosa, what is yours?"

"Isabel."

"And your sister?"

"Ania."

"My baby is called Katia." Replied Rosa.

Rosa knew that the woman struck by the club and thrown overboard was their mother and the man who protected them and died at the throttle was their father. She could not comprehend the images that would be going through their minds now and in the future.

No more talk took place between Rosa and Isabel, they both drifted off to sleep.

Rosa woke with both children pushing her and Isabel calling her name.

"Rosa, Rosa wake up."

Rosa opened her eyes to daylight, both children were pointing behind her, she heard the noise before she turned, a ships siren sounded. She turned to see a large grey vessel flying the American flag only twenty yards from the boat. As the boat drifted closer to the US Coastguard vessel one of the crew threw a rope to her. Placing the baby down on the blanket she tied the rope to a cleat. Two sailors on the coastguard vessel pulled the fishing boat alongside.

CHAPTER TWENTY-NINE

Mark woke first, she lay beside him, her tanned skin shining from the rays of light breaching the blinds. As not to disturb her he slid out of bed slowly and entered the en suite bathroom. Washed and shaven he returned to the bedroom, she was awake, leaning on her elbow and smiling at him. Apart from her hair being slightly ruffled she looked like she had been awake for a lot longer. Her seductive figure protruded through the light sheets that covered her to her waist, her breasts hung like firm ripe fruits. Lisa saw the way he was looking at her and smiled.

"Don't you tire?"

"Not where you are concerned."

"Well not before I have showered, if you are still game when I get back, you are on."

On her return they spent the next forty-five minutes amusing themselves with each other's body.

Mark lay back on the bed.

"Well that's the way to start a Saturday morning, beats a five mile jog."

"Maybe even ten miles." Joked Lisa.

He watched as she slipped out of the bed naked and walked towards the bathroom, he could not get over how beautiful she was.

Mark got up and slipped into a fresh pair of jeans and t-shirt. He headed for the kitchen to be met by Alice and Oscar, both queuing for breakfast. He said hi to them both and told them she would be with them shortly. Both animals just stared back at him with expectations of food in their eyes. The coffee was ready when Lisa appeared she rustled up breakfast for both pets and escorted Mark out to the veranda to drink his coffee.

He sipped his drink and held her hand; the scent of oranges hung in the morning air, the sky was blue and the sun warm, he thought to himself this is paradise.

"Happy?" Lisa said.

"Very."

He held her hand a little tighter.

His mobile rang twenty minutes later, it was Jeff.

"Hi Mark, sorry to bother you on your weekend away, but I have some news."

"Not bad?"

Jeff did not answer the question but went straight into the reason he was calling.

"I do not know if you saw the news today but the coastguard recovered some Cuban refugees early this morning, the report is that the boat was attacked by the creatures and ten people were killed."

"Where was this?"

"About fifty miles off the coast of Florida."

Lisa was watching Mark's face during the conversation and could see it was not good news.

"Mark the Admiral has ordered that Sabre, Arrow and Diamond advance the sailing to 1300 today."

Mark looked at his watch it was 1050.

"I have discussed your situation with the Admiral, they do not need you back for the sailing but they want you onboard Sabre when the operation begins. You need to be at Miami airport tomorrow at 1130, a military helicopter will pick you up and fly you to Orlando airport where Sabre's helicopter will be waiting to transfer you to the ship."

"I will be there."

"Anything you need me to bring for you." Asked Jeff.

"Just pick up some fresh clothes for me."

"No problem, enjoy the rest of the weekend."

Mark turned and gave a reassuring smile at Lisa.

"I am free until tomorrow."

"Good lets make the most of it. Thought I would take you down to see my yacht and then stop at a fantastic fish restaurant I know on the way back."

Mark was slightly curious why she did not ask about the creatures or the reason he had to leave early.

"Sounds good to me."

It took them twenty-five minutes to drive down to the marina where Lisa's yacht was berthed. The boat was a beauty, looking along her streamlined hull from stem to stern he saw the name Albatross decoratively painted on the stern. Stepping onboard, Mark gave a whistle of being impressed.

"Lisa, she is fantastic."

"Yes my pride and joy."

She eagerly took him below into the cabin area and showed him around. Everything was neatly stowed away and in pristine condition.

"Come on I will take her around the bay for an hour"

"What sailing?"

"No, we will take her out under power."

Lisa turned a key, which started a diesel engine, Mark slipped both the head and stern ropes and Lisa pushed the throttle slowly forward. She manoeuvred the boat out of the tight berthing with ease. As they reached clear water she increased speed and the yacht responded immediately, the streamline of the hull cut through the water with natural ease. Lisa steered Albatross towards a bay, Mark could see a number of yachts already in the area and a lot of activity going on at the beach opposite.

"What's going on over there?"

"Oh every weekend around this time of the year they have sailing competitions, looks like sail boarding today."

Mark could see dozens of colourful sails lying on the beach and a line of marker buoys about half a mile from the shore spaced about two hundred yards apart.

"Looks like they are going to start soon, will we watch for a while?" Asked Lisa.

"Sure."

She reduced the engine speed and slowly manoeuvred the boat to a position that would give them a clear view of proceedings. A loud klaxon sounded and they watched as people on the shore raised the sails of the boards and began to move out towards the first marker buoy. Dozens of sailboards were afloat and skimming the waves.

The leaders were about three hundred yards from shore and were heading towards the second marker buoy. The board in third place with a bright orange sail suddenly flipped upwards and the sailboard and person parted company. The upended sailboard dropped in front of two other competitors who both collided with the obstruction. Mark could see that all three of the competitors were on the surface and holding on to there stricken craft. He looked away back towards the leaders for a few seconds them returned his gaze to the three in the water. He could only see one person and he was frantically swimming towards shore.

Without removing his gaze from the fallen sailboards he spoke in a concerned tone.

"Lisa what is going on over there?"

She remained quiet but handed Mark a pair of binoculars.

He raised the binoculars and focussed in on the three sailboards floating on the surface. Against one of the white boards he saw red stains, he looked to the person swimming for shore, he had the person in view for a split second before the swimmer dipped below the sea and did not resurface. Lowering the binoculars he looked at the remaining sailboards, another four were lying flat in the water with no sign of the competitors. The safety boat was now driving towards the stricken sailboards at full speed.

He turned towards Lisa.

"Get the boat over there now."

Lisa pushed the throttle forward and Albatross responded immediately to the command.

Mark looked towards the safety boat it had reached two of the stricken craft and he could see the crew looking frantically for the competitors. As one of the crew hung over the rails of the boat to look closer at the sailboards it was then Mark's greatest fear became reality. From below the water rose a gigantic fearsome head, it snapped its open jaws shut on the crewman's head and dragged him overboard into the depths of the ocean. From that moment on chaos and panic took over as creatures began rising from the deep, flipping over sailboards and attacking the stranded swimmers. Mark looked around there must have been twenty sailboards lying prostrate on the water. The Albatross was now only a hundred yards from the area of devastation, Mark pointed out the closest swimmer to Lisa and she altered course in the direction he was indicating.

"Lisa go as close as you can, slow down but do not stop I will make a grab for the swimmer."

Lisa nodded.

Mark kneeled down on the deck of the Albatross and held on to a guardrail stanchion. He could see the swimmer clearly now, only twenty yards to go. Lisa slowed the boat down. The swimmer could see them coming and raised an arm. Mark grabbed the outstretched arm around the wrist and pulled it towards him, raising the young person enough out of the water for them to catch hold of guardrail. Lisa left the helm and rushed to help Mark. They could now see the survivor was a young female and could have been no more than fifteen years old. Together they both pulled the young girl to safety. Mark pointed to the girl to go below into the cabin area, Lisa returned to the helm and increased speed.

Mark scanned the area for another swimmer; there was no one to be seen. Lisa manoeuvred Albatross around the stricken sailboards of which Mark counted twenty-one. Other craft joined the search but the only competitor recovered was the young girl by Lisa and Mark.

Bringing the boat to a stop Lisa went down to the cabin area to comfort the girl. Mark stood looking over the area of devastation knowing that there was little chance of anyone else surviving. From below the surface of the sea, he caught sight of flashes of colour, the water was clear and the visibility in it was down to around thirty feet. The colours kept intermittently passing the boat, he made out the red shape of a creature and then he realised what the other colours were. What he was watching was the creatures returning to the deep with human body parts still clothed in the bright wet suits the competitors had been wearing. Mark called the safety boat alongside the Albatross and the young girl was transferred. Lisa stood on deck and watched her leave. She spoke softly and without direction.

"Her name is Carol her two brothers were in the race as well."

Mark put his arm around her.

"You saved her Lisa."

"Does it make up for the innocent people I have already killed?"

Mark now realised why Lisa had not mentioned the creatures all the time he had been with her. The huge loss of life at Jacksonville had probably driven home to her that she had created these monstrous killers.

"You have not killed anyone Lisa."

As he rested her head on his shoulder; he felt the warm dampness of a tear as her cheek brushed against him.

CHAPTER THIRTY

The total missing from the sailing regatta was twenty-two, the youngest being only fourteen years of age. Of Carol's two brothers, the oldest at nineteen, was named as missing, the other 17 year old made it back to the safety of shore. They drove back to Lisa's in relative silence, he held her hand most of the way but she was clearly lost in thoughts elsewhere. His greatest fear was that the press would come looking for Lisa after saving the girl, and if they did they would surely tie in the connection with her and the research centre, then her life would be hell. He knew the press could be utterly cruel and they would definitely paint her as the beautiful Doctor Frankenstein. When they entered the house he checked her phone to see if any messages had been left, thankfully there was none.

Mark poured a couple of drinks and sat next to her.

"Do not blame yourself, you were doing a job, if you had not done it someone else would have."

"But it was me."

"And it was what you were trained to do, you did not go out of your way to produce these creatures, it was part of a scientific experiment and due to a sequence of events it led to this. A sequence of events you had no control over."

She turned and touched him on the face.

"Take me to bed and let me forget this morning."

They made passionate and unrestrained love, it was different from the night before, he could tell she needed these moments of fervour to let her escape from the real world. Mark let her lead in every sexual movement, this sex was for her, he was just a compulsory accessory required to fulfil the objective.

A long period of silence followed and he held her in his arms.

"Sorry for that."

He hugged a little bit tighter

"You have nothing to be sorry for, I told you I will be around if you need me, and that means for anything."

The telephone rang and after the fifth ring Lisa picked it up, she was about to speak when Mark put his handover the mouthpiece.

"It may be the press, let me take it."

Lisa looked at him curiously and handed him the phone.

"Hello."

It was Jeff.

"Mark there has been a change of plan. After the attack today the frigates have been ordered to proceed at maximum speed to an operating area off the Florida coast."

Jeff went on to explain that Sabres helicopter would be in range tomorrow to pick him up directly from Miami airport at 1230. The three maritime aircraft would be based at Miami ready for immediate use. Mark put down the telephone and looked at Lisa she was sat on the same settee where they had kissed last night. This afternoon the sparkle in her had gone. Mark knew she was still running through this morning's incident and blaming herself. He kneeled down beside and put his arms around her neck he kissed her head and in a whisper said that they would get through this together. She forced a smile and put her head against his chest and cried.

The three frigates were each managing to maintain 24 knots on the route to their destination. On Sabre, Sharky was in the Operations Room doing final checks on the sonar system ensuring it was fully functional.

"Everything ready your end Chief?"

Sharky looked around it was Lt Cdr Emma Wright who had joined the ship shortly before they had sailed from Norfolk.

"All seems fine at the dry end, but it would have been nice to have given it a full test with the noisemakers deployed in the water."

Emma sat down on a seat by the main sonar system

"Do you think this is going to work?"

Sharky nodded.

"Sabre still has a score to settle with these creatures and everyone onboard has belief in the ship. Will the creatures respond to the transmissions? I do not know but if faith has anything to do with it then yes they will."

The telephone rang again at Lisa's home. Mark picked up.

"Hello"

"Hi it's Stella Coates here from the Herald, could I speak to Lisa Michaels please?"

Mark went silent for a few seconds thinking on how he was going to respond.

"I am afraid she is not available at present. Can I ask why you are calling her?"

Lisa looked at Mark from the settee. Mark put his hand over the receiver and whispered.

"Don't worry I will deal with this."

Stella Coates responded.

"Can I ask who I am speaking to please? I really wanted to speak to Miss Michaels regarding the incident in the harbour this morning. I believe she was there."

"This is a friend of Lisa's and unfortunately as I said she is not available at present."

"Well can you confirm that this Lisa Michaels is the same person that is the Senior Researcher at the Whitewater Bay facility?"

Mark's anxiety levels rose, they had made the link. He was being put on the spot and was struggling for a response. He had to end this call quickly.

"I am sorry I cannot answer that, I will let her know you called. Goodbye"

The reporter started to fire off another question but Mark hung up before it was finished.

"Was that a reporter?"

Mark nodded.

Both her legs were tight together and she was slightly crouched over them rocking her body slowly.

Oscar suddenly started barking, a few seconds later the doorbell sounded.

"Are you expecting anyone?"

Lisa rolled her head.

"I noticed a surveillance camera at the front door, where is it displayed?"

Lisa pointed to the large television on the adjacent wall.

Picking up the remote he switched it on and found the inputs. Clicking on CCTV a picture of those standing at the front door immediately flashed up on the screen. There were two people, a female with microphone in her hand and a young man carrying a camera. Mark could see more people coming down the driveway, at least two more of them were carrying cameras. He swore under his breath. He looked at Lisa who was just staring at the television; Mark pressed the off button on the remote control.

"Lisa I want you to take Oscar and go to your bedroom, I will deal with the people at the door."

Lisa nodded. Mark exited the lounge and returned leading Oscar by his collar, with his spare arm he held Lisa by her elbow and led her into the bedroom.

"Lisa please stay here and leave this to me."

She forced a smile towards him and mimed a thank you.

Mark returned to the lounge, he switched the television back on. There were at least eight people at the front entrance and three with cameras. The door bell rang again.

He approached the front door. On arriving he held the handle for a few additional seconds to gather his thoughts.

He opened the door. Before he could speak he was bombarded with questions.

"Is Lisa Michaels here?"

"Is it true that she created these creatures that have killed over one hundred people?"

"Why did she do it?"

"How does she feel being responsible for all those

young people that have died?"

Mark raised his hand to reduce the amount of questions being thrown at him. It gave him a small window to respond but he had to raise his voice to be heard.

"I am a friend of Miss Michaels and she is not available to comment on any of your questions at present. Now I would like you all to leave the grounds of the property or I will have to call the police."

As he stopped another barrage of questions were fired at him.

Suddenly the reporters got more excited and started firing their questions past him. He looked around and Lisa was standing in the hallway.

"Miss Michaels how does it feel to be responsible for all of those deaths?"

"Why did you create those monsters?"

Mark closed the door and leaned against it.

"Shit, Shit, Shit" he said to himself but deep down he knew it had only been a matter of time before the press linked Lisa with the creatures.

Mark put his arm around Lisa's shoulder and led her back to the lounge.

"Why did you come out Lisa?"

"Am I responsible for all of those deaths?"

"No you are not I explained to you it was something out of your control."

Tears were streaming down her cheeks.

As they passed the television he noticed the reporters were moving away from the front door but he could also see vehicles parked outside the main entrance. He led Lisa back to the bedroom and laid her on the bed. Returning to the lounge he found the connection for the telephone line and disconnected it. On the coffee table was Lisa's mobile he picked it up and switched it to silent. Returning to the bedroom he lay down beside her. He could feel the warmth of silent tears running over his arm. Mark stayed with her for over two hours until he knew she had fallen asleep. Raising himself slowly from the bed he covered her with a dressing gown that was hanging on the door. Oscar opened his eyes and looked at him then closed them again. Slowly leaving the bedroom he quietly shut the door. He made a coffee and sat in the lounge. On the large screen TV he could still see the television crews parked outside the main gate. He looked at Lisa's mobile, seven missed calls all marked unknown caller. It was 7:36pm that would make it passed midnight in London. He pressed fast dial to Admiral Lane. The Admiral did not sound like he had been woken.

"Hello Professor how are you?"

"Admiral I need some help."

Mark explained to him about today's incident and how the press had found out about Lisa and they were parked outside her home."

"She is not handling it well, she feels she is responsible for all of those deaths, I am worried."

"Well Professor I know you only call me when you have a plan so what is it."

Mark requested that Sabre's helicopter be diverted from Miami airport and pick him and Lisa up at her home. The rear garden had a clearance well capable of landing a helicopter.

"And where will we take Miss Michaels, Professor, back to Sabre?"

"No Admiral I think she needs to be around people that can look after her, her parents live not too far away, I was hoping we could drop her off there."

"Ok Professor give me an hour and I will get back to you once I see if it is feasible. I am sure we can sort something out. Oh I will need the addresses"

"Thank you Admiral, I will send you the details of Lisa's and her parents."

He returned to the bedroom and Lisa was lying awake, he sat on the bed beside her and ran his hands over her hair.

"We need to talk, I will go and make you a drink and if you feel up to it we can talk in the lounge?"

Lisa slowly nodded her head.

When she entered the lounge she had washed her face and brushed her hair. She sat next to him, he put his arms around her, and in return she pushed tighter against his chest.

"Lisa, I think you need to go and stay with your parents for a while."

She did not say anything, which he took as an agreement.

"What I need is the address and contact details of your parents."

She nodded and picked up her phone, she typed the password in and handed it to him. Mark looked through her contacts and found Mom and Pops. He noticed he was down as The Prof. He rang her parents and explained the situation, they readily agreed with Mark's plan and gave him their details. He also made a call to the gardener and someone called Sophia who was the cleaner. He arranged for them to look after Oscar and Alice whilst Lisa was gone. He then texted the addresses to the Admiral.

As promised within the hour the Admiral rang back.

"Right Professor, this is the plan. Tomorrow at 1230 Sabres helo will arrive at Miss Michaels address. The pilot will assess the landing position when he gets there. From there they will go to Miami airport to refuel. Miss Michaels will be transported by vehicle to her parents address. We are still discussing flight plans with Miami air control but I have given that problem to Admiral Hawkins to deal with so I am not expecting too much resistance."

"Thank you Admiral."

"No problem Professor, I hope Miss Michaels feels better."

CHAPTER THIRTY-ONE

Although he managed to get Lisa to bed before midnight, he knew that sleep did not come easy for her she still lay awake at 2am when he finally drifted off. The next morning he was hoping to wake up and find the reporters had given up and left but on checking the CCTV he could still see three vehicles and at least four people wandering around. It was going to be a long morning. Mark provided both animals with breakfast and let them into the back garden to exercise. On his phone he checked the internet to see what stories the papers were leading with. The incident at the beach was headlines. Within the story a picture of Lisa looked back at him. In it she was smiling and happy. Bold script beneath her picture read Harbinger of Death the report was blaming Lisa for all the atrocities the creatures had inflicted on the world. Other papers led with similar storylines and all mentioned her by name. Already there was mention of law suits against the research facility.

Lisa emerged from the bedroom just after 10am; on seeing Mark she gave him a pursed smile. He could tell she was not wearing anything under the thin blue dressing gown that was tightly wrapped around her shapely waist by a belt of the same material. This time yesterday that would have aroused him enough to whisk her back to the bedroom and she would not have resisted, this morning there was no thoughts of making love from either of them. She still looked tired, a tint of redness around her eyes provided evidence that she had cried more than a little during the night. He passed her his own coffee that he had made a few minutes earlier. Lisa had spoken very little with him since the reporters had arrived last night. He could feel her pain, the pressure and guilt she was feeling, particularly after seeing first hand the cruel and vicious deaths those creatures inflicted on innocent people. Mark knew that her life was never going to be the same, her sailing, the beautiful home and her research work was all going to end. If the reporters got their way as they usually did she would always be known as the woman that caused all those deaths. Moving close to her he held her against him. He slowly stroked her hair, she did not resist but neither responded to his affection.

"Lisa we are going to have to get ready for leaving."

She did not answer but nodded her head."

He led her back to the bedroom. Behind a sliding wardrobe he found a suitcase.

"Do you want to pack your clothes?"

She nodded again and started to slowly remove some items from the hangers.

"Where is your passport?"

"Why do I need my passport?"

It was the most words she had spoken to him since the reporters had called.

"You may not need it Lisa but you may require it at some stage so lets just be prepared for all eventualities."

She pointed to a bedside cabinet drawer. Mark removed her passport and placed it in a zipped pocket of the suitcase.

It was 1115 on HMS Sabre the helicopter was ranged on deck with rotors running. The signal was given by the Flight Deck Officer to lift off. The helicopter slowly rose from the deck. When clear it turned to Starboard and headed towards it destination 125 miles away in Miami.

Mark watched Lisa as she dressed, she was a beautiful woman. She pulled a pair of jeans over her tanned legs until they covered her black lace panties. He thought about the evening two nights ago when they first made love. He knew that it was going to be a long and hard road for her to get back to that woman full of energy, life and happiness. He watched her slip into a jumper. He recognised it as the jumper she was wearing the first day he had ever set eyes on her. It seemed such a long time ago now. He moved towards her and put his arms around her he gently kissed her on the lips, the fire had gone.

At 1220, the suitcase and Marks holdall were on the patio area. From the distance he could hear the distinctive sound of a helicopters rotor blade. Sabre's helo came into view shortly after. It was slowly circling, the pilot obviously looking for a safe place to land. He approached from the rear of the building avoiding the on looking reporters. About fifty metres away in a large clearing just to the side of the orange grove he landed. One of the aircrew quickly disembarked and ran towards Mark and Lisa, he was carrying two flying helmets which he handed to them to put on. He took Lisa's suitcase and escorted them back to the helicopter still with its engine and rotors running. By the time they had got in the aircraft, two reporters had sprinted to the rear of the building and were busy taking photographs. As the helo lifted off Mark could see two large cameras following their departure. In the helo Mark and Lisa sat next to one another, he held her hand tightly, but he could see her thoughts were far away.

It was only a few minutes flight time to Miami airport. The control tower authorised them to land immediately. Touching down the pilot shut down the engine, the reduction of noise was welcoming. The aircrew man assisted them both with getting out. When he took the flying helmet from Lisa, it struck home that they were going to part. Two vehicles pulled up, one tanker carrying aviation fuel and the second a black saloon car which parked a short distance away. He walked to the awaiting car with her. The driver got out and took the suitcase, he was well built wearing dark sunglasses even to a bystander they could assume driving was not his full time job. Mark took Lisa in his arms, holding her tightly he pressed his lips against her cheeks and whispered to her.

"It is going be alright."

She spoke softly

"Thank you for all you have done, I am sorry I ruined it all."

"You have nothing to be sorry for."

Tears began to waterfall from those beautiful eyes.

He could feel himself getting emotional and a tear started to form in his eye. The tear was tinged with guilt looking at this broken woman the emotion he felt was pity. She looked up at him and brushed her finger softly over his tear. Lisa kissed his lips, a kiss that that could only say goodbye. Turning she got into the car. He watched as the black saloon drove away, she did not look back.

CHAPTER THIRTY-TWO

They had been in the air for 45 minutes when the three ships became visible. At maximum speed the turbulence from the ships propellers left long white trails behind them. As they approached Sabre she reduced speed and altered course to give the helicopter the best approach from the prevailing wind. The flight deck looked incredibly small for the helicopter to land on, especially with the ship still moving through the water. The pilot hovered just to port of Sabre and slowly manoeuvred over until he was lined up with the centre of the flight deck and suddenly landed. On touching down the flight deck crew quickly moved in and placed lashing on each corner of the aircraft to ensure there was no chance of it moving. Mark remained in the helicopter until the pilot had shut down the engine and the rotor blades stopped. Before leaving the flight deck he waited for the pilot and aircrew to disembark and thanked them for their help.

In the hangar the Captains Steward was waiting and escorted him to the same cabin that he had used before.

"Sir, the Captain asked if you would like to join him for tea when you have settled back in?"

"Yes. Thank you. Give me five minutes and I will be with you."

The Steward nodded and left. Sitting down on the narrow bed he thought of Lisa, she would now be at home with her parents but he knew it would not take the press long to track their address down. Hopefully her parents would find her somewhere safe and private to stay until this whole affair had died down. The thought that the creatures may attack and kill again left him fearful that she would be persecuted even more.

He was awoken from his thoughts by the return of the Steward.

"Sir Are you ready?"

Although Mark was now familiar with the layout of the

223

ship through courtesy the Steward escorted him to the Captain's cabin.

The Captain took Mark through the plan. They were only a few miles from the planned operating area. Both the American warships would be streaming their passive arrays and monitoring the suspected frequencies that we expected the creatures would be using. Sabre would stream the noisemaker and start transmitting some of the known frequencies that were detected at Cape Fear. To avoid the American ships getting confused with what Sabre was transmitting and any reply from the creatures. Sabre would inform both the ships when they were transmitting and the frequencies being used. Anything outside those times or at different frequencies would be a reply from the creatures. All units hoped to be ready to commence operations within the hour. As on cue a message came over a small loudspeaker in the Captains cabin.

"Captain, Officer of the Watch, we are now in our operating area, reducing speed to 6 knots."

The Captain picked up a microphone alongside the loudspeaker and acknowledged the message. He finished off what was left of his tea and turned to Mark.

"Professor I think we should go to the Operations room and get this show on the road."

Entering the Ops Room it took Mark a few moments to adjust his eyes to the subdued lighting. Nearly all of the seats available were taken up by the crew at the displays. He noticed Emma Wright sitting alongside the main sonar system, she was typing away on a laptop that was connected to the digital sound enhancer. When she stopped typing he interrupted her.

"Hello Emma."

"Hello Professor, I heard you were back onboard."

"So are you all ready?"

"Well we have all the frequencies loaded and the translation programme set up. If we receive any reply it will appear on this display."

She pointed to a screen secured just above the digital

enhancer.

"The translator will display it exactly like it did at the analysis centre, frequency, meaning and the percentage of it being correct, however, we have never actually attempted this in real time or at sea."

He looked around for Sharky but he was not in the Ops Room.

"I thought the Chief would be here?"

"He is on the Quarterdeck; they are getting ready to stream the noisemaker."

Mark nodded he should have guessed as much.

A report came over that USS Arrow was in her operating area and streaming her passive array. Ten minutes later USS Diamond reported the same.

Over the loudspeaker he heard the Bridge order those on the Quarterdeck to commence streaming the noisemaker.

The Captain wandered over to Mark and Emma.

"Let the game commence."

Fifteen minutes later Sharky entered the Ops Room. He gave Mark a big smile and shook his hand.

"Good to have you onboard Sir."

"Good to see you again Chief."

Sharky took Mark through the plan. They were initially going to start the transmissions with the identified START and STOP frequencies. Those frequences would be identified by numbers 1 and 2 respectively. It saved the full frequency being reported to the other ships by reporting the number and time. If they had no joy with those transmissions they would start transmitting other frequencies that the translator had previously identified. Each individual frequency had been given a designated number which all ships were aware of.

The Captain called out for those in the Ops Room to remove their headsets and listen in.

"Team all units are in position and all of the equipment is operating. We will start transmitting the signal shortly, Chief Ward will be co-ordinating the transmission with the two American ships."

Sharky put on a headset and switched to external communications, he carried out a voice and time check with both the Diamond and Arrow. The Captain nodded to Sharky for him to commence the operation. Sharky called up both the other ships.

He prefixed each message with Sabres call sign Yankee–Two-Bravo

"This is Y2B transmitting Frequency 1 now out."

Sharky pressed the transmit button on the sonar control panel.

"This is Y2B transmitting Frequency 2 now out."

He pressed the transmit button once more.

One minute later Diamond and Arrow reported detecting both transmissions from Sabre.

Sharky transmitted the same messages and frequencies every three minutes.

At minute twenty nine USS Diamond reported a possible contact bearing 080 degrees. Emma Wright inputted the reported frequency into the translator to see if it corresponded to anything detected at Cape Fear. All eyes looked at the display.

The word GO flashed up with a percentage rating of seventy-six.

Sixteen minutes passed before both passive units reported another possible detection. The new frequency was quickly typed into the translator. This time the word HERE was displayed with a percentage rating of sixty-nine percent. With both units detecting the last frequency the bearings were immediately plotted on the chart to get a cross cut. The Captain looked at where the position put the swarm. It was showing as only three miles off the coast of Florida. Mark looked at the chart and an awful thought came over him. He called out anxiously.

"What time is high tide in that area and is there any sewerage buoys near by?"

The Captain called up to the Bridge requesting the information.

The Bridge responded within ten seconds.

"Captain Sir, high tide is in fifteen minutes and there is one sewerage buoy in the vicinity."

The Captain looked at Mark. "They are coming ashore?"

Mark nodded.

"Roger Bridge where is it opposite?"

"Sir it is opposite Miami North Beach lots of holiday resorts there."

The Captain switched to external communications and transmitted to all ships.

"This is Yankee-Two-Bravo it is suspected that the swarm is heading for shore, landing area will be North Beach all units bring helicopters to immediate notice. Standby for further orders."

He called to the senior communicator.

"Get me headquarters in Norfolk on a secure line."

The Captain stopped to gather his thoughts for a minute before deciding on the next course of action.

"Officer the Watch get hold of the Royal Marine Officer tell him I want his men ready to deploy in fifteen minutes with weapons and extra ammunition."

The Communicator called out.

"Sir Norfolk on the secure line button 4."

The Captain switched to button 4 and gave Norfolk a brief on the developing situation. He finished off by requesting to land fully armed Royal Marines on American soil.

"Bridge as soon as the marines are ready I want them in the helicopter and airborne heading for North Beach, but do not land until we have authorisation from Norfolk that they can deploy."

"Roger Sir, helicopter is now at immediate notice, they can take eight Marines at a time."

The Captain called up USS Diamond and requested them to send their helicopter to transport the additional Marines. He also requested USS Arrow to fit a heavy machine gun to their helicopter for air support."

The Officer of the Watch reported that eight marines were onboard the helicopter and asked permission to launch the helicopter.

Immediate permission was granted.

Flying time from Sabre to North Beach was going to be sixteen minutes.

The Captain turned to Mark.

"When they meet the Marines, and try to retreat, what do you think they will do if they get back into the sea?"

"They will probably move pretty fast towards deep water."

"That's what I thought."

Turning to the chart table he looked at the water depths. The depth remained constant at about 40 metres for a about a mile out then it dropped to over 100 metres.

"I am going to set up a kill zone just here." And pointed to an area just short of the 100 metre mark.

"If any escape I want the maritime aircraft to saturate this area with depth charges. Work out how long it will take then to get there at a speed of?"

He looked at Mark.

"Usual speed is 11 knots but I think they will be going faster trying to escape so I would use 16."

"16 knots it is" said the Captain.

The plotter used his dividers to work out the time it would take them to arrive in the kill zone.

"Sir it will be seven minutes from leaving the beach."

Mark smiled to himself, it had been less than ten minutes ago that they had worked out they were coming ashore and the Captain had not only the defence in motion but the attack plan in place should they choose to retreat.

The Captain turned to his Warfare Officer.

"Recover the noisemaker; inform Diamond and Arrow to recover their passive arrays. Once they are recovered bring all units to two miles off North Beach."

Diamonds helicopter had picked up the remaining Marines and was now heading to join Sabres helo. Arrows helicopter was airborne and heading to North Beach fitted with a heavy machine gun.

The communicator called out.

"Captain Sir, Norfolk on secure communications button 4."

The Captain selected the secure communications. He addressed the caller as Sir so Mark assumed he must be speaking to a more senior Officer. The Captain recited what he had already put in place to the caller. He finished with a yes Sir will do.

Once again the Captain called for all those in the Operations Room to listen.

"Okay, that was Admiral Hawkins on secure communications. He is happy with the plan and has authorised the landing of our Marines. The nearest US military unit is forty-five minutes away. Currently the Police are trying to get people out of the danger areas of North Beach and will be supporting the Marines. Arrow's helicopter will be patrolling the beach area with the heavy machine gun. Both Sabres and Diamonds helicopters will carry out surveillance once they drop off the marines and directing the Marines to any creatures sighted. The three maritime aircraft are getting airborne now. In the event of the creatures escaping back to the sea, we will saturate an area with depth charges that we predict they will to be passing through. CPO Ward if it is a big swarm then we may be able to pick them up on active sonar so lets get a sonar crew closed up."

Both Sabre and Diamonds helicopters flew down the shore, they could still see people walking along the sea front. Police cars were driving up and down stopping pedestrians and telling them to get clear of the beach area. As Sabre's helicopter reached a part of the beach there was a large populated area with people enjoying outdoor meals. There must have been two hundred people congregated there. The pilot pointed them out to the marines. Lt Davies the officer in charge of the marines signalled to put them down. The helicopter hovered just off the ground and all eight marines disembarked. Diamonds helo carried out the same manoeuvre shortly after, bringing all twelve Marines together. On reaching the first group of people they spread out forming a line about five yards apart from each other. Initially the public were curious and stared at the Marines and the high calibre weapons. Not many were moving as directed, some were still eating and drinking and others joking amongst themselves. The Lieutenant raised his automatic weapon to the air and fired off a rapid volley of shots. This greatly assisted in gaining the peoples attention. They began moving through the crowds shouting at them to clear the beach area. As they reached groups who were still reluctant to move another volley of shots would be fired to encourage them. The twelve Marines were herding the crowd like sheep inland to their cars and hotels. Two police cars pulled up and four officers joined the Marines in controlling and dispersing the crowd of people. From the front of the crowd the farthest point away from the Marines the sound of chaos and screaming suddenly erupted. People were turning around and running back towards them. In their panic they were knocking over other people that were still trying to return to the safety of their hotel and vehicles. The Marines tried to stop those from returning but they just barged past them back towards the beach. More and more of the crowd started turning around and running back towards them. The first indication that the people were in danger was when they saw a screaming body being thrown above the crowd.

All the Marines brought their weapons to the ready and started moving through the crowd of people at pace. On breaking through the crowd they gained their first sight of the creatures. Eight of them were devouring the victims they had brought down. The Marines started engaging immediately. The eight huge creatures did not retreat they moved towards the threat at great speed, jaws wide open and huge fangs showing. Bullets were ripping into them, parts of their flesh were being left in their trail as they advanced towards the Marines. The noise from all the weapons was deafening, the last two creatures got to within five yards of the Marines before their advance stopped. Some of them had taken over twenty hits to the body before succumbing to their wounds. Lt Davies looked behind him at the crowd of people. Some had stayed within the safety of the Marines and Police others were running in all directions looking for a place of safety.

Behind the carcasses of the creatures there were seven bodies on the ground, some were reasonably in tact others had limbs and heads missing. Lt Davies flipped down a headset and switched the communications switch to all units. On Sabre the transmission came over the loudspeaker in the Operations Room.

"42 detachment, we have encountered eight of the creatures all destroyed, can confirm seven known fatalities amongst civilians, no loss to military or law enforcement. The creatures somehow managed to get behind us and attacked towards the beach."

Captain Piper looked at Mark.

"Only eight where are the bloody rest of them got to, and how the hell did they get behind the Marines position?"

Mark realised they were using the same tactics as before, the first creatures were driving the people towards another group.

"Captain let the Marines know to expect an attack from the beach, it's a trap."

Before Sabre could get out the message, the Marines heard single gunshots coming from the beach area. They could see a lone Police Officer firing towards the sea. The Marines sprinted towards the Officer to support him. Before they could get to him the Officers weapon ran out of ammunition. Less than fifteen yards from him were over a dozen creatures moving very quickly across the sand. People were running in all directions hampering the Marines in their attempt to open fire. The Police Officer turned to run, he was too late two of the creatures had already got within striking distance and rose from the ground towards him. The first landed on his back bringing him to the ground, the hooks from its underbelly latched on and sliced into his body. The second locked on to his right arm, amputating it in one bite. The Marines now had clear visibility to open fire, they engaged with the automatic weapons, the creatures would not retreat they kept advancing like they were possessed by demons. They were making ground towards the Marines faster than they were dying. Suddenly even louder gunfire erupted. Arrow's helicopter appeared from behind the Marines position and started firing the heavy machine gun into the advancing hoard. As the larger calibre bullets starting hitting them, huge lumps of flesh from the creatures were being thrown into the air. One was completely cut in half by the gunfire but still managed to slither a few yards before stopping. With the support of the machine gun the Marines were now winning the battle. The final creature got to within four yards before its head totally disintegrated from the number of bullets hitting it. As the last one dropped the Marines were reloading their weapons in anticipation of another attack.

Lt Davies surveyed the area of devastation, sixteen creatures dead. The lone Police Officer looked like the only casualty. Amazingly all of the civilians had managed to escape. He switched to transmit on his microphone.

"All unit's there was a second attack from the beach, total of sixteen creatures destroyed. One known fatality is a Police Officer."

Captain piper responded.

"Captain of Sabre speaking is there any sight of the remaining creatures?"

"Negative Sir. We are going to patrol farther up the beach and see if we can pick up any trace of them. Sir we are using up a lot of ammunition killing these creatures, can I request we are re-supplied?"

"Roger, will recall our helo to resupply you with ammunition."

The Captain turned to the helicopter controller.

"Bring the helo back for a transfer of ammunition to the

Marine detachment.

The controller acknowledged and called up the helicopter to return to Sabre.

The Captain leaned on the chart table and looked at the chart of the North Beach area. Without looking up he spoke to Mark.

"Professor that is twenty-four of them dead, if your prediction is correct it leaves over fifty of them unaccounted for, any ideas?"

Mark joined the Captain at the chart table. He picked up a pencil and marked the area of beach the Marines had encountered the creatures. It was a very long and flat beach with numerous places they could have come ashore.

"Going back to your previous question on how did the first creatures get behind the Marines without being seen. There were a lot of people walking around out there surely they would have been sighted them prior to the attack?"

As they were both pondering the question Lt Davies reported in.

"All units believe we have found further evidence that more creatures have come ashore approximately two hundred metres farther down the beach from the others. Have found trails in the sand leading to a very large drainage pipe."

"That's your answer Captain they got off the beach through a drainage pipe which probably exited in the inner harbour.

On the chart it showed the North beach was a sea peninsula with a large inner harbour on the other side of it."

The Captain nodded and called up all the other units.

"This Yankee-Two- Bravo, we suspect that the remaining creatures have managed to access the inner harbour via the use of drainpipes. The inner harbour is to be included in the search areas."

He them called up Lt Davies.

"Lt, how many drainage pipes can you see?"

"We have two within one hundred metres of us Sir."

"Right Lt I am getting the helo to bring out two heavy machine guns, I would like them set up facing those entrances. The US military are due to be with you in the next fifteen minutes, once they are there you can handover to them to conduct the searches."

"Roger Sir will do."

Looking back over the chart the Captain said to no one in particular.

"That's the front door closed on them."

The Helicopter controller called out to the Captain.

"Sir we have three American helicopters approaching ETA in seven minutes, they are each carrying twelve Marines."

"Roger HC, provide them with a brief on what we have in the air. Once they are at the scene instruct Arrow and Diamond to bring their helos back for refuel and keep them on deck at five minutes notice."

The Captain called up Lt Davies.

"Lt, there will be thirty-six US marines with you in the next ten minutes. Give their Commanding Officer a handover and you and your men remain on the beach guarding those drainage pipes."

Lt Davies acknowledged the order.

The Captains Steward came into the Operations room and asked if the Captain would like tea or coffee. It amused Mark that in the middle of a battle with the creatures they were still considering whether to have tea or coffee. The Captain said he would take tea and have it in his cabin.

"Professor will you join me please?"

As the Captain left the Operations room he asked the Operations Officer to take over and to let him know if there is any change in the situation.

The tea did taste good to Mark.

"Professor where do you think they have got to?"

"I thought we would have heard or seen evidence of them by now so I can only come to one conclusion, I think they are aware that there is a serious danger with the

234

Marines and they are lying low for a while. They could still be in the drain pipes but my bet is they are somewhere at the bottom of the inner harbour."

"You think they are that tactically aware?"

"I had a suspicion that when the two swarms joined up together that one of the creatures was dominant I think they are following orders."

The Captain nodded his head twice. Mark could see he was thinking what decisions he would be making if he was the creature in charge.

"It makes sense what you are saying Professor, I think that would be my course of action in their present situation. Stay low and evaluate the situation."

A message came through from the Operations Room.

"Captain Sir, the US marines are on the ground now and are conducting searches of all areas. They are setting up a Command centre in one of the hotels."

"Roger Ops has the helo delivered the weapons and ammo to our Marines yet?"

"Yes Sir, delivered and helo is on her way back. Sir Admiral Hawkins is on secure communications and wishes to talk with you."

Mark returned to the Operations with the Captain and listened as he went in to discussion with the Admiral providing him with an up to date brief on how the Operation was proceeding.

"Yes Sir in discussion with Professor Yates we believe they are holed up in the inner harbour. We have the flood drains covered by the Royal Marines in case they try to return to the sea via that route. Your Marines are patrolling other sectors."

The Admiral must have then asked about casualties.

"Eight we know of seven civilians and one Police Officer."

The Captain went in to a period of listening to what the Admiral was saying, with the occasional yes sir to acknowledge he was agreeing to the instructions being passed. The Captain made the final statement.

"Yes Sir, I will discuss that with Professor Yates and keep you informed."

He put down his headset and beckoned Mark to join him.

"The Americans have set up a Command Centre at the Hotel Rouge, Admiral Hawkins would like you to join the Commanding Officer in the Command Centre and provide advice on the creatures. This is the first time these troops have encountered them and he wants to make sure they are aware of what they are up against."

Mark nodded.

"How are you with a weapon Professor, I would like you to be at least carrying a sidearm whilst you are ashore?"

"I have handled a weapon before and know the basics how to aim and fire."

"Good, can you be ready in thirty minutes?"

Mark returned to his cabin and packed a few items into a small holdall. He slipped into a flying suit and sat on his bed. He thought back to Lisa and wondered how she was managing. The change in her worried him, he now realised why she never talked about the creatures in those two days it had obviously already been eating away at her long before the attack against the surf boarders. This latest attack would not be long in making the news and the loss of more life would make her feel even guiltier. He was interrupted from his thoughts of Lisa by a heavy knock on his open door. A tall and very domineering figure of a Chief Petty Officer stood there taking up most of the width and height of the door.

"Hello Sir, Chief Wilson the Captain informed me you required a sidearm whilst ashore."

He held a browning pistol and two spare magazines in his huge hands. He took Mark through the loading and unloading procedure and making the weapon safe and armed. Mark put on the belt provided and clipped the pistol into its holster.

Before leaving the Chief got Mark to sign a book to say

he had received the weapon and spare magazines.

A second knock at the door followed shortly after. It was one of the aircrew.

"Sir, we will be ready to leave in five minutes, can I take your bag?"

Mark thanked him and followed him towards the flight deck.

CHAPTER THIRTY-THREE

It was less than a ten minute flight from Sabre to the hotel. On the way he saw the Royal Marines on the beach with the two machine gun positions directed toward the drainage pipes. One of the Marines obviously recognised it as Sabres helo and gave a friendly hand signal. Three ambulances were in attendance on the large grass area where the seven civilians and the Police Officer had lost their lives. The boardwalk on the peninsula was empty of people apart from groups of marines patrolling the area. On the roadway leading to the hotel he could see a roadblock being set up. Two coaches were exiting the area. Mark assumed them be full of holidaymakers being transported to somewhere safe. Flying over the inner harbour he looked down, it was large, probably over mile square hundreds of small and medium sized boats were tied up along its perimeter. They touched down on a large lawn area outside the Hotel Rouge. Disembarking he made his way to the entrance where four armed military personnel stood on guard. After explaining who he was one of them escorted him through the main entrance and into a room that he assumed in normal business would be a function room for parties or weddings. There were six people in the room, all were US military, they had set up a table with charts on it which Mark assumed to be of the holiday complex and North Beach. Around the charts were empty and half filled coffee cups. On a table opposite lay four automatic rifles, helmets and combat jackets. Before he arrived at the table he was approached by one of the soldiers, he wore the rank of Major.

"Professor Gates I assume, I am Major Scott Jackson.

"Hello Major it is Professor Yates not Gates."

"Sorry Professor someone must have written the message down wrong."

Major Jackson had a strong American accent. Apart from the Southern drawl Mark could never work out what part of America accents were attached to. All he knew was that some were easy to understand and others more difficult. Major Jackson fell into the more difficult group. He was early forties and had the usual US army haircut. He looked strong which complemented his six foot two build.

"Well Professor I understand from Headquarters you are quite knowledgeable on these creatures?"

"Yes I am fairly acquainted with their tactics and what they are capable of."

Mark walked over to the table where the chart was to see what information they were putting on it. There was a few numbers written in areas which he assumed to be patrolling sectors and apart from a coffee cup mark that was about it. They were missing where the drainage pipes were and where the Royal Marines were set up with the machine guns. He thought the Captain of Sabre would go ballistic if his crew presented this to him as a piece of intelligence.

"Major you are aware that we suspect the creatures are holed up in the inner harbour and how they got there?"

"Yes we got that message, came through some drains and your Marines have got that exit covered with heavy machine guns."

Mark diplomatically asked if they could show them the drains on the chart, one of the other soldiers pointed an area out. Mark picked up a pencil and drew both drains in and on the beach wrote Royal Marines machine guns.

"Major the entrance to the inner harbour, do you know how wide that is."

"Yeh it is less than thirty feet across, but it has a pair of flood gates, which doubles as a bridge which we have closed, so they cannot exit that way."

"Is there any other way out of this harbour apart from that entrance?"

"Nope, that and the drains appear the only way out."

Mark looked all round the harbour on the chart. In one of the far corners of the chart was marked the wording Salt

Creek and a wavy line.

"What is this Major?" pointing to Salt Creek.

"Oh that is a very small creek that runs out of the harbour into the salt water marshes."

"Has anybody checked it out?"

"Yeh I sent a couple of our guys over there to have a look."

Mark had to take a few seconds to try and compose himself before he responded.

"Major, twelve Royal Marines met eight of these creatures and just managed to stop them. We still have well over fifty on the loose. Two soldiers will not stand a chance if they come across them. Right now these creatures are like caged animals looking for an escape route they are very intelligent and can take a man's head off in one bite. It may be worth while checking on those two soldiers and maybe reinforcing their position. If the creatures locate that creek it could be an attractive option or even their only option for them to make their way back to the sea."

Mark traced the creek with his finger, it led on to saltwater marshes but they could easily cross over those and get back to open water on the other side of them. It did look an attractive option.

The Major went quiet for a few moments assessing on how he should respond, he was aware that this guy had the ear of the Admiral in charge of this operation and did not want to act arrogant and look stupid if by chance this guy was right.

"Good point Professor."

He called to a Sergeant to radio up the two checking out the creek and told them to wait until reinforcements arrived.

Mark looked at the chart again and pointed to the beach they would most likely head for if they did go through the saltwater marshes exit.

"Major if they do use this as an exit I believe they will head directly through the marshes to this beach here. It may be worthwhile setting up a defence line to intercept them if they do."

The Major nodded and called to his Sergeant again.

"Let's set up two heavy machine gun posts on this beach and see if we can get power over there for floodlighting, it is going to be dark in the next three hours."

Mark had already thought that they had less than three hours of daylight left and it would swing the advantage to the creatures when the sun went down. Around the harbour there was quite a bit of street lighting but the beach area would not give the marines clear visibility for their targets until it was too late. Somehow he was going to have to force the creatures hand before it got dark. He thought back to when Sabre first encountered the creatures and how they had used explosive charges to stun and kill some. The water here was too shallow to use depth charges and would probably cause immense damage to the harbour and boats but maybe they could use charges less powerful to force them into moving. Turning he said.

"Could I run an idea past you Major."

The Major listened attentively to what Mark was saying and kept nodding in agreement.

The Major's tactical experience came in to play now Mark could see his brain working through every scenario if the creatures did make a break for it. The Major called his Sergeant over to join the discussion. They would need all defences in place and ready before they started the operation.

"Sergeant once those machine gun points are ready on the beach call back the troops from salt water creek and allow the creatures to exit that way if they desire. It will be a lot easier to take them out on land. And support those machine gun points with an additional six marines. Let me know when everything is in place?"

The Sergeant acknowledged with a "Yes Sir." He doubled off to make the necessary radio calls.

The Major called out again to his Sergeant.

"And I want two armed helicopters in the air for support, so let's get them refuelled and ready now."

Mark called up HMS Sabre and requested to speak to Sharky Ward.

The Chief came on the radio.

"This is Y2B Chief Ward speaking over."

"Chief it is Professor Yates speaking, when you encountered the creatures in Plymouth you used charges to bring them to the surface, do you think we could use the same method here?"

"Yes Professor it should be possible but looking at the chart you have a big expanse of water so it would be a bit of pot luck on you hitting them. Unless ...."

Mark broke in before the Chief had finished thinking.

"Unless what Chief."

"Unless we use larger charges and set them off simultaneously Sir."

"How large a charge Chief, we have lots of boats in the harbour."

"Sir if we went for five pound charges being set off in fours then that should provide good coverage and not affect too many surface vessels. The coverage is increased if they are dropped a distance apart but explode roughly the same time. Each explosion causes a pressure wave that when they collide result in a crushing effect for anything within that area."

"Please tell me Sabre has these charges available Chief."

"We carry sixteen five pound charges in the magazine Sir."

"Excellent can you request Captain Piper to talk to me?"

"He is right beside me Sir passing you over."

Mark took the Captain through the plan and requested that the charges were primed, ready and delivered to shore within the hour.

The Captain agreed to his requests and wished him luck.

Major Jackson had stood next to Mark throughout the conversation and was rubbing his hands together and smiling.

"Professor I am getting a warm feeling about this plan."

Mark smiled and thought he was warming to the Major also.

The Sergeant called out.

"Sir, the machine gun points are set up on the beach and reinforced with an additional six marines. Both helos are refuelled and armed. I have pulled back the platoon from salt water creek and redeployed them to other areas."

From outside the building you could hear the noise of helicopters coming into land. Looking out of the window Mark could see Arrow's and Diamond's helicopters all settling on the large lawn area. Forty five minutes later, Sabre's helo touched down beside them carrying sixteen five pound explosive charges.

CHAPTER THIRTY-FOUR

It was 1725 and sunset was less than two hours away. In the large function room over twenty people gathered. They were all talking amongst themselves waiting for the brief on the operation to begin. Major Jackson look around those in attendance, deciding everyone was there he walked to the front.

"Gentlemen can I please have your attention. We are running out of daylight and we want this show on the road as quickly as possible."

The crowd became quiet with just the occasional cough.

"As you may know we strongly suspect that those creatures killed earlier this afternoon were part of a group of roughly eighty. We believe that the remainder of the swarm are lying low in the inner harbour. If we allow them to stay there and make their escape during the dark there is a good chance some of them will be successful and make it back to the safety of the sea. We do not intend to give them that opportunity. I am going to hand you over to Professor Yates who has come up with a plan.

Mark walked forward and looked around the group of people in front of him, he recognised a few, Sabres flight crew and the Royal Marine Lieutenant.

"Gentlemen, the plan is that we are going to drop explosives into the inner harbour to try and persuade the creatures to make a break for it. There are three options for them to escape. One is how we suspect they entered the harbour by use of the large storm drains. The second is where they attacked the people earlier today and the third is via the salt water creek. The storm drains will be covered by the Royal Marines detachment, the attack area will be covered by US Marines and the beach leading from salt creek will also be covered by US Marines. If the creatures do go by salt creek we will let them proceed through until they get to the beach area. If we try and take them out in the salt water marshes they will have a lot of cover and it would be very difficult to destroy them as a group. The plan is to let them continue on to the beach, where the Marines will be waiting for them. Two armed helicopters will be monitoring the situation and will proceed to assist in destroying the creatures if called upon or suspect they are needed."

Mark paused for a few seconds for any questions.

"The dropping of the explosions will be carried out by the three helicopters from the ships and one US Marine Helo. This has to be a co-ordinated attack with all four helos dropping the explosives together at set ranges. HMS Sabres helicopter will call out the co-ordinated drop of explosives. Each helicopter cannot be more that fifty yards from each other to ensure the explosives have maximum affect. We have sixteen 5lb charges available giving us four opportunities to panic the creatures into making a run for it. These creatures have come across helicopters before and it has never been a pleasant experience so I suggest you make as much noise as possible for a few minutes before dropping the charges which should get them nervous before the charges go in. Is there any questions?"

A Captain attached to the US Marines raised his arm.

"Professor if they all make for the same exit, do you think we will be able to stop them?"

Mark nodded.

"In the event they all go for the same exit, both armed helos will provide support which should give enough fire power to destroy them. If any do make it back to sea then we have the Maritime aircraft on station for another two hours, they will saturate a pre-designated area with depth charges which should finish them off."

Major Jackson stepped forward again.

"The Royal Marines will be call sign Bravo one, salt water beach Bravo two and the third area Bravo three. The armed helicopters will go under the call sign Hotel one and Hotel two. The weapon carrying helicopters will be Whisky one to four. I would like everyone reporting in as soon as they are ready which I expect to be in no more 15 minutes."

Mark broke in.

"Gentlemen for those that have not come across these creatures before please do not underestimate them. They are extremely intelligent killing machines. The Royal Marines reported this morning that they would not retreat and kept attacking even though they were being slaughtered. Please show no mercy towards them and ensure they are all dead before approaching. We cannot afford for any to make it back to open water. Thank you and good luck."

Within ten minutes all Bravo units had reported in, and all six helos were in the air. All the helicopters were flying low and in formation over the inner harbour. Mark wondered what was going through those creatures minds lying at the bottom of the harbour listening to the familiar noise of helicopters above them. He was hoping it was getting them extremely edgy.

Major Jackson got on to the radio to all units.

"We will commence the operation in five minutes all helicopters take up position for first delivery of explosives.

On board HMS Sabre the Operations room was full of people wanting to listen in on the proceedings from ashore. The Captain looked around and could see in their faces that they wanted to have their revenge on these creatures. He turned to the on watch communicator and asked him to switch the radio circuit to the ships main broadcast so the whole ships company could hear how it was proceeding.

The next transmission came over the loudspeaker.

"This is Whisky One all helos in position for drop."

"This is Command proceed when ready."

The four helicopters hovered forty feet off the water all were in position making a tight box fifty yards apart. The Observer on Sabres helo Whisky One gave one final check of their positioning seeing it was accurate he called out over the air.

"Standby drop now, now, now."

On the last now, all four simultaneously dropped the grey oblong cases containing the explosives. A few seconds went by and the explosives went off, three all together and one just slightly behind. Four spouts of water rose in the air. The helos could clearly see the shock waves transmitting out from each detonation until colliding with each other and forming another water spout in the centre of the box. All eyes in the helicopters were on the area of impact praying for some tell tale sign that they had been on target. Suddenly something was spotted moving rapidly in the water towards the storm drains.

"This is Whisky one movement sighted in the water, moving towards Bravo one position out."

"This is Bravo one roger out."

"This is Command can you see how many."

"Negative but it does not look like many Whisky One out."

One of the armed helicopters moved nearer Bravo one position in case they required support.

"This is Whisky one, have clear visual now, two creatures entering the storm pipes towards Bravo One out."

"Bravo One roger out"

The Royal Marines had both machine guns and automatic weapons ready. The creatures exited from the storm drains at amazing speed. Immediately all weapons engaged. It was a futile attempt. Both creatures were torn to shreds as a hail of large calibre bullets ripped into them. They had barely reached ten yards from the exit before coming to a stop. Bullets continued to hit them after they stopped forcing their carcases even nearer to the exit of the storm drain.

"This is Bravo One, two creatures destroyed out."

"Roger Bravo One, Whisky One commence with second drop of explosives."

"Whisky one Roger out."

All four weapon carriers moved fifty yards forward in

unison. Hovering forty feet above the surface, Whisky One called out for the explosives to be dropped. This time it appeared that they all went off simultaneously, the pressure waves from each explosion moved out like synchronized dancers coming together in a crescendo. All eyes were once again on the surface. The observer on the Arrow's helo pointed to movement in front of them. Two long red streaks were moving at amazing speed towards Bravo Three position. The pilot pressed his radio transmission button.

"This is Whisky Three two creatures heading towards Bravo Three position out.

"This is Bravo Three copied out"

The Marines at Bravo Three all cocked their weapons and stood ready to engage.

The two creatures came ashore on a short strip of sand which led to the large expanse of grass. As they breasted the grass, the Marines opened fire. It was another slaughter twelve automatic weapons engaged them in rapid fire. The creature's bodies bounced around the ground from the number of the bullets hitting them.

Bravo three reported in both creatures destroyed.

Major Jackson turned to Mark.

"Another two, I was expecting more."

Mark nodded in agreement with the Major.

"I would have thought they would have tried to escape in force."

Mark tapped the chart table softly with his forefinger in thought. And the penny dropped.

"Major have you ever watched the movie Zulu?"

The Major looked at him curiously thinking it was a pretty strange time to discuss movies."

"Major it is what the creatures are doing they are testing your defences to see which is the safest route, the same tactics the Zulu chiefs used."

"You think those creatures are that tactically aware to try something like that?"

"Major one of those creatures down there is in charge

and believe me they are extremely aware of tactics. How much do you bet at the next dropping of explosives they will head towards Bravo Two's position at Salt Water creek. If they get ashore there the rest will follow."

"I have not known you long Professor but I have learnt not to bet against your hunches."

"All units this is Command, we believe the creatures are testing our defences and the next two will head for Salt Water creek. Do not engage them let them come ashore, we will deal with them when they cross the marshes and reach the beach. Both helicopters Hotel One and Two standby to reinforce Bravo Two on my command. Out"

Both Hotel One and Two acknowledged.

The Captain on Sabre smiled at his Operations Officer.

"I can just see the Professor coming up with that idea."

"How many Marines have we at Bravo Two Major?"

"Twelve total and two machine guns, the armed helos will be providing support."

"Well they may be meeting over fifty of these creatures very shortly."

The Major sucked slightly on his bottom lip and opened communications to Bravo Two.

"Bravo Two how much open ground between the marshes and your positions?"

"This is Bravo Two approx twenty five yards clear firing range over."

"This is Command have you got an option to extend that distance?"

"This is Bravo Two we can go back another ten yards which will put us on the high tide mark."

"Roger Bravo Two you have five minutes extend the clear firing range the extra ten out."

"Whisky One this is Command commence next drop out"

Sabre's helo acknowledged and directed the other three aircraft though the same procedure. After the explosions the helicopters lifted higher in the air to get a better view of any movement.

Diamonds helo made the call.

"This is Whisky four, two creatures sighted moving towards Bravo Two position out."

The Major smiled and winked at Mark.

"This is Command when they come ashore do not engage, I repeat do not engage the creatures unless you are in immediate danger. Bravo Two remain silent as possible I do not want them to hear anything that will get them suspicious. "

"Bravo Two copied out."

"What do you think Professor?"

"If they play their usual game, one or both of the creatures will have a look around and then go back into the water and report all clear."

"Do you think they will go as far in as the beach to check."

"That's why I have my fingers crossed Major, I hope not."

Mark looked at his watch, he had started his stop watch on Whisky four reporting the creatures had left the safety of the inner harbour that was four minutes and thirty-six seconds ago.

"Major I think we had better drop another pattern of explosives in a minute otherwise they may get suspicious why we are delaying."

"You are crediting these creatures one hell of level of intelligence Professor."

"Believe me Major you cannot underestimate them."

"This is Command, Whisky One, commence next explosive drop.

"Whisky One roger out."

All four helicopters took up their position at equal distances apart. On the order they all dropped their final charge.

Before the explosives hit the water Whisky four called out.

"This is Hotel Four, one creature returning from Bravo Two position. Out."

All four explosions detonated in unison again. Before the water disturbance from the explosives had settled a streak of red like a long wide torpedo was seen passing under the helicopters.

Whisky One, reported first.

"This is Whisky One, multiple creatures heading towards Salt Water creek, estimate over fifty out."

"This is Command, Bravo Two standby they are heading your way. Hotel One and Two be prepared to provide support."

Both Hotel One and Two manoeuvred to approach Bravo Two's position from the sea which would give a clear firing range from behind the Marines position.

"How long do you think it will take them to get across those marshes to the Beach Professor?"

"Five maybe six minutes if they move at speed, which I think they will."

It took them only five minutes twenty seconds for the first one to reach the sand. They were travelling fast, probably the maximum speed they could go at. The Marines opened fire as soon as the creatures broke cover from the marshes. The heavy machine guns had the creatures in a crossfire and were inflicting massive damage to their bodies. The Marines were firing directly on to them as they tried to advance over the beach. From behind the Marines the two Helicopters took up position and started raining down high calibre bullets from above. Some of the creatures had made it twenty yards on to the beach but all were going much slower from the amount of bullets entering their bodies. Two who appeared to be least wounded made rapid headway through the dead and dying towards the Marines. At ten yards from their goal they were met with a stream of bullets from automatic weapons. The creatures came to a grinding halt, only moving as other bullets slammed into them. More were streaming out from the marshes trying to make it to the safety of the sea. All of them met the wall of death before their second slither across the soft sand. Firing continued for another minute after the last creature had left the marshes. As the marines walked around the carnage, intermittent shots were fired if they came across any that showed possible life. Major Jackson and Mark could hear the horrendous amount of gunfire very clearly even being so far from the scene of action. A few seconds after the last shot was heard, Bravo Two reported in.

"This is Bravo Two all creatures destroyed, no casualties, out."

Mark and the Major gave each other a high five. Onboard Sabre you could hear a call of celebration through out the ship.

Major Jackson spoke into his microphone.

"All units remain on alert until we complete a full search of the area. Hotel One and Two conduct a visual search of the marsh area to make sure there were no stragglers."

Mark took a deep breath, hoping that it was all over and all the creatures were destroyed.

"Major I am going to take a walk."

"Professor I would prefer if you remain safe until we get the all clear."

"Thank you Major but I think I will be okay."

The Major turned to two Marines.

"Marines escort the Professor and keep him safe."

Mark did not argue with the escort. When he got outside he asked if they would mind if they went around all the sites that the creatures were killed. Both Marines nodded. At Bravo one the Royal Marines were still in position along with some US Marines. The Marines from Sabre recognised Mark and greeted him. He looked at the two recent kills, both had sustained massive damage to their head and bodies. Walking farther down the beach they reached Bravo Three position, the two killed there had similar injuries to the ones at Bravo One. One of the creatures was lying on its back, Mark knelt down and pulled it over. The body was still flexible and slightly warm.

"Anything wrong Professor?" asked one of his escorts.

Marked rolled his head. "No nothing wrong, just curious."

They crossed the bridge over the entrance to the harbour which was the quickest way to the beach head at Bravo Two. You could still smell cordite in the sea air from the number of bullets that had been fired. One part of the beach was totally covered with the carcasses of the creatures. Although Mark would normally feel regret for sea life killed on this scale, he felt no remorse for them. The film of them killing those young people was still vivid in his mind. He walked around the bodies of the creatures, stopping and looking at some more closely, occasionally stooping down to move one. Both the Marines escorting wondered why he was taking such an interest in the dead creatures. On the way back he stopped at the waters edge of the inner harbour, staring at the still water. As he looked on something in his gut was telling him that what he was thinking was true and he was not being paranoid about it, that bastard was still down their, waiting. It had sent all of these creatures to their death so it could survive.

CHAPTER THIRTY-FIVE

In the Command Centre, Major Jackson and three other soldiers were sat at a table drinking coffee. As Mark entered the Major raised his hand and waved him over to the table.

"Coffee Professor? I am going to give it another 15 minutes and then start the clear up of the carcasses before it gets too dark."

Mark nodded to the coffee and pulled up a chair at the table. He turned to the Major and looked at him with a concerned look.

"I think there is at least one still alive."

The comment delayed the Major on pouring the milk into Mark's coffee.

"Sorry Professor, are you sure?"

"Not sure but I suspect there is at least one still in that inner harbour."

"Because?"

"Amongst this swarm there was one creature that we tagged with a transponder. I have been around all of those killed today. None of them have that transponder on."

"Yes but it could have come off or been destroyed during all of the shooting, some of those creatures were torn to shreds in the gunfire?"

"Possible but somehow I do not think so. I think that those creatures we killed today were sent out as insurance, if they made it to the sea then it would prove it was safe, if they did not then we would assume that was all of them. We would pack up our gear and leave allowing any other creature to exit by whatever area they wished without risk."

The Major ran his fingers through the front of his hair stopping at the top and to scratch his head.

"Professor I know you think these creatures are super smart but you are saying that they are willing to sacrifice themselves for another, that's one hell of a discipline system amongst them."

Mark thought back to the time when they were tracking the creature with the transponder. The erratic behaviour in the tracking and the changes of speed it was not chasing fish it was challenging for the dominance of the swarm and it was bloody victorious.

"Major, I need for you to trust me on this, there is at least one left out there."

"Well Professor, luckily I had no plans for tonight, give me any suggestions how to get this bastard for we have less than ninety minutes of daylight left."

"Do we know what time the next high tide is?" Asked Mark.

The Major called out to a soldier who was putting some charts away.

"Do we know when the next high tide is?"

The soldier stopped what he was doing and ruffled around in a case and pulled out a laptop. After a few seconds he replied.

"Sir 2125 hours."

Looking up at the clock Mark saw that was just over two hours away.

"If it thinks the area is clear that is when it will leave, the sea will be at its closest to any of the exit points."

"So we have three exits Professor which would be your first choice?"

"The way they entered by the storm drains, it is the shortest and most protected route. At high tide mark the exit is only a few yards from the sea. If it gets through the drains it can be in the water within seconds of exiting."

Mark realised this was not going to be easy. With such a short distance to cover once the creature exited the drain it could still make it to the sea before it took enough bullets to stop it. They were going to have to slow it down or stop it whilst it was in the drain.

"Major have you got an explosives expert amongst your men."

"Yes Sergeant Reece is our ordnance expert, I will

255

bring him in."

The Sergeant arrived in the conference room within five minutes he was roughly five feet ten with short cropped hair which looked like it would be fair if allowed to grow his face had the look of granite about it with each feature having been chiselled in place. The Major called the Sergeant over to a table where he and Mark were sitting.

"Sergeant we have a problem and hopefully you can come up with a solution."

They explained the expected route of the creature and the need to stop it before it hit the beach.

"How long is the drain Sir?"

"About thirty feet. And there are two of them, about 100 yards apart."

"Would you prefer a triggered explosion?"

"What would you recommend Sergeant?"

"Well Sir if we go for a remote and we time it wrong then it could possibly get out before we reacted, with the triggered then it would guarantee the explosion would go off at the right moment, so I would recommend the triggered, it will just take a little longer to set up."

"How long?"

"For both drains about forty five minutes no more than an hour."

"Okay Sergeant let's go for the triggered explosion on both drains, let me know when it is all set up."

Mark knew that the creature would not easily fall for a trap and would probably be carrying out its own surveillance of the area well before it was planning to exit. The Sergeant was already exiting from the conference room and Mark called out to him.

"Sergeant all of your work has to be completed on the beach side away from the inner harbour I am sure the creature will be monitoring the drains for sometime before it decides to leave, we cannot let it see anything suspicious."

The Sergeant looked at the Major, who responded.

"Make sure no Marines approach the drains from the inner harbour side and keep any noise down to a minimum."

"Yes Sir."

"Well Professor, the explosives will be ready within the hour, any other recommendations?"

"Yes Major we need to start withdrawing most of the marines and ensure all helicopters are on the ground. I will go with what your suggestions are on essential personnel to take the creature out should it choose another exit?"

Mark and the Major discussed the plan over the next twenty minutes. One camouflaged machine gun point would be situated at each of the other exit points the marines would be using night vision sights. A further two marines would act as spotters a safe distance from the drains and report if the creature made any move towards them. Within the hour Sergeant Reece had reported back that both drains were now rigged to explode should anything cross over the trip wire that was situated roughly half way through them. Mark looked at his watch sunset in twenty minutes and high tide in thirty five. The Major called up all units who were still operational and carried out a radio check. On completion he ordered that all movement and radio contact to be kept to a minimum.

"Now we wait Professor."

Mark nodded, he looked out of one of the large conference room windows, the sun was dropping behind the horizon the sky was a deep shade of red. The phrase red sky at night sailor's delight ran through his head. Now everything was in place he started to question himself, was he being paranoid was the creature with the transponder lying with the rest of the carcasses. Part of him wished it was the other part wanted it to crawl into those drains and get blown to pieces. He only wished he could see the look on its evil face when it realised it had walked into a trap. He looked at his watch again twenty-five minutes to high tide. He checked his watch a further six times before it pointed to 2125 and high tide. No-one had reported any movement from any of the lookout points. His watch moved past 2130 and still no reports. The Major looked at Mark as if wanting an explanation. The time passed 2140, fifteen minutes past high tide. A click on the radio broke through as if someone was going to transmit, all ears tuned towards it, a few seconds passed and then a report from the drains lookout came through.

"Possible movement in water at southerly drain out."

A whole minute ticked past.

"Confirmed holding visual on one creature in the vicinity of southerly drain out."

This time it was over two minutes before the next transmission came through.

"Creature out of the water entering southerly drain out."

The next transmission reported the creature had entered the drain. No explosion happened, it had been thirty seconds since it had entered, it should be on the other side by now. The Major looked at Sergeant Reece for an explanation, but the Sergeants expression did not change. Suddenly a huge bang shook the windows and a flash lit up the inner harbour area. A wry smile crept over the Sergeants face.

It had been over five minutes since the explosion. The Major and Mark escorted by two marines walked to the site of the explosion. Four bright beams from their torches flickered in front of them. They could still smell residue from the explosion which hung heavily in the warm night air. Breasting a small grass embankment they stepped on to the sandy beach and made their way thirty yards further along to the scene of the destroyed storm drain. The explosion had managed to collapse the drain and the boardwalk above it had dropped into the void. The exit was blocked by a mixture of cement, rubble and sand that had been forced from the beach in the explosion. Mark climbed up on to the boardwalk and looked down at the crater the explosion had left. It was filled with similar rubble as the entrance along with timber and some metal framework from the boardwalk. Checking the inner harbour side it showed the same signs of damage and blockage as the beach exit. The Marines checked around the beach area for any sign that whatever entered the tunnel had not made it out. The only marks visible on the small strip of sand was that of the Royal Marines from earlier in the day.

"Well Professor whatever went in there did not make it out."

"Definitely looks that way Major."

"You think that is all of them destroyed now?"

Mark nodded.

"I am fairly certain."

"Well I am going to leave a detachment of Marines patrolling the area overnight just to make sure Professor."

A wooden bench overlooking the sea was situated a few yards away from the area of the explosion. Sitting down on it Mark looked out to sea he could see the lights from the three warships at anchor two miles away. He cast his mind back to the first time he had come across the creatures and the people that had since lost their lives. Recalling how many lives he could have possibly saved if he had noticed quicker the similarities in the attacks. It still riled him how he had failed to notice each attack being at high tide. His mind settled on Lisa and his feelings for her. She was the spark in this whole saga that had rekindled feelings he had not felt in many years. A tinge of anger and frustration passed through him knowing deep inside things would never return to how it was. He felt guilty and selfish, was he thinking of himself, it was she that had suffered the most, her beautiful mind and wonderful life destroyed. From deep inside he still retained a slender hope that maybe one day they could rediscover those wonderful times together, but he knew he would only be a constant reminder to her of the mayhem and deaths caused by those creatures. The Major woke him from his thoughts.

"Professor I am going to head back to the command

centre and give a final brief to the other units, you coming along?"

Mark looked at the Major and gave him a tight smile.

"I will come along later I just need some time to myself."

The Major nodded as if understanding he had interrupted Mark from his thoughts.

"I am going to station the two marines up by the entrance to the boardwalk, you need them shout."

"Thank you Major I will be fine."

Mark felt an urge for a large straight rum to help him get his head together. He was tired, physically and mentally for the past six months these creatures had played a major part in his daily life. Now finally the swarm was destroyed his thoughts could only relax by reflecting back on the entire series of events. His mind kept drifting back to Lisa he knew he had fallen in love with her that day in Washington. After that night even the mention of her name ignited feelings that he could not describe. Making love with her was something wonderful that could only be felt by being intimate with someone you truly love. He placed his head in his hands and swore to himself as if to release the tension and regret that was building to explosion point. He raised himself from the bench to return to the hotel complex and find somewhere he could get some alcohol. He took one last look out to sea at the warships, their anchor lights glistening like stars. He thought of Sabre's crew and the part they played in destroying those creatures he felt a very strong attachment to the frigate.

He was just about to turn away when he heard a noise like a rock falling, then nothing total quietness apart from the sound of waves gently lapping against the beach. Mark stood perfectly still straining his hearing to pick out any unfamiliar noise. A whole minute went past with nothing heard then suddenly another rock falling. Walking over to the crater in the board walk he shone his torch into the opening. No movement it looked exactly like it did before.

He clicked the torch off and stood motionless concentrating on all of the sounds around him. The next noise sounded like a larger rock falling and it came from the beach area. Walking down from the grassy area he stepped on to the soft sand, switching on his torch he scanned the immediate area in front of him. Nothing it was all clear. Walking farther along the beach he reached the storm drain that had been destroyed. Slowly he scanned each section. By torch light it all looked normal until a small block of cement started tumbling down the rubble. As another piece of rubble fell his senses went on full alert. He unclipped his holster and withdrew the pistol. He shone the torch on his weapon to check it was not switched to safe and cocked it. For the next three minutes it went totally quiet.

He was beginning to think it was probably some loose rubble that had just dislodged itself, when a much larger piece began to move, not rolling but being pushed out of place. As the cement block reached its extremity, gravity took over and it quickly tumbled down, hitting the sand with a thud. The absence of the block of cement left a dark cavity in the rubble about the size of a football. Mark moved closer, his pistol firmly pointing at the hole. From within it he could hear heavy breathing, like someone struggling to bring air into their lungs. Another piece of rubble fell from the cavity. The breathing was joined by a noise of movement from within the dark hole. He shone his torch into it, the movement suddenly stopped and the breathing got shallower. He moved the beam of light around the hole and it reflected back a bright yellow glow like it was shining on an opal. Mark knew exactly what it was, an eye. He aimed his pistol pointing it directly at the yellow glow. The creature realising Mark's intentions gave one final push to clear the debris, its head pushed fully out of the cavity. The speed of which the creature responded to the threat caught Mark unaware, he stepped back his footing sinking into the soft sand and unbalancing him. He fired the pistol but it only nicked the top of the creatures head. The creature pushed again getting around six feet of its body out of the cavity. Mark raised his pistol again aiming at the head but the creature responded by swinging the freed body and head towards Mark striking him across both legs and knocking him to the ground. The torch flew out of his hand landing just short of the creatures head. For a split second he got full view of the grotesque head. One side had all the skin ripped away displaying the jawbone and the rows of gruesome teeth. The neck had a huge chunk of flesh missing from it. The creature heaved the body out again nearly twelve foot of it was on the beach. One more heave and it would all be on the beach. It was not concentrating on Mark it was making the priority to reach the water, another five yards and it would succeed. He raised his pistol fully focussing on the head he fired and hit the target. The creature started swinging its head around in a huge arc. The rest of the body fell from the rubble. The whole body was now on the beach. Mark fired again hitting it just behind the head. The creature's movement became slow and laboured, it was getting confused and started moving along the beach rather than towards the sea. Recovering his torch he followed the creature. It stopped, low shallow breathing was the only sign of life. The creatures body had been badly damaged in the explosion, huge lumps of flesh were missing from numerous places on the body. Part of the tail was only connected by a thin piece of muscle and skin.

The two marines that had been stationed at the entrance of the boardwalk came sprinting along the beach to join him. Mark held his hand up to indicate for them to hold fire. He wanted to look this monster in the eye when he fired the fatal bullet. Looking down at the dying creature it's eyes flicked opened, it tried to move its head in the direction of Mark but it only had the strength to slide it a couple of inches across the sand. Mark raised his weapon and fired it directly into the head twice. The creature jolted then lay perfectly still. Blood from the bullets exit points soaked into the sand. Running the beam of light from his torch along the body of the creature he found what he was looking for. Exactly where Alan Dempsey had placed it was the transponder, still held securely in place with the surgical staples.

CHAPTER THIRTY-SIX

Mark remained in Norfolk another five days, during that time he called Lisa's parents home seven times. Six calls went unanswered with no facility to leave a message, on the seventh attempt someone picked up the receiver. It was the house maid, she reported that the family were not available and she did not know when they would be returning. She agreed to let the family know that he had called if they contacted her. Initially she did not want to take his contact details but finally agreed. The tone of her voice did not fill Mark with confidence that she would fulfil the deal of passing on his mobile number and email address should the Michaels family make contact with her.

On his final day in America Mark met up with Jeff and Kate. They were still working out of the same building but different offices. Jeff had arranged a private lunch for them in the Officers quarters which was apparently made easier with the fact that Admiral Hawkins was also attending. On entering the reception area of the Officer quarters Mark saw Kate and Jeff sat in comfortable leather chairs. It was good to see them both again. When they sighted him they rushed over, strong handshakes and pat on the back from Jeff and hugs and kisses from Kate followed. Kate kept a friendly arm wrapped around his waist.

"Its great seeing you again Mark, I was hoping it was just going to be a friendly lunch together but Jeff must be bucking for promotion asking the Admiral along."

Jeff shook his head and smiled.

"Look I just mentioned to him that we were meeting for lunch and he asked if he could join us, I wasn't going to say no to an Admiral."

Smiling Kate pushed him in the ribs.

"Yeh if you say so Jeff."

A steward approached and asked if they were the party for lunch with the Admiral. He advised them that the

Admirals driver had rang and he was on his way and would be with them in fifteen minutes.

"Just time for a quick drink" Said Jeff

Entering the adjacent bar area they ordered three straights, rum for Mark and two bourbons. Kate raised her glass.

"Let's hope we can all get together again, we make one hell of a team. Even if it's just another chance to see Mark with just a towel on."

Other Officers in the bar turned and looked towards the group of three as they chinked the glasses together and downed them in one.

"You started without me."

Heading towards them was Admiral Hawkins.

Jeff still clearing the residue of bourbon from his throat answered.

"Sir, sorry we were not expecting you for a few more minutes."

"Commander relax I always give out the wrong time I am arriving catches people out. So what are we drinking?"

Jeff looked like he was stuck on what to say so Mark stepped in.

"I am on rum and I think the other two are bourbon Admiral."

"Rum sounds good to me Professor, Steward two rums and two bourbons please."

They spent another twenty minutes in the bar and each finished off another two drinks. The lunch went very well. The Admiral was excellent company coming out with some very amusing stories. Between the main meal and the sweet the Admiral tapped his spoon on the table for attention.

"I would just like to thank you all for the good job you did in destroying those creatures. I am sure if we did not have this team in place, a lot more innocent people would have lost their life's, so thank you."

Jeff said thank you and Mark and Kate nodded in support.

The Admiral continued.

"Professor in recognition of your service to the United States of America you have been put forward for the Presidential Medal of Freedom, which I can confirm is fully supported by the White House."

A smiling Kate and Jeff stood up and congratulated Mark. Mark himself felt slightly embarrassed but responded.

"Admiral, I am honoured to be considered for the award, but what was achieved would not have been possible without this small but excellent team. It has been a great pleasure working with Commander Winters and Kate and indeed yourself who has fully supported everything we asked for no matter how ridiculous it may have seemed at the time. If ever I can be of assistance in the future it would be a privilege to be asked."

The Admiral nodded and took another drink from his glass.

"I have also asked Admiral Lane to recognise the part HMS Sabre played in all of this. She is one professional warship with an excellent Command Team."

All nodded in agreement.

The steward approached them and asked if they were ready for the sweet course. The Admiral answered.

"If there are no objections I suggest we skip the sweet and go and try a few more shots in the bar?"

All three nodded in agreement.

CHAPTER THIRTY-SEVEN

He had been back in England two days when the email arrived from Lisa's parents.

Dear Mark

We would like to thank you for the kindness shown towards our daughter Lisa. I am afraid she has taken the events over the last few months badly and is still finding it difficult to come to terms with them. We are spending sometime in Europe with her. She is receiving the best help but the doctors have advised it may be a long road back.

At this present time we kindly request that you do not attempt to make contact with her. As parents we will always be there for her. We love our daughter so very much and you can understand how it feels for us seeing her in so much pain.

Thank you so much for your help.

Aaron and Linda Michaels

Mark read thru the email at least four times. He knew what her parents were asking made sense. Seeing her again could have a very negative affect on her recovery. In his heart he knew that it was over, he was always going to be a reminder to her of those tragic events. He poured himself a large straight rum and thought of their night in Washington together, the night he fell in love with her. Since the death of his wife this was the first woman that had made him feel like that. He swallowed the drink in one. The glass smashed into numerous pieces as he threw it against the wall.

The Admiral had invited him down for lunch the following

weekend. As he pulled up the gardens were in full colour from the spring flowers. Daffodils stood proudly in and around the tree line, tulips provided a splash of colour at the front entrance. The old northerly wall was transformed into a waterfall of violet and pink from the aubrietia plants growing between the cracks. As he exited the car the front door opened and the Admiral and Mary along with Buster stepped out to greet him. The Admiral with a broad smile stretched out his hand and gave him a firm and friendly handshake.

"So good to see you again Professor."

"And you to Admiral."

Mary looked just as radiant and full of energy as the last time they had met. She gave him a friendly hug and a kiss on the cheek.

They enjoyed a lovely lunch with no mention of the creatures.

Afterwards Mary left the Admiral and Mark to talk.

"Any news of Miss Michaels Professor?"

"She is somewhere in Europe with her parents."

The expression on his face and the way the Admiral nodded, Mark new that he did not need to explain any further.

"And Sabre Admiral how is she?"

"She is currently in Plymouth on a leave period, but you will not be aware that Chief Ward was on the promotion signal to be promoted to Warrant Officer, in fact once he is promoted I am arranging for him to be on my warfare staff."

"Excellent news and well deserved. And the Captain?"

"John has another six months with Sabre but I am sure there will be an attractive posting for him at the end of that. And you Professor, how are you doing?" The tone of the last question indicated that it was not small talk.

The question caught Mark unawares. Some nights he would think back at what he could have done differently to avoid some of the attacks. He often thought of Lisa and he had noticed himself that he had been drinking more than his usual. The Admiral looked at him awaiting an answer.

"I think I have changed since I first met you Admiral, I have seen people die horrible deaths and occasionally think back if there was anything I could have done to have stopped it happening. I also met a wonderful woman who I will not see again. But I am dealing with it."

The Admiral paused before replying.

"Yes Professor, when we first met I do not think anyone could have predicted where it was going to lead and the affects on so many people. I can say with some certainty that if it was not for you there would have been many more people affected. As for the lady in question I do feel for you, and it is going to take time to ease the pain."

Just as the Admiral had finished, Mary entered the room carrying a tray of tea. All three of them sat in the conservatory drinking from china cups and discussing nothing in particular. Mary told of how much she liked the Caribbean when the Admiral was posted as Senior Naval Officer there. Mark said he loved the place and would often spend his free time in Tobago where the beaches and slow life style helped so much in him re-charging his batteries. The Admiral suggested that Mark should consider taking a break there in the near future. Mark smiled at him.

"I think that may be a good idea Admiral, a very good idea."

Three weeks later Mark was sat at Pigeon Point beach enjoying the sun and watching the pelicans diving for fish. He had a cold rum and coke in his hand and he felt more relaxed than he had in a long time. As he finished his drink, his mobile rang. It was the Admiral.

"Hello Admiral, checking up on me?"

"Hello Professor just wondering how long you are intending to stay out there?"

"Oh another week maybe ten days."

"Look Professor I hate to ask you this but a problem

has popped up and I think I will need your help again. My staff checked the flight times and they have tentatively booked a seat on one returning in two days time. Totally up to you Professor I do not want to spoil your break."

A smile broke over Marks face. When the Admiral said tentatively he knew that meant booked, once again he decided to take the line of least resistance.

"That will be fine Admiral it will be good working with you again."

"Excellent Professor I am having a chap from the British Embassy drop off a file for you to read. My staff will contact you with the flight details."

Still smiling to himself Mark ordered another rum and coke.